TWISTER'S WAKE

Randall Reyman

A Cyrus Brandt Novel
Book 1

ISBN: 9781980864080
KINDLE DIRECT PUBLISHING

Cover design by Randall Reyman
Cover photograph by Greg Fombelle

**For more info, go to
www.randallreyman.com**

1

Liz pushed herself up from the ground where she had been lying for several terrifying minutes. She was trembling, and as she rose slowly to her hands and knees she wondered if she should try to stand. Struggling to her feet, she staggered momentarily in the wet grass to right herself. Mud and plant debris covered the front of her jean jacket and pants, and she brushed it off as she looked behind her to check on her Jeep Cherokee. It stood where she had left it, apparently undamaged.

Liz could hear the emergency siren sounding from town, and she tried to remember if it had been sounding earlier. Looking to the east, she could see the massive funnel cloud about a mile away. It was still on the ground, moving slowly away from her, grinding its way through the corn and soybean fields in its path.

She had been halfway through her mail route, hurrying to outpace the storm, when her rearview mirror suddenly took on an ominous blackness. The tornado must have touched down about a quarter mile behind her, and with it had come a deafening and frightening roar. Seeing the monster was edging closer to her, she instinctively had slammed down hard on the brakes, veering toward the shallow ditch and bringing the SUV to an abrupt stop. Forcing the door open against the resisting wind, she had run toward the culvert just ahead and stumbled, falling headfirst into the wet ditch. That's where she'd stayed until the danger passed.

"Son of a bitch! That was too damn close," Liz muttered as she balanced on unsteady legs, trying to regain some semblance of composure.

She stood there for about a minute, waiting for her eyes and mind to refocus. Luckily, the twister had veered across the road just behind her, entering the soybean field to the south. She could see the wide swath of debris, consisting mostly of tree branches, weeds, and fencing that its force had left behind. There was something else out there, too. What was it? Looking more closely, it looked like trash strewn across the field, and it took only a couple of seconds for her to realize what she was really looking at.

"Goddamn it! Ya gotta be kidding me!" she blurted as she stood shaking her head in disbelief. The wind forces of the twister had sucked a large portion of her undelivered mail through the Cherokee's open window and distributed it across the field like confetti.

Taking a deep breath, Liz stalked back to her vehicle to slip out of her shoes and into her Wellingtons. She grabbed a large mailbag out of the back and traversed the ditch, pausing briefly to contemplate the job ahead.

"I don't remember this in the damn job description," she grumbled as she picked up a Walmart flyer stuck in the mud next to her foot. She stuffed the flyer into the mailbag.

As Liz strode into the soybean field, an old pickup truck pulled out of the driveway of a farmstead half a mile up the road. The truck was now heading her way.

2

500 Hz. Or maybe a bit more, 550 perhaps. It didn't really matter because it wasn't the frequency so much as the decibel level that made the town's emergency warning system effective. But here, five miles out, he found it barely audible, its intensity greatly attenuated by the distance.

Cyrus Brandt cautiously ascended the wooden steps from the basement and paused on the linoleum landing. "Come on, Molly. It's OK. Come on, girl. Everything's fine," he called.

The big yellow Lab slowly crept up the stairs, tail between her legs, her body trembling with each guarded step.

"That was kind of scary, wasn't it, Mo girl?" Cyrus scanned the first floor of the farmhouse as Molly followed him through the living room toward the front porch. Everything appeared to be in its place as he walked out the door onto the porch and gazed upon the flat Illinois landscape.

Was there a flatter place on Earth? He doubted it. As a kid he'd never really thought about that. It was later that he began to encounter people from places like Colorado and California who were quick to offer unwelcomed critiques of the Illinois terrain, revealing their disdain for the tedium of this land. Screw them, he thought. Cyrus found mountains to be a pain in the ass. Why the hell would you want to live in a mountain range if it meant you couldn't ever see the horizon, or you had to drive an hour to go twenty miles as the crow flies? No, Cyrus didn't want to live like that. To him, even the undulating landscape in a Grant Wood painting with its bulbous breast-like hills was a bit too rugged. He liked his landscape flat or flatter.

Cyrus had been away for several years, but he was glad to be back now on the smooth Illinois plains. This was his true home, where he could let his eyes behold the earth falling away in all directions into the horizon at its proper eight inches per mile, framing the vast dome of heaven in every direction.

Cyrus stood and surveyed the surrounding area, looking for evidence of storm damage. He could hear the siren still screaming faintly from the town of Elby. The world seemed eerily quiet aside from the siren, and Cyrus noted that the windsock in the front yard was hanging limply on its pole.

3

Everything had taken on a serene calmness, contrasting sharply with the ferocious wind and rain of the storm just a few minutes ago.

He walked to the west end of the porch and looked toward the driveway where his dad's old Ford F-150 pickup was parked. It appeared to be fine, which was a relief. Cyrus and his dad had put a lot of miles on that truck, hauling rock or crop seed or tools or whatever needed hauling. It was well-worn and rusted now, but Cyrus still loved that truck. His dad had purchased it new at a time when trucks were procured simply to serve a utilitarian purpose. It had few unnecessary amenities, unlike the pickup trucks nowadays that were decked out like a Lexus and comparable in size and cost to many small homes. Why people would buy those huge, lane-hogging obscenities Cyrus couldn't understand, especially when they were driven primarily by Valium-tight mothers transporting their overnourished and underexercised children to school and back.

During his time in Iraq, Cyrus had heard about the growing popularity of roadworthy Humvees back in the States. Cyrus had seen plenty of the military M998 versions of these vehicles. And long after his deployment, Cyrus had become increasingly aware of the devastating damage done to many of them by IEDs in the continuing Gulf conflicts. He could envision the aftermath of such attacks: the mingling of smoke and sand and blood, the limbless bodies, the disfigurement of young men and women. So it was no surprise that the sight of the *civilian* Hummers just brought back unsavory memories of events he was trying hard to suppress. The current oversized truck models were simply the progeny of those earlier war monsters. He hated that.

Cyrus scanned the outbuildings scattered around his farmstead. The barn, tractor shed, garage, chicken coop, and other livestock buildings had been empty for years. They were now just vestiges of an earlier age when life on the family farm was a viable prospect. Though in need of paint, the buildings were all still in reasonably sound structural condition, and Cyrus was relieved to see they had survived yet another Illinois spring storm. The only damage he could see amounted to tree limbs scattered about the yard, and one linden tree that appeared to be uprooted and lying on the ground next to the barn.

He turned his attention to the field south of the homestead and realized that one of his buildings hadn't survived this storm after all. The old corncrib in the field across the road lay in ruins. It was now strewn in splinters across the field, as if someone had violently kicked a toy model made of Popsicle sticks and papier-mâché. Like the other buildings on the farm, the corncrib had been empty for years, so it was no great loss. Still, Cyrus would need to get out there and clean up all the debris to make the field suitable for cultivation again.

Eight months ago, Cyrus would've never imagined that he would be living in his boyhood home again. But when his mother died last October and left him the old farm, everything changed. The forces holding him in Ohio were rapidly deteriorating. He was going through a nasty divorce, and it didn't help that he was becoming increasingly frustrated with his professional life. If there ever was a reason to pull up stakes and start over again, his mother's death offered him the opportunity to do so. Perhaps, he'd thought, moving home would help him regain some of the mojo from his youth and get his life on a better course.

Cyrus was well aware that his decision to move back home was rather ironic. For the six years since his father's heart attack, his mom had lived a lonely life in this house without the companionship of her loving husband, who had been by her side for some forty-eight years. As an only child, Cyrus understood his responsibility to look after her following his father's passing. Though Cyrus tried to call her regularly, it was never quite enough, and he knew it. The clutter of his life in Ohio caused him to eventually become more and more immune to his mother's appeals for him to call or visit. Now she was gone, and he would forever carry the guilt of knowing that it took her death to finally bring him home.

Cyrus was just about to turn and go back into the house when he noticed a vehicle parked in the ditch about a half mile down the gravel road to the west. He could barely make out a person in the field next to the road who appeared to be picking up litter and putting it in a bag.

3

Liz noticed the old truck as it got closer, but she continued her task, collecting envelopes, flyers, letters, and magazines. It wasn't until the truck pulled to a stop next to her Cherokee that Liz sighed deeply, and reluctantly walked toward the tall, lean man who was standing there observing her.

When the man realized what he was looking at, he called to her, "Well, it looks like you have your work cut out for you this morning!"

"No shit, Sherlock," Liz replied, her voice full of frustration. "Sorry, …yeah, you're right on that account. Nothing like a tornado to ruin a perfectly nice morning. Hi, my name is Liz."

"Nice to meet you, Liz. I'm Cyrus Brandt."

"Yep, I know who you are. I've been delivering your mail for the last few months, you know. You must be Mrs. Brandt's son. Sorry to hear about your mom's passing. She was a great lady. Always left me a real nice gift in the mailbox at Christmastime."

"Thanks. Yeah, she was special. I wish I'd thought more about that before she died, rather than after. Now it's a bit late."

"I know what you mean. Both my parents passed a few years ago. Even though they weren't model parents, not a day goes by that I don't wish I could talk to them again."

Cyrus watched as Liz tried to pick detritus from the front of her jacket. He put the woman at around fifty-five, showing signs of a life that had pulled no punches. She exhibited a bit of the added bulk that comes with aging, but she carried herself well, shoulders back, eyes paying close attention. She was studying him now, and he could sense the gears working under that disheveled graying hair.

Finally, after an awkwardly silent moment, he said, "You're probably wondering if I'm here to stay. The answer is, I'm not sure." And he wasn't sure. He had been living in the old farmhouse for a few months already, and he was no closer to deciding his future than when he'd arrived. His jigsaw puzzle of a life had been strewn out in a big, disorganized heap, and he hadn't even begun arranging the pieces according to shape and color, let alone assembling them into a recognizable image.

"Until I think of someplace better to go, I guess you'll have to continue delivering my mail to that old house up the road there," he said, gesturing toward his farmstead.

"Happy to do it. The last thing I want to see is another abandoned farmhouse on my route."

Cyrus was well aware of the economic downturn throughout the rural Midwest. Most of the small farmers were out of business now, either retired or dead. Their kids had moved on to other lives at the urging of their parents, who had seen this coming. Most of these farms had been sold off—or, if kept in the family, rented out—to large-scale operations that had more up-to-date equipment suited for working large tracts of land. It was all corn and soybean production now, and many of the old farmhouses sat abandoned and decrepit.

Cyrus's mother had held onto all of the family's original 160 acres and had made a cash rental agreement with a nearby farmer, who had promised her yearly payments based upon the harvest. Cyrus simply continued this arrangement, which he figured would provide him with a means to survive at least for the foreseeable future.

Liz finally turned back to the field and said, "Well, that stuff won't jump into this bag by itself. I'd best get back to it."

"Do you have another bag?" Cyrus asked, eyeing the back seat of the Cherokee.

"Oh, that won't be necessary. I can manage."

"No, I mean it. Molly and I've got nothing else on our plate this morning. Besides, I wouldn't want anyone to miss out on receiving their *Cane County Examiner* in a timely manner."

"Yeah, you sure wouldn't want that to happen," Liz replied with a hint of a smile. She pulled an empty bag from the back of the vehicle and said, "Here you go. Knock yourself out." Then, as an afterthought, she added, "I really appreciate the help, Mr. Brandt."

"Just call me 'Cy.' I don't put much stock in formality." Then he looked down at Molly and said, "OK, girl, let's go help rescue the U.S. Postal Service."

4

About six miles east of where Liz and Cyrus were pulling mail from the damp soybean rows, a man's body lay twisted, propped awkwardly against a wire fence amid a patch of morning glory that was spilling out into the adjacent cornfield. For the last couple of days, the body had been lying in a shallow ravine on the other side of the field, half-buried in the side of a creek bed. The twister had picked it up that morning and carried it about five hundred yards before unceremoniously dropping it here next to the county road.

The victim, a man in his mid-sixties, was clearly visible from the road even though the weeds shot up obliviously all around him. The body was missing much of its right hand, probably taken by a scavenging coyote, and the man's face was mostly gone, a yummy bit of soft tissue for some critter's repast. The deep crimson gash across the front of his throat and the brown dried blood covering the front of his shirt revealed much about the man's recent history.

5

An hour and a half later, Cyrus stood on the road watching Liz drive back toward town in her Cherokee. She would need to head back to the post office in Elby to re-sort everything before she could resume her route.

Cyrus reflected on his encounter with Liz. It appeared that he had perhaps made a new friend. That's what people do, he thought, as they morph from *visitor* to *local*. Was he becoming part of the community? Maybe that jigsaw puzzle was putting itself together.

Cyrus found an old towel in the pickup and cleaned off Molly's muddy feet before they both hopped into the pickup and drove back toward the house. Instead of pulling into the drive, Cyrus decided on the spur of the moment to continue straight past his house and head toward town. It was past lunchtime, and he thought he might stop at Annie's diner for a bite to eat.

Since coming back to the area, Cyrus had taken a liking to a modest café on Main Street called Annie's Place. He had known its owner back in high school. A couple of years Cyrus's junior, her name was Annie Bales then. She was a rather gangly but attractive girl who had definitely inherited the talk gene. He remembered having a bit of a crush on her, though he had never let her know it.

Now Annie had moved gracefully into her early thirties, still retaining many of the qualities Cyrus had admired so many years ago. Her gift of gab hadn't changed. But there was a lot about her that had. Many years of cultivating that relentless smile had etched tiny crow's feet at the edges of her bright hazel eyes. What once was a teenager's body with more bone than muscle had ripened into one of lithe female proportions.

In college, Annie had bounded from major to major, searching for her passion, before she finally settled on a liberal arts major so she could forage at will in diverse and fertile fields. How she ended up back in Elby after college was a mystery, even to her. It took marriage and the inescapable weight of life to finally corral her.

Annie and her husband had opened the diner soon after they were married and successfully kept it going through some rough economic times. Then, about five years ago, Annie had lost him in an auto accident out on Highway 38, when a sheet of black ice had sent his car plummeting through a guardrail into an unforgiving ravine. She had been operating the diner by herself ever since, and living in the apartment right above it.

Cyrus pulled up to the curb outside the diner and rolled the windows down halfway. "You stay put, Molly . . . and no barking! I'll be back in a jiff."

Molly had come with the farm. Once his parents' dog, now his, Molly had become a constant companion for Cyrus these last few months. But the diner was one place where Molly wasn't allowed. She didn't seem to mind, though. There was a lot to see on Main Street as she waited in the pickup for Cyrus to return.

Cyrus walked into the diner and noticed that most of the lunch crowd had already left. He took a seat at a table in the back as Annie walked toward him with a glass of ice water and a cup of coffee.

"Well, look what the cat dragged in," she said as she set them down in front of him.

When Annie leaned over the table, Cyrus couldn't help but notice that the top button of her white blouse was open, and he caught sight of the tops of her two spherical and silky-looking breasts held captive by a low-cut bra. Annie quickly turned and walked away, and Cyrus observed that hers was a physique of enthralling arcs and vectors, fluctuating as she moved like the collective orbits of imagined solar systems. As he watched her move, the term *high tensile modulus* (a term heralding back to his life in academia) came to mind. The term described the effect of stress on an object, and he could see little if any evidence that Annie was at all affected by the strain of her labor. He watched with rapt attention as she moved effortlessly from table to table like a poster child for Newton's first law of motion. Cyrus couldn't help but fantasize how someday he and Annie might enjoy testing Newton's third law together as well.

How long had it been since he'd been with a woman? Certainly not since his wife had left him. The breakup had really knocked the wind out of his sails. He had married Janice just after grad school, and he had been a devoted husband. Unfortunately, she hadn't been quite as devoted. When she left him for another man, it was a major blow. He wasn't sure he

10

could ever trust another woman with the type of commitment he'd once shared with his wife. Even now, as he watched Annie move gracefully about the diner, he doubted that he was ready for another woman in his life. Any serious relationship between him and this waitress with the smiling hazel eyes was probably just a distant fantasy.

As Annie passed by with a pot of coffee, Cyrus motioned for her to lean in as if he had a secret to reveal. "Hey, you might want to button that top button before some customer decides to throw you down on their table and have you for lunch."

"Who's to say I didn't leave it unbuttoned on purpose?" she replied smiling as she quickly buttoned it back up.

This kind of good-humored jousting had become the norm when he showed up at the diner. Annie and Cyrus both genuinely liked each other, though this light repartee was as far as it had ever gone.

Then she asked, "What'll you have today, hon?"

"Well, if you're not on the menu, I guess I'll just have the special, whatever it is."

"It's the hot roast beef sandwich. You can't go wrong with that."

"Sounds good, and bring a piece of that cherry pie with it."

The front door creaked open, and in walked a solidly fit man wearing what Cyrus took to be some kind of law enforcement uniform. Over six feet tall, and displaying a holstered weapon on his hip, the officer exuded an air of authority that permeated the diner, turning every head in his direction and causing a momentary lapse in all conversation.

Cyrus was surprised to see Annie meet the man with a wide smile and a kiss on the cheek. "Some customers get special perks, it appears," Cyrus said under his breath, but intentionally loud enough for Annie to hear.

"Say hello to Sheriff Thomas Bales, Cy," she said with an obvious tone of pride. "It's good to have a big brother who's the law in this county."

"Well, I'll be damned. It's about time I ran into you," said Cyrus. "I've heard a lot about you from Annie. All good, of course."

Cyrus could clearly see the resemblance as he studied the sheriff's face. Annie and her brother shared many of the same facial characteristics; the same smiling hazel eyes, the high cheekbones that supported a sleek, pleasant countenance.

"You know, Tom, I still remember you from high school," Cyrus recalled. "You were a couple of years ahead of me, but everybody knew Tom Bales, Mr. Basketball of Tri-City Consolidated High School."

Tom a bit embarrassed, smirked, "Wow, that was a long time ago, a lifetime ago. Now I'm just sheriff of this quiet little county."

"This is Cyrus Brandt, Tom. He's back home, living out at the old Brandt house outside of town," Annie said.

"It's good to meet you, Cyrus. Oh, and I'm awfully sorry about your mom's passing last year. What was it, October?"

"Yeah, thanks, appreciate it." Then he added, "Come on over and have a seat, Sheriff, unless you're meeting someone else."

"I'll join you for a bit," Tom said, "but I need to get out on the road assessing the damage left by that storm this morning. Annie, could you whip something up for me quick-like?"

"Hot roast beef sandwich is the special, and it's coming right up," she sang as she headed for the kitchen.

"Perfect, and could I talk you out of a cup of coffee, too?" Tom asked as he took a seat opposite Cyrus and set his hat on the chair next to him.

Cyrus's curiosity was getting the best of him. "So how does a Mr. Basketball become a sheriff, if you don't mind my asking?"

"Well, it's not a very interesting story. Went to the community college because they had a program in law enforcement. That's how it started. Eventually I served as a cop over in Springfield, and when the deputy sheriff position came open here in Cane County, I came home to stay. Got married. Had two great kids. When Sheriff Gaines retired five years ago, I sort of inherited the job with the help of the voters of this county.

"I can't really complain. I've made a pretty nice life for myself. I feel like I'm actually making a difference here. People seem to like me, for some reason. And hell, it's pretty quiet in these parts. It's a lot less stressful than patrolling the streets in Springfield with all that gang activity."

"And I'll bet you enjoy some other perks, like free food at your sister's diner, too," Cyrus added.

Annie had returned with their plates and set them on the table. Overhearing Cyrus's last comment, she said, "Hey, haven't you heard the saying that there's no such thing as a free lunch? Tom pays in many other ways. Trust me."

"Yeah, she's right about that," Tom responded with a crooked smile. "And what about you, Cyrus? It must be, what, twenty years since you left town?"

Cyrus became pensive as he spoke. "My story isn't exactly a success story. After high school, I went to U of I. I really liked being in college, and I just kept going until I got a Ph.D. to hang on the wall and collect dust."

"Holy shit!" Annie blurted out. Cyrus hadn't noticed that she'd returned with his pie and was standing next to the table listening intently to his narrative. "Well, well, well. We've got a doctor in the house. Whoopee doo!"

"I'd like to speak to the manager, please. I have a complaint about the staff at this establishment. They're very rude," Cyrus shot back with a wink.

"You think the staff is rude? Wait till you meet the manager. Oh, wait, that's the same rude person," she replied, smiling. "So, are you some kind of brainiac or something?"

"No, just a guy who went to school for a very long time. You might say I've done more schooling than Dory the Fish."

"What's your area of expertise?" asked Tom, ignoring Cyrus's lame joke.

"Oh, let me guess, let me guess!" Annie was animated now. "Animal science? Sociology? No, wait, I know. Archaeology, like Harrison Ford in Indiana Jones?"

"No, I studied physics," Cyrus replied quietly, almost apologetically.

There was a pause as Tom and Annie took that in. Tom finally said, "What does a person do with a Ph.D. in physics, if you don't mind my asking?"

Cyrus took a deep breath, paused, and then stared into his coffee cup. "I'll tell you exactly what that person does. Before he even gets the degree, he joins the National Guard to help pay for his schooling, and he gets sent to Iraq for eleven months to kill a bunch of Iraqis. Then he comes home, finishes his schooling, and tries to get a cushy research job, which doesn't materialize.

He finally lands an adjunct teaching position at a small sucky college in Ohio and works there for peanuts for several years, thinking if he excels in his teaching he'll get a full-time job, but since his area, which is physics, isn't attracting enough students, he's told a full-time line isn't in his future at the sucky college. Then he gets depressed and his wife leaves him for the dean of the business school, who of course is a lot happier and makes a lot more money, and then his mom dies and he says 'screw it' and moves back to his boyhood home to see if he can make a new start. That's what a person does with a Ph.D. in physics. Any questions, class?" Cyrus finally took another breath and looked up.

Tom and Annie were silent for several pregnant seconds, not knowing what to say.

Finally, Cyrus broke the tension by saying, "Aw, hell, you can't expect life to always be a bowl of frigging cherries. This tastes great, by the way, Annie," he continued as he shoved a spoonful of mashed potatoes into his mouth.

Just then, the diner door flew open and Cyrus looked up to see Bill Fry, the manager of the Ace Hardware store situated next to the diner. Cyrus could also hear Molly barking excitedly outside in the pickup.

Cyrus and Bill did not know each other very well, but Bill knew the barking dog belonged to Cyrus, and he said, "Mr. Brandt, could you do something about your dog out there? He's disturbing the few customers I have this afternoon."

"Sorry. I'll get right out there." Cyrus pushed his chair back, stood, and threw some bills onto the table. Turning to the sheriff, he said, "Good talking to you, Tom. I'm sure I'll see you around soon."

"Have a great day. And don't you worry about this piece of pie. I'll put it to good use."

Cyrus rolled his eyes. "I'm sure you will, Sheriff Bales." With a quick wink to Annie, Cyrus was out the door to the street.

It didn't take long for Tom to devour the pie Cyrus had left behind, and he was soon back in his office down the street from the diner checking for any new reports of damage or injuries from the tornado. His cell phone beeped.

"Sheriff Bales. Can I help you?"

"Hi, Tom. This is John. How's it going out there in God's country today?"

"Hey, man, I'm just living the dream. What's up?"

John Corbit was an Illinois State Police trooper assigned to Tom's county. The two kept in fairly close touch, sharing information such as suspicious activity, which was rare, and accident reports along Route 38, which ran through the middle of Tom's county. The two men had become close friends through the years. Most of their on-duty interaction took place over the phone, but sometimes their paths intersected at accident scenes on Cane County roads and highways.

"Well, first of all, I just wanted to touch base with you about the twister this morning. We haven't seen much evidence of traffic disruption due to storm damage in your area. The path of the tornado seems to have been mostly south of Elby through the cropland. We've got a few downed trees and farm buildings blown down, but no injuries. Do you have anything to report?"

"Not thus far, but I'm just about to head out and take another drive around the area where the tornado touched down."

"Sounds good. Hey, Tom, the other reason I'm calling is to get you up to speed on a recent development regarding that prison break in Pontiac. We have reason to believe the two escapees stole a car and headed south, in your general direction. Someone reported they'd seen a car matching the description traveling on a back road toward your county. We have no idea if these guys are still in the area, or if they've passed through. The trail has just gone cold, like they disappeared off the face of the earth. There's probably nothing to be concerned about, but I just want you to keep your eyes open. I'll send over all the information we have on these guys. Let me know right away if you see or hear anything, OK?"

"Will do, John. Thanks for the update. And give my best to Beth and the kids."

"Thanks, Tom. Talk to you soon."

Tom had seen a bulletin a week or two back about the two inmates who had escaped while being transferred from the Pontiac Correctional Center to the prison in Tamms. That's about all he knew, and he hadn't given it much thought until now. Both Pontiac and Tamms were high-security prisons, and he remembered from the original notification that these two escapees were violent offenders and considered very dangerous. Tom resolved to study the information John was sending over as soon as he could get to it. But right now he needed to deal with tornado damage control.

6

Cyrus spent the next morning picking up the remnants of his destroyed corncrib in the field across from his house. He had hooked the old John Deere tractor up to an aging hayrack and driven the rig out into the field to get started. It was a beautiful June morning, with cumulus clouds drifting overhead and the smell of clover and honeysuckle in the air. He had almost forgotten how much he loved the smell of rural Illinois in the spring and summer months. It was good to be home, he thought.

He was able to put much of the smaller debris on the hayrack, but he had to unhitch the wagon and use the tractor to drag some of the bigger roof sections to the side of the field. He would get around to dismantling those later, but at least they were out of the way for now.

As Cyrus headed back along the fence line toward the road, he spotted a large tractor slowly pulling a large implement along the road in his direction. Cyrus continued driving toward the gate that provided field access from the road and finally brought the John Deere to a stop. As the large rig got closer, Cyrus recognized that the driver was Leo Kotaska, who farmed much of the land in the area, including Cyrus's one hundred and sixty acres. Leo was pulling a large cultivator, ostensibly intended for use in the field where Cyrus had just finished his cleanup work. Leo deftly maneuvered his huge Case tractor and cultivator into the field and pulled up next to Cyrus.

"Morning, Cyrus," called Leo through the open window of the tractor cab. "What're you doing out here?"

"Hey, Leo. Just cleaning up the remnants of my corncrib." Cyrus could hear polka music blaring from Leo's tractor radio. He recognized the unmistakable sounds of a wheezing accordion and a staccato snare drum.

Leo turned to look out where he expected to see the corncrib but saw only the remnants of a rock foundation where the building had stood.

"What the hell happened to it?"

"Tornado. It came right through here. It barely missed the house. Didn't you hear the siren?"

"I did hear the town siren earlier, but I didn't know anything actually touched down. I guess I should have been paying better attention, because you know what they say . . . *Mackerel skies and mares' tails make tall ships carry low sails.*"

Cyrus didn't let on that he had no clue what Leo meant by that. He knew Leo was an eccentric fellow who often quoted odd sayings and philosophical axioms. Usually they were on the order of Mark Twain witticisms or H.L. Mencken social dogma, but sometimes Leo would reach back in time for some quirky little adage as he'd done today. Cyrus figured this little saying had something to do with weather patterns and decided to pretend that he knew exactly what Leo was talking about.

"Yeah, I guess so," Cyrus said noncommittally. "So what have you got on the CD player today? Sounds like the usual polka stuff."

"Usual? Hardly that, Cyrus. This is a recording from the finals of last year's Nebraska Invitational Polka Competition. It doesn't get much better than this," Leo asserted as he reached to turn up the volume on the dashboard. He proceeded to move his head back and forth to the beat of the music in a sort of head-banging movement, done in a way that only polka aficionados could pull off.

Cyrus stifled a laugh and sat there smiling, pretending to show a deep appreciation for what he was hearing. "Nice stuff," he finally managed with a straight face.

"Have you guys been gigging much?" Cyrus asked, raising his voice over the loud music. Cyrus knew that Leo led his own band, called Leo's Polka-Time Boys. He had never heard them perform, but Leo had talked a lot to Cyrus about *the Boys*, as he called them. The group seemed to have a decent following of fans, and they played regularly for events around the Elby area. Leo was the leader of the band and played the clarinet. Cyrus knew Leo could get around on the clarinet pretty well because he'd once observed Leo playing the thing as he was harrowing the field next to Cyrus's house, steering the tractor with his knees while he repeatedly beat the "Clarinet Polka" into submission with the old licorice stick.

"We've got some gigs coming up. We're playing for a sixtieth wedding anniversary party this weekend, and we just booked a gig for August over at the State Fair in the Ethnic Village. We're really looking forward to that one. Maybe you can come and hear us."

"Yeah, maybe," Cyrus said without an iota of sincerity.

"You really should come. The band's really going to be up for that state fair gig. We'll be taking the polka to a whole new level, I promise. You'll have a great time. Besides, you know what Bob Marley said about polka music, don't you?"

"Bob Marley said something about polka music?" Cyrus asked incredulously as he listened to the Kearney Polka Ramblers burn their way into the last chorus of "In Heaven There Is No Beer."

"Well, not actually polka music, but music in general. He said, *'One good thing about music; when it hits you, you feel no pain.'*"

"Hmm. OK, if you say so. But did Bob Marley ever happen to hear you play the clarinet?" Cyrus replied with a playful grin.

"What do you mean?" Leo asked suspiciously.

"Well, you know what Mark Twain said about the clarinet, don't you?"

"What's that?"

"He said, *'A gentleman is someone who knows how to play the clarinet and doesn't.'*"

Leo shook his head, saying, "No, I think he was talking about the banjo, if I remember correctly."

"Oh, . . . whatever. Clarinet, banjo, what's the difference?"

"Huh?"

"Just playing with you, Leo. See you later." Cyrus winked and tipped his cap to Leo before driving the tractor and hayrack through the gate, over the road, and up his driveway. Leo sat in puzzlement, head cocked to one side, as he watched Cyrus disappear past the barn to the back of the farmstead.

Cyrus spent the next ten minutes unloading the debris into a large pile behind the barn. When he had finished, he parked the hayrack where he had found it and drove the tractor back to its shed. As he walked back to the house, he continued down to the road to grab today's mail from the mailbox. Standing by the mailbox, he could see Leo now crisscrossing the bean field with his cultivator.

Cyrus began to sort through the various catalogs and flyers. What he was really looking for was not there. He wondered when he would receive his final divorce papers. A few days ago,

Janice's lawyer had left a message on his voice mail indicating the papers were on their way and he should be receiving them any day now. He was glad to hear it. He just wanted this whole divorce mess to go away.

He hadn't been very smart in dealing with the divorce, and while his wife had retained a lawyer to represent her, Cyrus had decided to go it alone. That had been a big mistake, and he had lost many of his financial and physical assets when all was said and done. Still, he was now anxious to get this entire distasteful process over with and behind him.

The next morning Cyrus arose late, having had a few too many beers the night before. The sound of polka music still bouncing around in his head and the anxiety over the divorce had gotten the best of him. Alcohol consumption had seemed like an obvious remedy at the time. In retrospect, with his head aching, he wasn't so sure. He popped a couple of Tylenol and decided to head into town for something to eat. Maybe if he got some food in him, he'd feel better.

Cyrus parked down the street from Annie's diner. When he walked into the brightly lit restaurant, he saw Annie and another waitress clearing dishes from the early breakfast crowd.

"Hey, guys," he said, trying to act upbeat, his eyes squinting in objection to the diner's blaring fluorescent lights.

"You look like shit, Cyrus," Annie said.

"Gee, thanks. I always love being greeted that way."

"You OK?"

"Oh yeah, I'm great. It's just that last night I tried to enhance Sam Adams's next quarter earnings."

"Say what?"

"Oh, nothing. Just had a little too much to drink last night."

"So, you were out partying, huh?"

"Yeah, Molly and I were really tearing it up at my house during the wee hours."

"Boy, you need to get a life," Annie remarked.

"Yeah, I'm going to do that one of these days. Could you fix me a couple of eggs over easy with a side of bacon? Maybe some toast? And coffee, lots of coffee."

"No problem. Coming right up," she said as she walked off toward the kitchen.

A few minutes later, Annie came back with Cyrus's breakfast and placed it on the table in front of him.

"You know?" she said. "It looks to me like you need to enlarge your circle of friends beyond just that dog."

"Whadaya mean? Molly is great company. She never argues with me and always agrees with my political views. That's the kind of friend I like. Of course, I suppose it wouldn't hurt to hang out with members of my own species."

Annie nodded as she turned to go. Cyrus called after her, "Hey, Annie, you're a member of my species, right?"

"Hmm. Not sure yet. The jury's still out on that one."

"Well, I was cleaning out my freezer the other day and found a couple of steaks that need eating. I was just thinking maybe you'd like to come over to my place Sunday afternoon and keep me company while I throw those suckers on the grill. Maybe you can tell me how to get my life together. What do you say?" He stopped abruptly, somewhat surprised with himself at the invitation he had just offered.

"Are you asking me on a date, Dr. Brandt?"

Scoffing, Cyrus replied, "Oh, come on, of course not. I just can't eat both of those big old steaks by myself, and as much as I like that dog, she for damn sure isn't getting one of those. And don't call me *Dr. Brandt!*"

"Hmm . . . well, I guess the diner is closed on Sundays, and I don't have any plans. Sure, why not? What can I bring, Professor?"

Cyrus shook his head in disapproval and said, "Don't bring anything, smart-ass. You cook for me all the time. The least I can do is reciprocate. Why don't I drive to town and pick you up at say four o'clock? You live upstairs, right? I could meet you out front."

"I have a better idea. Since this isn't a real date, I'll just drive over myself, OK?"

"OK. Do you know where my place is?"

"Yeah, I went by there the other day to pick up my weekly supply of eggs from Sally Hampton, who lives just up the road from you. As I drove by I waved at Molly, who was lounging in your front yard. I'm surprised she didn't mention that she'd seen me," Annie said with a smile.

"Molly isn't much of a talker. Not like you," he shot back.

21

"Yeah, well, maybe it's time you found a friend who actually speaks real words," Annie said. She quickly spun around and headed off to the kitchen, saying, "I'll see you on Sunday around four, then."

Cyrus admired her as she walked away. Annie Branson had a lean, firm body that moved with the grace of a dancer. She seemed even athletic, with her assured and quick gait. Annie's dark brown hair was cropped short, and it gently tossed to and fro as she moved about the diner. Even in her work uniform, she was a strikingly beautiful woman, Cyrus thought. But what had he just done? Why had he asked her to come over to his house? What was wrong with him? He had already told himself he wasn't ready for another relationship. The wounds were way too fresh.

7

Sheriff Thomas Bales stood on the side of the gravel road, staring at the corpse that lay before him in the weeds. George Pence, who lived just down the road, was talking. ". . . So I decided to come out today to work on this fence line the twister took down, and that's when I found it. It's pretty ripe, isn't it?"

"Yeah, looks like he's been dead a few days." Tom walked back toward his car for some privacy and made a call on his cell phone to the office. "Sarah, Tom here. We need the coroner to come and fetch a body out here near the Pence place. And if you can get ahold of Robert Backus tell him to get out here. He'll want to see this." He gave Sarah specific directions, then returned to where George was standing, staring at the grotesque sight in the ditch.

Tom took a cursory glance around the area, looking for anything interesting that might answer the questions now taking shape in his head. He noticed Pence slowly edging closer to the body with morbid fascination. "Please stay back, George. I don't want you compromising any evidence."

The body was in pretty bad condition. One hand was missing, and the face was badly mutilated. The body was leaning oddly against the barbed wire fence and was dressed in what appeared to be some kind of uniform with a brown shirt and gray pants. Tom suddenly noticed something that gave him pause. He turned away from the scene and reached again for his phone. "Sarah, did you get ahold of Robert yet?"

"Yes, Tom, he's on his way."

"Good, and would you tell the coroner to hold off for a while? We need some time to look this over. Thanks."

Agent Robert Backus was a Crime Scene Investigator assigned to Tom's county. For several years, he had worked as an Illinois State trooper patrolling the myriad of Illinois roads and highways. Eventually, he transferred to the position of CSI for this region. Tom had worked with him before at the occasional crime scenes that presented themselves rather rarely in this sleepy county.

Robert drove up in his cruiser about twenty minutes later. "Well, look what we have here. It seems like your day just became a lot more interesting," he remarked as he pushed the car door closed and walked to where Tom and George were standing.

"Yeah, it seems so," Tom replied without looking Robert's way.

"What do you see so far, Tom?"

"Well, first of all, you see that brown shirt? Well, that's not a brown shirt. That's dried blood, and lots of it. And check out the laceration across the neck. It's partially hidden under that matted grass. This guy had his throat cut."

"Hmm . . . looks that way," Robert replied as he moved closer to the body.

"And you know what's really weird about this?"

"What's that, Tom?"

"I don't see any evidence of anybody being around here. It's as if the body was just dropped here from the sky."

Robert turned to George Pence. "Have you seen anything odd, anybody suspicious around here the last week or two?"

George directed his gaze upward as he thought. "No, not that I can recall. This is a fairly isolated road. I'm about the only one who uses it, mainly to get to my fields and back. As a matter of fact, I came by here just about three days ago with my cultivator to work this field, and I don't recall seeing anything here. I think I would've spotted the body then if it was here."

Robert muttered to himself, "So the body has been here only a couple of days, but its condition would indicate that it's been out here far longer than that. Forensics will give us a better idea about that." Then he turned to Tom. "Any thoughts?"

Tom took a moment to look west from where he stood. "I think I know how this guy got here. Look that way." He pointed westward. The tornado's path was still visible, although not obvious to the casual observer. "We're right along the path of the twister. That guy had a wild ride to get here, it seems."

Robert said, "Yep, looks that way. The twister may have dropped him here, but the twister didn't cut this guy's throat."

The sheriff simply nodded, recognizing that natural forces had nothing to do with the demise of this victim. There was nothing natural about the jagged incision dissecting this unfortunate man's throat. This crime was the result of a quite unnatural act; an act that only could have been perpetrated by a

24

sick and dangerous killer; a killer who was most likely still in Tom's county.

8

Annie turned into Cyrus's driveway at exactly 3:55 on Sunday afternoon. Cyrus stood next to his charcoal grill on the patio as he watched her pull to a stop and get out of her car. Annie was wearing a short-sleeved, multicolored blouse with very tight jeans. He had never seen her in anything besides her work uniform before, and he was momentarily struck by the sight of her.

"What are you gaping at, Doc?" she said as she walked up the sidewalk.

"Oh, nothing. I just thought, I don't know, I don't know what I was expecting. But you clean up real good," he said, and then he grimaced at making such an awkward remark.

"Well, I couldn't decide between my old brown gunnysack or this blouse and jeans. So I decided to save the gunnysack for a special occasion," she quipped.

"Ha, ha, very funny, and don't call me *Doc!*"

"Yeah, whatever," Annie replied. "Can I help with anything?"

"No, everything's under control. Go grab yourself a beer from the fridge in the kitchen."

Annie walked up the steps into the kitchen and headed for the refrigerator. On the kitchen table she noticed some things Cyrus had prepared for dinner: potato salad, baked beans, and a bowl of sliced fruit. She took a few steps into his living room and was surprised to see everything neatly in its place, very clean and tidy. She had expected to find a house strewn with empty beer cans, old McDonald's wrappers, and some kind of nerdy science journals on the coffee table. But Cyrus's place was immaculate. She muttered to herself, "He'll make someone a good wife one day."

Annie walked back outside with her beer and joined Cyrus by the grill. "Gee. You cook, you clean, you do physics. You're kind of weird."

"Yeah, that's me, weird," Cyrus replied. "My mom taught me how to cook before I went off to college. A messy college roommate taught me the merits of cleanliness. And the physics part? Well, that's just me being curious about the big questions, I guess."

"My big question is why your wife left someone who cooks and cleans like you do."

"It takes more than that to make someone happy, I guess."

"I suppose so."

Cyrus threw the meat on the grill and closed the lid. The smell of the simmering steaks enveloped them as they sat at the picnic table Cyrus had set with a red plaid tablecloth and utensils. The panorama around them was an expansive vista of dark earth as far as the eye could see, coming to life with row after row of corn and soybean seedlings swaying gently in the early summer breeze.

"It's really beautiful out here, isn't it?" Annie said.

"Yep. I'd forgotten just how beautiful it was until I came back and experienced the planting season again. I should never have left in the first place."

"Well, I don't know about that. You know as well as I do how tough this life can be. You had to take your shot. It just didn't work out like you'd hoped."

"Boy, that's for sure. OK, that's enough about my life failings. Let's get to eating this stuff."

Annie brought the side dishes out to the picnic table as Cyrus finished up the steaks. They spent the rest of the afternoon together making small talk and discussing Elby and some of its more interesting people. It had been a long time since either of them had spent time like this, socializing one-on-one with a person of the opposite sex. Still, the dynamics of anything beyond simple friendship were not in play today. Though the circumstances surrounding the end of their marriages had been quite different, the emotional scars remaining were similar.

As the sun peeked through pink and purple wisps of clouds and fell toward the flat Illinois horizon, neither Cyrus nor Annie felt able to penetrate the emotional barrier separating them. It didn't really matter, though. It was enough to just pass the time together, pretending they were two ordinary people living two ordinary, happy lives.

9

The coroner's staff had arrived at the scene and was attending to the body as George escorted the two law enforcement officers through his soybean field, backtracking the path of the tornado. They walked about a half mile to the west and came upon a dirt path that shot out perpendicularly from the road and bisected the field, ending at an outcropping of trees about five hundred yards to the south.

Tom looked down at the road and saw some recent tire tracks that had mostly been washed away by the storm. Looking at George, he said, "What's at the end of this road?"

"Nothing but a shallow creek that runs through my property."

"Have you been down this road recently?"

"Nope."

"Well, somebody has." Tom said as he started walking down the road, with Robert and George right behind him.

The tracks seemed to end just short of the trees, and the two law officers split up to search the area. Once they made their way through the tree line, they encountered a small creek that had eaten a ravine about five feet deep in a circuitous route through the cropland beyond. They searched the area, one on each side of the creek. After about five minutes, Tom heard Robert yell, "I think I found something."

Tom and George found Robert looking down the side of the ravine just below him. Robert said, "It looks like someone dug a hole in the side of this bank, and it's been fairly recent, too."

Tom looked more closely at the site. "Whatever was buried there appears to have been exhumed, maybe by a coyote or a dog or something. See the tracks there?" Then Tom pointed to some scraps of cloth half buried in the mud. "Those look like they match the slacks of the victim. I'll bet you a fiver that some critter dug up that body, and the twister carried it over to the road."

"Well, it kind of looks that way," Robert replied as he took pictures with his cell phone. When he had taken enough photos, he joined Tom on top of the embankment.

Tom said, "OK, let's get back and talk to the coroner when he gets here. Hopefully he can get some prints off the one hand that guy has left."

Robert stopped walking and turned to the sheriff. "Tom, you can check the missing persons database if you want, but I think I know who this guy is."

"Oh, yeah?"

"When I worked down in southern Illinois, I assisted in transferring inmates from the Marion Correctional Center to other prisons. Those gray slacks our victim is wearing? They look a lot like the ones those inmates wore. I think this guy might be one of the escapees from Pontiac I told you about. Maybe those two guys had a falling-out."

"That's one hell of a falling-out, if you ask me," Tom replied as he started back toward the road.

10

Cyrus spent the next day continuing his cleanup of the farmstead. Though he had already taken care of most of the corncrib debris across the road, he still had plenty of fallen limbs to get rid of, as well as the linden tree that had been uprooted. He looked around and finally found his dad's old Stihl chainsaw in the garage and determined to get it running. He assumed the chainsaw would be tough to start because it hadn't been used for several years, and when he tried to start it, his fears were confirmed. Cyrus managed to find an empty gas container, and he poured some gas into it from the lawn mower gas can. Then he added some two-cycle oil he found on the workbench. After multiple tries yanking on the pull cord, the old chainsaw reluctantly sprang to life.

He let it run for a minute, then shut it down and placed it in the back of the truck. Next, he proceeded to drive around the farmyard, cutting up limbs and putting them in the back of the pickup. By noontime, he had taken care of most of the fallen limbs, but he hadn't even started working on that linden tree.

Molly had been hanging around him the entire morning, as if this was some great adventure. "Let's go, Molly," Cyrus said as he tossed the chainsaw in the truck bed with the branches. "That's enough for one day. Let's unload these branches and then get cleaned up and head into town for some lunch." It occurred to Cyrus that he had been eating quite a few of his meals at the diner recently. He admitted to himself now that it wasn't the food drawing him there, but the woman who served it to him.

Thirty minutes later, Cyrus and Molly were in the pickup heading down the driveway. In ten minutes, they had made their way to the edge of town. Soon they were parked in front of Annie's diner. Cyrus shook his finger at Molly. "No barking this time, and I mean it." Molly looked at Cyrus with her huge brown eyes as if she knew exactly what he was saying. Cyrus hoped to God she did. "I would love to sit and enjoy a nice, relaxed meal for once, OK?" He cracked the window and closed the car door behind him before he walked toward the door of Annie's Place.

He looked back at Molly one more time, giving her a stern look and a finger point, before he disappeared into the diner.

The place was busy today, and no tables were available. Cyrus took a seat at the counter. Annie, who was taking an order at one of the front tables, looked over his way and gave him a quick smile.

At that moment, the door opened and Tom walked through it. He took a seat next to Cyrus and righted the coffee cup that was facedown on the saucer in front of him.

"How's it going, Sheriff?" Cyrus asked lightheartedly.

"Don't ask."

"What's up? Don't tell me Elby is in the middle of a major crime wave or something," Cyrus joked.

"So I guess you haven't heard. You must be the only one left in town who hasn't."

"Heard about what?"

"Found a body outside of town by the Pence farm. Actually, it's not too far from your place."

"No shit?"

"You remember hearing about those two guys who escaped up at Pontiac?"

"Yeah. So?"

"We think this body might be one of them. That means the other escapee might be here in the area somewhere. This whole thing has me a little on edge right now."

"I can't say I blame you. What're you going to do about it?"

"Well, we're waiting for verification of the victim's identity from the office in Springfield. If this is indeed one of those escapees, I need to start looking around, seeing what I can see. But I have a lot of area to cover, with not a lot of staff. The State Police are on it too, but still . . ."

"Well, you can't do much till you get the report from Springfield, so you might as well try to relax and enjoy your lunch."

"Easy for you to say."

Annie walked over and filled Tom's cup with coffee, asking, "What are you two boys having today? The special is meat loaf, in case you were wondering."

"That'll do fine, Ann," said Tom.

"For me too, if you'd be so kind," Cyrus added with a smile.

Tom's cell phone buzzed, and he abruptly excused himself and walked out the door to answer it. A minute later, he returned and sat back down to the meal Annie had just brought. He said, "Well, the report just came back. That body we found was one of the escapees, all right. Now I have to start wondering where that other guy is. If he's the guy who killed this one, and I have to assume he is, we're looking for one bad piece of work."

"So what're you going to do, Sheriff?" Cyrus asked.

"Start looking for him. He could be holed up anywhere in the area. Hell, he could be hanging out in your barn for all we know. Now I'm wishing we'd hired another deputy sheriff when I took over for Sheriff Gaines. I've got two deputies, but we really could use some extra help with this guy on the loose."

Annie heard what Tom had just said and sat down next to him, saying, "Maybe Dr. Cyrus here could help you out. He's not doing much these days but sitting out at his place watching the crops grow."

"I'm doing just fine out there, thank you very much," Cyrus said. "And stop calling me *Dr. Cyrus*!"

Tom turned to Annie, saying, "No disrespect to Cyrus, but we need trained personnel to do this kind of work, people who can handle themselves in tough situations, people who know how to do investigative work, that sort of thing."

Now Cyrus felt like he needed to defend himself. "Well, you know, Tom, I've always considered myself more of a lover than a fighter. But I found out over in Iraq that a lover can turn into a fighter pretty damn quick. Before I was sent over there, I trained as a military policeman. In Iraq, I was on a lot of security details, but I saw plenty of action, too. I can handle myself all right. And in my academic field, I've always been a curious sort, asking lots of questions and not stopping until I found the answers. It seems like that's the kind of person you might be looking for."

"Hmm. You really think you might be interested in helping out?"

Cyrus now began seeing this as a challenge. "I might."

"Of course, we'd have to get a background check done on you."

"Of course. For all you know, I might be a serial killer."

"If you were military police, I imagine you had plenty of firearm training."

"Been around guns all my life. I did a lot of hunting when I was a kid, back when there was actually some game to be had in these parts. And yeah, you're right; my Iraq experience taught me more than I really need to know about handling weaponry."

"Do you have a gun now?"

"Yeah. I keep a Glock 19 around for security. It's a nine millimeter and holds fifteen rounds in the clip. It's a nice little piece, and I'm pretty handy with it, if I do say so myself."

Annie sighed and shook her head. "I guess I'll go attend to my customers. All this man-talk about your big bad guns is likely to give one of you a hard-on, and I don't want to be around to see that."

Cyrus and Tom watched without expression as Annie walked off, twirling a dishcloth in her hand. Tom said, "If you're serious about this, Cyrus, stop by my office tomorrow and we can talk more about possibly making it happen. Like I said, the department really could use a hand with this investigation. We're going to need a lot more help out there canvassing the area to see if anybody has seen anything. Can you come by around ten tomorrow morning?"

"I'll be there with bells on," Cyrus replied. Then he added, "Hey, Tom, now that we've got that settled, how about buying me that piece of pie you owe me?"

"Gee, Cyrus, I would, but I really need to run. Lots to do, you know, protecting and serving. See you tomorrow morning, then?" Tom replied as he walked smiling out the door.

11

The next morning, Cyrus was up early and decided to go for a run. He figured he'd better get off his duff and get back in shape if he was going to be a part of the Cane County Sheriff's Department.

"No time like the present," he said to Molly as they headed west from his mailbox at a lumbering pace. It was a beautiful morning. A soft wind gust enveloped them in the smells of the abundant flora, both wild and domestic, thriving around them.

Thirty minutes later, Cyrus made it back to the driveway and looked to see where Molly had gone. He spotted her jumping over the ditch from the opposite field to the road. Molly had something in her mouth, and Cyrus watched her as she proudly walked up to him with her quarry. Cyrus reached down and retrieved some pieces of paper from Molly's mouth. "Looks like somebody's junk mail. I guess Liz didn't find all of her mail out in that field after all. Good girl, Molly. Good job."

He patted the dog on the head, and the two of them walked up to the water hydrant near the house to have a quick drink. The hydrant consisted of a spigot attached to a pipe which rose about three feet above the ground, and below it was an old well that had been there as long as Cyrus could remember. He thought back to the days when he was a boy, and would come back to the house after working in the fields, looking forward to a cool drink from that spigot. He pulled the handle upward, and soon cold water came spewing forth from the spigot. Cyrus filled Molly's bowl and then bent over to put his mouth under the running water. When his thirst was quenched, Cyrus left Molly at her bowl and walked toward the house to sit on the front steps. That's when he heard his phone ringing from the kitchen. He stumbled up the steps and made it to the kitchen by the second ring.

"Hello?"

"Hey, Cy, it's Annie. I was just thinking since tomorrow is Thursday, usually a slow day here at the diner, maybe I could make a picnic lunch and come out to your place around noon. My gals at the diner can hold down the fort for me. I know you're meeting with Tom later today, so maybe you can tell me about all the crimes you've solved by the time I see you. What do you say?"

Cyrus paused a moment, thinking about the significance of this conversation, and then said, "Yeah, I guess that would work. Sure, why not? I don't know yet if Tom will need me for anything tomorrow. So I'll tell you what, plan on it unless I call you this afternoon, OK?"

"Sounds good. Talk to you later," Annie said before hanging up.

Cyrus put the phone down and stood there wondering about this unexpected development. This sounded a lot like a real date to him. It made him feel good in a visceral way, in spite of his trepidation about getting involved with anyone. He walked out to the porch steps and sat down. Molly loped over and rested her head in his lap.

"Well, Molly girl, it looks like maybe you're not the only female who appreciates my finer points." Cyrus gazed straight ahead for a long time, staring out into the soybean field but seeing only the slippery slope that potentially lay ahead.

At precisely ten o'clock in the morning, Cyrus entered the sheriff's office and stopped at the front counter.

"Hi, Cyrus," Tom said. "Say hello to Sarah." Tom gestured toward the woman working at the desk behind the counter. "She's the one who really runs this place. I'm just here for decoration."

Sarah looked up at Cyrus and said, "Oh, don't listen to him. He just says that stuff so he doesn't have to give me a raise. You must be the famous Dr. Cyrus Brandt who Tom has been telling me about."

Cyrus replied sheepishly, "Well, I wouldn't say I'm famous, and I don't care much for that *doctor* business, but yeah, that's me."

"Have a seat, Dr. Br . . . er, Cyrus, that is, and I'll take you through this paperwork."

Twenty minutes later, Cyrus sat down in front of Tom's desk. Tom said, "OK, so here's the deal, Cyrus. Of course this is all pending your background check results, but I'm not anticipating a problem, given what I know about you. Now, since you haven't completed the training like my other guys, you shouldn't be carrying a gun. You'll need to have more certified firearm training before you can start carrying. We'll see about getting that training as you go. But I'm thinking that your military police experience may help to fast-track you through that requirement. The thing is, I really need some help right away, as you know."

"Sounds good to me. I'm just happy to help. When do I get my fancy new uniform?"

"Well, that probably won't happen. But we do need to get you a badge so people see you as an official representative of this office. We'll also let you use that Hyundai SUV out back with our markings on it.

"And regarding that gun of yours: until you finish your training, just keep it in your vehicle. I'm confident you will never feel inclined to use that thing. If anything dangerous comes up, I mean anything, you contact me, got it? The last thing I want to see is my temporary deputy waving his gun around."

"Don't worry about that, Sheriff. I've had enough gunplay for one lifetime."

"Glad to hear it. Now let's talk about this guy we're looking for. First of all, for all we know, he's long gone. If I were him and slit a guy's throat in this county, I wouldn't stick around. Still, we know the two of them stole a white Mercedes sedan that some lady left running outside her house in Pontiac, and we haven't been able to locate it. The last time it was spotted was when someone saw it headed down Highway 38 in our direction. That's what makes me think he may still be in the area, holed up somewhere. I hope I'm wrong, but we won't know till we canvass this whole area for information, suspicious activity, that sort of thing. Basically, I think our main goal right now is to find that car.

"The victim we found over near the Pence farm was a guy named George Fromm. He was doing time for aggravated assault and drug dealing in the Rockford area. Forensics indicate his throat was cut, but we already knew that. He'd been buried about a half mile off the road for a week to ten days before we found him. His body was apparently picked up by that twister and then deposited where we found him. The fellow he escaped with, who apparently killed him, is a felon by the name of Byron Patterson. He was doing a life term for sexual assault and

36

murder. He is a really bad, dangerous dude. If you encounter him, don't fuck around. You back off and call me right away. Don't take any chances."

"OK, OK, Tom. I got it. I won't pull a Dirty Harry on you, I promise."

"OK, good. That desk over there by the window? It's yours if you need it. I'm going to give you this file on Patterson, but don't take it out of the office. You might want to study it to see the kind of guy we're dealing with here." Tom handed the file to Cyrus.

"OK, I'll leave you to it. You can stick around and study that as long as you'd like. If you need anything, just ask Sarah. I'm going to head out and continue looking around. You can stop back late tomorrow afternoon, and we'll develop a search grid to use the next day. Do you have any questions?"

"No, Tom, but I'll let you know if I do. Thanks."

Cyrus spent the rest of the morning looking through Patterson's file. Patterson was indeed a nasty piece of work. His life had been a constant string of incarcerations, each leading to an eventual release, followed by more and more heinous crimes, until finally he'd raped, shot, and mutilated a female attendant at a BP gas station on Interstate 80. Now Cyrus wondered if this deputy sheriff thing was a wise career move for him. "Hopefully, this guy is in another state by now," he muttered to himself, "and he's someone else's problem."

12

Annie showed up right on time, precisely at noon. Grabbing her purse and picnic basket off the back seat, she scurried up to where Cyrus was standing. "Hey, Doc, beautiful day for a picnic."

Cyrus hesitated for a moment and then replied, "Listen, little girl. If you call me that again, I'm going to send you and that picnic basket back to town."

"Yeah, right," she responded. "OK, Deputy, let's get this party started." Molly walked up to Annie, wagging her tail with a wild abandon. "Hey there, Molly. You're a good girl." And then she said to Cyrus, "See, Cyrus, at least your dog likes me."

Shaking his head, Cyrus took the basket out of her hand and led Annie and Molly to the table, which he had covered with a crisp tablecloth. He set the basket on the table and looked inside. He began pulling out sandwiches, plates, table service, covered bowls of coleslaw and fruit salad, potato chips, a couple of cloth napkins, two bottles of water, and finally, two pieces of cherry pie.

Cyrus looked at Annie and said, "Ah, finally, the pie you owe me."

"Well, actually, I don't owe you any pie. I believe it's Tom who owes you a piece of pie."

"Oh yeah, that's right."

They sat down together and began arranging the food in front of them on the table. Annie said, "So, speaking of Tom, how did it go at the sheriff's office today?"

"Well, you know, we discussed top secret stuff about the cases under investigation. I could tell you about them, but then I'd have to kill you."

"Come on, really. Tell me how it went."

Cyrus swallowed a piece of his sandwich and replied, "Tom's still waiting on my background check, but otherwise I think we're good to go. I have to say, though, after reading the case file on this escapee we're looking for, I'm not sure I want to be running into this guy anytime soon. He's a nasty one."

"Do you really think he's still in the area?"

"Not sure, but I have a feeling Tom thinks so. That's why he's taking me on in the first place."

"What's the plan?"

"Well, I think we'll meet tomorrow at his office to work that out. I'm assuming we'll be canvassing house-to-house in the rural areas to find out if anybody has seen anything suspicious."

"That sounds time-consuming."

"Yeah, I know. But Tom won't be satisfied until we do that. He doesn't want someone as dangerous as this guy hanging around his county. He's a good sheriff, Annie."

"Yeah, I know. He really cares about the people around here, and he takes his duties very seriously. This county is lucky to have him."

As Cyrus and Annie finished their meal, they chatted and looked out upon the expanse of cropland surrounding Cyrus's house. Annie shared memories of her life with her husband and the aftermath of his death. Cyrus opened up about the circumstances surrounding the demise of his marriage. They were becoming more comfortable in each other's company, more willing to share both the joyful memories and the painful ones. They could feel an important kinship developing, and it felt good. Very good.

Finally, they cleaned off the picnic table and proceeded inside to the kitchen. As they stood next to each other at the sink rinsing off the dishes, the conversation again took on a more playful tenor. Cyrus said, "You know, Annie, this is looking more and more like a real date."

"Aw, hell, Cy. Just loosen up, OK? You can call it a date if you want, or you can call it a lonely hearts club meeting. I don't really care," she said with a wink and a smile. "You know, we can mope around the rest of our lives, or we can take life by the balls and shake it. I think we should consider doing the latter."

"That kind of hurts just to think about."

"You know what I mean. Life is just passing us by, and here you and I are sitting in some kind of black hole of despair. We need to come back out into the light eventually, and I say the sooner the better."

"Nice little metaphor, except for a couple of things. Did you know a black hole isn't really dark when you enter it? Scientists now believe it's really quite bright in there."

"So now you're going to start entertaining me with physics fun facts? Wow, you really know how to show a girl a good time. And besides, according to my experience watching Star Trek reruns as a kid, I once saw Captain Kirk take the Enterprise into a black hole and . . ."

"Yeah, yeah, yeah. All of that's a bunch of malarkey. In reality, the gravitation is so strong in a black hole that when light enters, it can't escape. It just bends and bounces around in there. Theoretically, if you ventured beyond the event horizon of a black hole, you would see an amazing light show once you made it inside."

"Well, la-dee-da, Mr. Brainiac Physics Guy! I'll look forward to seeing that someday. Maybe you can take me there."

"Well, actually, you wouldn't enjoy it very much, because if you made it inside the black hole, your body would be stretched to the thickness of a noodle and then you'd cease to exist."

"I don't think I'd like that."

"No, you wouldn't look good as a noodle. You look fine just the way you are."

Annie gave Cyrus a playful elbow to his midsection. "Well, listen to you, Cyrus Brandt. That may be the first real compliment you've ever paid me."

"I guess maybe there's hope for me after all."

"Maybe, indeed," Annie replied.

13

Byron sat on the sofa in the living room of the two-story home. He had been there for ten days, trying to decide his next move. For now, he figured he was safe. No one would suspect he was hiding there as long as he kept the lights off and the curtains drawn. He had been able to find enough food in the cupboards and refrigerator to sustain himself, and he had been able to find an adequate hiding place for the white Mercedes behind the pole barn. He was fairly certain he had sufficiently disposed of Fromm's body, and it wouldn't be found in the foreseeable future. So at least for the time being, he felt relatively secure. Still, he knew an intensive manhunt must be underway since his escape, and both the state police and the local sheriff's department would be on high alert, aggressively searching for him.

This was not uncharted territory for Byron. He had been in this situation before. His life had been a continual cat and mouse game between him and the law, and he had learned much from his earlier mistakes that had resulted in his recapture. This time, he hoped to use what he had learned to retain his freedom as long as possible, maybe even indefinitely. If he could just escape from this area and get as far away as possible, he thought, maybe he could assume a new identity and survive as a free man in some faraway, isolated place.

He didn't like this feeling of being hunted. He much preferred being the hunter. Wasn't that what life was really about—either being the hunter or being the hunted? Those were your only real options. He knew what it was like being both of them. As a boy, he had learned early on that he preferred one over the other. His parents had given him up for adoption, releasing him into a world that thoroughly enjoyed hunting him. The scars from those difficult early years remained as he moved into manhood, developing the skills that allowed him to take instead of be taken from, bully instead of being bullied, kill instead of being killed. He considered the world something to be utilized for his own profit, and women for his own pleasure. *Survival of the fittest* was his mantra. It was a law of the natural world, and he had developed the animal instincts to survive in that world.

Byron stood up and walked to the window, cautiously peering through the small opening in the curtain to check for any traffic coming from the north. He walked to the opposite side of the room and checked in the other direction. Nothing. That was good. Since it was getting toward evening, he switched off the TV and double-checked to make sure all the lights were off. Then he turned on the radio that he had placed next to the La-Z-Boy recliner, and sat down.

He would stay there until morning, waking occasionally throughout the night to take note of any slight noise that he heard outside the house. This had been his routine for ten nights now, and he was anxious to make his next move. But he wasn't going to make this decision alone. There were others involved in his plans, and together they would devise a careful and deliberate strategy.

14

Cyrus woke up late the next morning, put on a pot of coffee, let Molly out the front door to do her business, turned on the TV, and sat down in front of CNN to see if the world was still in one piece. All of this had become something of a ritual the last couple of months, although more often than not he would forego the TV. Cyrus was tired of seeing news about small-minded, self-serving leaders imposing their will upon the people who put trust in their leadership. Why couldn't the people in charge be the best of us rather than the worst? Lately, Cyrus found that he would awaken in the morning in a good mood, but by the time he had watched the news he would be in a rather dark place. He was realizing now that his desire to stay connected was becoming less important than his need for a little tranquility in his life. After all, did the world really need his attention while it was fucking itself up? No, it could do that all by itself.

Today, however, Cyrus did turn on the TV and take note of another day's worth of people fucking up the world. Strife in the Middle East? Nothing new about that. Republicans stonewalling Democrats? Let them kill each other. Another shooting in a school? Just old hat in a country that loves its guns.

Cyrus turned off the TV and decided to work off some of his angst with a short run. As he got dressed and made his way out of the house, he spotted Molly sitting proudly by the door with another piece of muddied mail hanging from her mouth.

"Found some more mail, I see. Good girl," Cyrus said as Molly released it into his hand. "I'll put this one with the rest of them."

Molly had been finding more of these, and Cyrus now had a pile of eight or ten pieces of mail on his kitchen counter that he planned to leave at the post office soon. Thus far, none of it seemed terribly important—mostly catalogs, flyers, and letters to "current occupant."

As Cyrus took the letter to the kitchen to place with the others, his cell phone vibrated. It was Tom calling.

"Yeah, Tom. What's up?"

"I guess we're good to go here. Your background check came back, and it shows you apparently haven't committed any murders lately."

"Boy, that's a relief. So do you want me to come into town today?"

"Yes, we really need to get you sworn in and started. When can you get here?"

"Give me a chance to change, and I'll be there as soon as I can. I'd say thirty minutes?"

"Sounds good. See you then," said Tom as he disconnected.

Cyrus walked into the sheriff's office a half hour later and noticed Sarah at the copy machine. She was about sixty years old and had been Sheriff Gaines's office assistant for many years. When Gaines retired, she had considered doing likewise, but when Tom came on board, she knew the two of them would get along just fine, so she had decided to stay on and help him transition into the job. Tom was very grateful for her decision, as she had proven to be invaluable in the day-to-day business of the Cane County Sheriff's Department.

"Morning, Sarah," Cyrus offered.

"Hi, Cyrus. Tom is out back if you're looking for him."

"Thanks," Cyrus replied as he continued to the back of the office and out the back door. Tom was sitting inside the department's Hyundai SUV. The driver's side door was open, and Tom had just started the engine. He grabbed a few pieces of trash off the floor of the vehicle and got out without turning the engine off.

Tom said, "I thought I should get this thing ready to roll. If you're going to be going around asking questions, people will feel more at ease if you pull up in an official department vehicle."

"Makes sense," replied Cyrus.

Tom reached in to shut down the engine, and then he tossed the keys to Cyrus. "Let's go in so I can tell you what I need you to do."

Tom sat down behind his desk and waited until Cyrus was seated in front of him. "I haven't heard a peep from the state police, so apparently there have been no sightings of the white Mercedes. Patterson could be hiding out somewhere around

44

here. Or, if he stashed the car somewhere, he may have gotten a ride out of this area. One thing is for sure: we need to find that car. That's our priority right now. Without that, we don't have a clue what happened to this guy."

Tom thought for a moment and then continued, "So here's what I want you to do. Focus your attention in the rural area south of town for now. Just ask people if they've seen anything suspicious. Ask about the Mercedes, inquiring in particular about the days when Patterson was first thought to be in the area. Snoop around a bit, but remember that you're representing the law here. You need a warrant to search any private property. If you find no one home, just walk around and see what you can see. You don't need a warrant to look in a window or two. If you see anything interesting, I mean *anything*, give me a call and I'll take it from there. Oh, and make sure you display that badge I gave you. If you take your handgun, keep it in the Hyundai and don't plan on using it, OK?"

"Got it, Sheriff."

"OK, Cy. Let's get you sworn in and on the road."

15

Cyrus put the Hyundai in gear and headed south out of town. He had a lot of ground to cover, and he had decided to start with a search of the conservation area down by the river. As he drove up and down the access roads, dodging the numerous potholes and occasional fallen limbs, he wondered about the possible scenarios that could have played out these last few days. Maybe Byron Patterson had just kept driving that Mercedes right through Cane County and continued for hundreds of miles without being detected. It was possible. But not probable. More likely, he'd stashed the car somewhere—but where? If he had parked it somewhere like this wooded area, what would he have done next? Was he living out here in the woods somewhere? Highly unlikely, Cyrus thought. At least not for very long. He might have gotten a lift from some unsuspecting stranger and managed to get out of the area.

Cyrus's greatest fear was that Patterson had entered someone's home and was holding them captive, or worse. Still, it seemed implausible that this could happen without someone else noticing. People around these parts were pretty knowledgeable about their neighbors' comings and goings. Someone would certainly have noticed something by now.

So all Tom and his deputies could do was wander the countryside hoping to spot something. They knew this could be a big waste of time, but what was the alternative? They couldn't just sit in the sheriff's office and wait for the phone to ring.

Cyrus drove on, covering mile after mile of gravel and dirt roads, homestead after homestead. He had grown to love the vast landscape of the Illinois prairie, but now it seemed like this task Tom had given him would take forever. There were just too many roads to check. Many of them were merely access roads to tracts of cropland. How could he possibly check them all? Still, he drove on, carefully annotating the map that was spread across the passenger seat.

By mid-afternoon, after four hours of searching, Cyrus drove back into town. He had covered much of the area along the river and had stopped at a couple of homes to ask questions. But now he needed a break. He decided to stop in at Annie's for a cup of coffee before heading out again to continue his search.

The diner was empty except for Annie and the cook, who were hanging out in the kitchen. Cyrus sat down at the counter as Annie walked up to greet him.

"Hey, stranger," she said. "Been solving any crimes lately?"

Cyrus just shook his head. "This law enforcement thing isn't as exciting as TV makes it out to be. It's pretty boring out there, and I've just barely started."

"Well, try running a diner if you think you have it bad."

"OK, point taken."

"What can I get you?"

"Just a cup of coffee, and maybe some company. I've mostly been driving around the county talking to myself for the last four hours."

"Did you learn anything during those conversations?"

"You are real funny," he said as he turned the coffee cup right side up and placed it on the saucer for Annie to fill. "I've been focusing my search on that bottom road in the woods along the river. When I leave here, I'll be moving east toward Oakton until I run out of light. Then tomorrow I'll be heading to Springfield for my firearms training. After that, it's back to covering my search grid."

"Tom's going to work you like a dog if you let him, you know."

"I know, but he really wants to solve this case, and he won't expect more of me than he expects of himself."

"I suppose not."

"Tom did mention that he was going to give me Friday afternoon off, so I'll at least have that to look forward to."

"Well, if you can't find anything to do, I know a gal who could make herself available to hang out with," Annie said as she leaned her elbow on the counter.

"Are you asking me on another date?"

"Hey, remember what I said about grabbing life by the balls? Besides, people who know me know I'm a sucker for a man with a badge. Let's not call it a date. Let's just say you'll be keeping me under surveillance."

"Surveillance sounds good. Sure, let's do it. Do you want to come out to my place again, or would you rather do something else? I'm wide open for ideas."

Annie said, "I don't mind coming out there. We can keep Molly company. I can grab some KFC on the way out there. How's that sound?"

"Fine. It's settled. Show up any time after 3:00 or so, OK? I've been meaning to do some target practice, and I should be done by then."

"Well, look at you and your big bad gun," Annie taunted.

"Hey, with that guy still on the run, I'd rather be safe than sorry."

"Yeah, you're right. I shouldn't make light of it. Maybe I'll come out early just to watch, if you don't mind."

"That would be great. I'll be out back behind the barn if you show up early. OK, I'd better get out on the road before Tom sees me flapping my jaw in here. How much is the coffee?"

"On the house for law enforcement officers."

"Much obliged, ma'am." Cyrus got up, gave Annie a little nod and a smile, and walked out the door.

16

The week leading up to Friday seemed like an eternity to Cyrus. He got up each morning and was on the road by nine o'clock. Except for short lunch breaks, he continued on his search grid until dusk every day. When he got home, he reported in to Tom by phone. So far, no one had noticed anything unusual or suspicious, and no one they talked to had seen a glimpse of the white Mercedes they so desperately wanted to find. They had managed to cover only about one-third of the area, and Cyrus knew they had much work ahead of them.

On Friday, Cyrus was up and on the road again at nine o'clock. He was now gradually working his way to the southwest of Elby. He had managed to find a few people at home when he stopped to inquire, but more often than not, his knock on the front door was met with silence. When that happened, he proceeded to check the property, looking discreetly in the garage or any building that could house the vehicle he was looking for. Finally, at around noon, he called Sarah to check in and then headed for home.

As he drew close to his farmstead, he could see a pickup truck parked on the road in front of his house. He pulled up behind the vehicle and rolled down his window to peer ahead at Leo Kotaska, who was apparently carrying on a conversation with Molly in the middle of the road.

"What the . . . ?" Cyrus muttered under his breath as he got out to investigate.

Leo was kneeling down, stroking the head of the Labrador and speaking to her in soft tones. Cyrus noticed that Leo was holding a handful of letters in his left hand.

"What's going on, Leo?" Cyrus asked.

"Hi, Cyrus. I was just passing by on my way to a rehearsal with the Boys, and I saw your dog crossing the road with this in her mouth." He handed the letters to Cyrus. "I thought it might be something important."

Cyrus nodded his head, saying, "Yeah. She's been bringing me that stuff ever since the twister came through here. It was blown out of the mail delivery truck down the road."

"Bummer. Maybe that's why I haven't yet received this month's IPA Newsletter."

"IPA?"

"International Polka Association. If Molly finds that, be sure to let me know."

"Will do, Leo. So you say you're on your way to a rehearsal?"

"Yep. The band is trying out some new material for the gigs we have coming up."

"New material? You mean people are still writing new polkas?"

"Well, actually, we're learning some old classics that we've been meaning to get into our repertoire, like the 'Beer Garden Polka' and the ever-popular 'In Heaven There Is No Beer.'"

"Leo, why is it that every polka seems to focus on beer and beer drinking? Most popular songs I hear on the radio are more about things like love."

"Isn't it obvious? Have you ever danced a polka?"

"Can't say I've had the pleasure," Cyrus replied with a smirk.

"Well, if you had, you'd know that it's impossible to sing romantic lyrics into your dance partner's ear while you're dancing the polka."

"Oh, I see what you mean."

"Now, beer. That's something you can really sing about at full volume as you high step it along the dance floor. Get it?"

"Yup. Got it."

Cyrus had turned to walk toward his Hyundai when Leo called after him, "Well, this is something new, isn't it?"

"What do you mean?" asked Cyrus as he turned back around.

Leo gestured toward the Hyundai and then pointed at the badge attached to Cyrus' belt. "Looks like you've taken up a whole new line of work."

"Afraid so. I'm just helping out for a while. The department is a bit short-handed, and I thought it might be of some service."

"Actually, I heard something about that through the grapevine already. The wife heard it from her sister, who heard it from the cousin of the hairdresser who does the sheriff's wife's hair."

"Wow. That's quite an information network you have going there."

"Well, you know how word circulates in a community like this. I think it's great that you're helping out, doing your civic duty and all. Besides, I suppose it probably gets pretty boring just sitting around the house pondering the big physics questions of the universe."

"I've been thinking less and less about that stuff recently. Maybe my days as an intellectual are behind me. I'll leave it to you to ponder those questions during your long hours on the tractor seat."

"Nope, can't do that. It'd be kind of hard to drive a tractor, practice the clarinet, and ponder the truths of the universe all at the same time."

"Yeah, I suppose so."

"Besides, I've never been one to search the vastness of the universe to discover my truths. As Sartre once said, '*the meaning of life isn't something discovered, but something we create.*' I like that notion of creating my own meaning."

"Hmm. I'll have to think about that," replied Cyrus, and he would.

"You do that. I'll see you later, Cyrus. The Boys are waiting on me." Leo walked to his pickup, got in, and drove on to his rehearsal.

Cyrus pulled the SUV into the driveway and stopped next to the house. He walked to the front steps with Molly at his side and found two more pieces of mail that the dog had deposited there earlier.

"Good girl, Molly. You may have a bright future in the postal service if you keep this up," Cyrus said to her. He picked up the letters and went inside.

Forty-five minutes later, he was in the back area of his property setting up tin cans on a downed tree limb. He had dragged the limb in front of a small ridge that jutted out from the long pine-tree windbreak.

Cyrus had purchased his Glock 19 handgun back in the days when he had first joined the National Guard. He had become familiar with firearms during his youth on the farm, but that experience was primarily with rifles and shotguns. When he had begun receiving further firearm training in the Guard, he'd decided to purchase the handgun for security reasons. At least that's what he had told himself. He hadn't used it much through the years, except for the occasional target practice that helped him retain at least a minimal skill level. The gun itself felt good in his hand. It was well-balanced, easy to use, and very reliable. But like most handguns, it was difficult to fire accurately at a target. Now, in his current position as a deputy sheriff, he figured he had better improve on what skills he already had with the weapon. If he ever had to use it, he wanted to be damn sure he would hit his target. His life could depend on it.

Cyrus took a position about thirty yards from the target area and filled the clip with fifteen rounds. He raised the weapon and fired off three rounds in rapid succession, hitting none of the tin cans.

"I've got some work to do," he muttered to himself.

Annie had been standing nearby, leaning against the side of the barn. She said, "Hey, deadeye. Doesn't look like those tin cans are in much danger today."

Cyrus gave her an expressionless sideways glance. Then he raised the weapon and fired three more rounds at the target area. One tin can exploded off the log and landed several yards away.

"One out of six ain't bad," Annie said.

"You think you could do any better?" Cyrus said as he turned to face her.

"I suppose I could try, if you show me how," she replied coyly.

Cyrus's guard came down a little, and he said, "Sure, come over here. Let me show you how to hold it."

Annie walked over and awkwardly took hold of the weapon. Cyrus said, "Now be careful. Always assume it's loaded, and never point a gun where you wouldn't want to shoot it, OK?"

"OK. Show me how I should hold it," she requested. Cyrus put his arms around her to help her hold the gun properly and point it toward the target. Cyrus could feel the dampness of her hair. It smelled of citrus, and he surmised that she had just washed it before driving out here. He took in all her sweet smells as he reached around her body, showing her how to bring the weapon up with both hands.

"Now I'll let you take a shot," he said as he released his grip on her wrists and stepped back.

Annie looked back at Cyrus and gave him a wink. "You know, Cy, I think I'll check something first." Then she adeptly discharged the clip from the Glock, took note of the rounds left in the clip, and deftly shoved it back into the gun. Without hesitation, she turned toward the target, lifted the weapon, uttered something quietly to herself, and fired four rounds at the tin cans—hitting three in rapid succession. Then she turned to Cyrus and handed him the gun. "Something like that?" she asked with a mischievous grin.

"What the . . . ?" blurted Cyrus. "You little scamp. Where did you learn to shoot like that?"

"When you have a brother in law enforcement, you learn a thing or two," she responded with a satisfied smile. "Tom used to take me out shooting all the time. We haven't done it for a while, though. I'd almost forgotten how much fun it is."

"I noticed you said something before you fired. What was that all about?" Cyrus asked.

"I said *peanut butter*," Annie replied.

"Huh?"

"I learned that from a shooting instructor I had once. He told me to say *peanut butter* to remind myself that my trigger movement should feel like I'm moving my finger through peanut butter. That helps me squeeze the trigger nice and slow. It also distracts me from anticipating the recoil, which is a common mistake. So I always say *peanut butter* as I'm squeezing the trigger. It seems to work for me."

"I'll say," agreed Cyrus. "I may have to try that."

Cyrus and Annie spent the next hour in playful competition until Cyrus finally said, "OK, lady. You win. I concede to your superior skill on the firing range. But I'm not relinquishing my badge to you, and I'll have to insist on a rematch soon."

"Anytime, gunslinger. Now, what do you say we dig into that fried chicken?" she replied.

As they walked back toward the house, Annie slipped her hand around Cyrus's arm. Cyrus said nothing, but he felt a surge of something he hadn't felt for a long time. What was it? Desire?

They reached the house and walked inside. Cyrus ejected the clip from the Glock and double-checked to make sure there wasn't a live round left in the chamber. He set the weapon aside on the countertop.

Slowly and deliberately, he said, "I don't think I've ever met a woman quite like you, Annie. You cook, you shoot, and . . ."

"Whoa, stop right there, buster," she interrupted. "Couldn't you just say I'm beautiful?"

"I was just about to get to that, if you'd give me half a chance."

"Oh, sorry, Professor."

Then she turned and, without warning, kissed him gently on the mouth. Her lips were supple and inviting, and Cyrus pulled her close against his body. "Wow," he said softly. "That was a nice reward for not much of a compliment."

"I guess you've learned something valuable today. File that away for future reference."

"OK. Then let me also say you smell fantastic, and you're a hell of a good kisser."

"That'll work," she said and kissed him again, this time letting it last much longer.

They held each other for a long while. Annie's cheek rested against his chest and Cyrus buried his nose in her hair, taking in the fresh smell of citrus. He hadn't held a woman for a long time, and she felt good in his arms. Still, taking the next step would come with consequences. Were the consequences worth this one moment of desire? He wasn't sure. One part of him didn't give a shit about the consequences. That part of him only wished for implacable pleasure. But the disciplined, scientific part of him was well-rooted in the nature of cause and effect. If the *equal and opposite reaction* component of Newtonian physics had shown him anything, it was that once events were put in motion, things could be forever changed—not necessarily for the better. And of course there was the question of his emotional fragility. Was he really ready for this so soon after Janice had left him? Probably not. Hell, the divorce papers hadn't even been processed yet. What was he thinking?

Cyrus sighed deeply and gazed glassy-eyed out the kitchen window. He thought about his marriage and the love he'd thought he once had for Janice. He had been in grad school at the time. Young and naïve, and totally engrossed in his studies. Janice was working at the coffee shop around the corner from the Physics and Astronomy Library. Was it love? He'd thought so at the time, but in retrospect, he now had his doubts. She had offered him a convenient diversion from his studies, and he figured she had seen in him someone with the potential for a stable future. The sex was good, and they got along.

Maybe that should have been enough. But then again, maybe he didn't really know what love was. Was it more than a combination of sex and convenience and just *getting along*? If so, he really couldn't call their marriage a love-based one. In the end, that was probably why it fell apart. There just wasn't enough there to bind them together through the tough times. Maybe they had never really been in love at all.

"What are you thinking about, Cy?"

"Oh, nothing, really. I was just kind of thinking about generalities. About life. About love.

"Since the breakup of my marriage, I find myself hoping that love is more than what Janice and I had. It just has to be. I thought I loved her. I'm not sure I believe that anymore. I'm not sure our relationship ever grew beyond what we had in the very beginning. I think people who are really in love have something better than that. Something that gets better with age. I wonder if the best kind of love develops at a slow simmer, allowing feelings to steep and infuse, resulting in a sort of consommé of the soul. I know that must sound pretty stupid."

"Not so stupid, I don't think," Annie interjected quietly. "My husband and I had a love like that. We had dated in high school, but when I went away to college, our relationship cooled way down. It wasn't till I came back home that we realized how much we had in common. We started dating again, and it felt really good. Then after we got married, good became great, and great became awesome. It took about three years before our relationship had fully flowered. It was about five years after we were married that Todd was in his accident, and our love was snuffed out just like that, in the blink of an eye."

"I'm so sorry, Annie," Cyrus whispered, as they continued to hold one another, bodies pulled tightly together, faces hidden in the embrace.

"I guess I was a little too forward a moment ago, Cyrus. Since Todd died, living alone hasn't been easy. It's downright lonely sometimes. I let the moment get the best of me. I'm sorry if I made you uncomfortable."

"It's OK, Annie. I'm flattered, actually. At any other point in my life, I would've been wondering how I got so lucky. But right now it seems I have some demons to exorcise. Maybe we both do. What do you say we give each other some time, OK?"

"I'm good with that. Maybe we can let that *consommé of the soul* simmer for a while," Annie said, smiling up at him.

17

Bob and Mary Barnett returned home in the late afternoon after having been away for eleven days. They had been visiting Bob's parents in Missouri and had intended to stay for a full two weeks. As they pulled into their driveway and stopped next to the house, Bob turned to his wife and said, "I'm sorry, honey. I know that wasn't what you envisioned for our visit, and I didn't mean for it to happen again, but when Dad starts going on and on about his political views, I just can't stand it sometimes. I had to say something."

"But Bob, you do that every time with him. Can't you just let it slide?"

"Apparently not, I guess," he replied dejectedly.

"Well, at least we had eleven days without an argument between you two. That must be some kind of record."

Bob just shook his head as he opened the car door and got out. He opened the rear door and pulled out two large suitcases. With both hands full, he left the car door open as he carried the luggage to the front stoop. Mary gathered the rest of her things and followed him up the sidewalk to the house. Bob lifted the bags as he started up the front steps.

Suddenly he paused and said, "Take a look at that. Somebody has been tampering with the latch on the door." He set down the suitcases and peered through the small window of the door but saw nothing suspicious. When he pushed gently on the unlocked door, it swung open.

Bob and Mary looked at each other worriedly. "You think somebody's in there?" Mary whispered.

"I doubt it, but it sure looks like someone broke in at some point while we were gone," Bob said to reassure her. "You stay here while I take a look." Bob slowly opened the door all the way and stepped into the kitchen.

"Bob, be careful. Maybe we should call the sheriff."

"I doubt whoever broke in here stuck around. They're certainly long gone by now, I'm sure." But Bob wasn't really *that* sure as he crept nervously through the kitchen and turned the corner into the front room. He came back into the kitchen a few seconds later and said, "I don't see anything amiss. I'll be right back. I'm just going to take a quick look upstairs."

Mary stood on the front steps and watched from outside the door as Bob turned and headed for the staircase. As she waited for him to come back, she scanned the area outside the house. Everything seemed just as they had left it several days ago. Turning her attention back through the door to the staircase, she called, "Bob?" Bob did not reply. "Bob, is everything OK?"

She thought he should be back by now. Why wasn't he back yet? "Bob?" she cried out with much more urgency.

Mary entered the house and edged cautiously through the kitchen, her eyes darting nervously from side to side. She reached the staircase and peered upward. "Bob?" she called, almost at a whisper.

She slowly stepped up onto the first step and held firmly to the stair railing. Just as she raised her foot to mount the second step, a large hand forcibly covered her mouth and an arm gripped her body, squeezing her so tight it was difficult to breathe. Mary struggled, kicking to free herself as she screamed through the attacker's hand. Then she felt the hand release from her mouth and deliver a sharp blow to the side of her head. Everything went black.

***

Patterson walked into the living room and looked cautiously out through the curtains. He didn't see anything that concerned him, so he turned around and walked back up the steps to the master bedroom. He stood in the doorway staring at the terrified young woman who was gagged and tied to the bed. Mary's wrists were secured to the bedposts on either side of the bed, and she had pulled her legs up to her torso in a vain attempt to protect herself from this monster. Patterson could hear her crying faintly through the rag that was duct-taped in her mouth.

"Now, don't you worry none. I'm not going to hurt you, not so long as you cooperate," he said.

In his right hand he held a knife with a short but deadly blade, which he was nervously wiping on his slacks. He walked up to the side of the bed where Mary lay terrified and trembling.

He laid the blade flat on her cheek, caressing her with it. She quickly pulled her head away and let out a muffled scream.

"Don't worry, my dear. I'm not going to cut you with this. Not if you do just as I say."

He reached under her skirt and she began to kick desperately trying to repel his advances, but she was tied securely and had nowhere to go. He finally got ahold of her underpants and ripped them violently from her body, throwing them into the corner of the room. "There. That's better," he said calmly. The woman was now screaming hysterically into the wad of cloth in her mouth, which muffled the desperate sound to a dull moan.

"None of this would've been necessary if you hadn't returned home early from your little trip," Byron said as he paced next to the bed, watching her struggle. "I would've been gone from here if you'd stuck to your damn schedule."

On the other side of the wall, in the next bedroom, lay the body of Bob Barnett. His throat had been cut, and he lay covered in blood in the corner of the room where his killer had let him drop.

18

Cyrus was driving back home after a long day searching for the white Mercedes. He would check in with Tom soon, and then see what he could whip up for dinner. He was anxious to get home and out of this SUV. He could feel a pull in the muscles in his lower back, and he knew that the pain would only get worse if he didn't stop soon. What he needed was a cold beer and a warm shower, and he would be as good as new.

Cyrus turned onto the blacktop south of town and headed for Elby. This particular blacktop bordered the area he would be searching the next day. Just after he turned onto the road, he passed a newer two-story home where he noticed a sedan parked next to the house. The rear door on the driver's side was slightly ajar, which he found unusual. But he assumed that whoever lived there must be in the process of loading or unloading the vehicle. He took note of the name on the mailbox as he drove by. It simply said *Barnett*.

19

Cyrus was up early the next morning. The sun was still hiding below the horizon when he had completed his household chores and filled Molly's water and food bowls. By the time he started for town, it had risen and the Hyundai cast a shadow in the ditch to the left of the road. Cyrus watched the shadow as it danced along in the roadside vegetation at sixty miles per hour. He suddenly remembered what he had noticed at the Barnett home the evening before, and he decided to take a little detour down that blacktop to drive past their house.

As he neared the Barnett home, Cyrus slowed down and stopped in the middle of the blacktop in front of the Barnett place. The sedan was still parked next to the house, and the rear door was still open slightly.

Cyrus backed up a bit and then pulled into the driveway, parking just behind the sedan. He grabbed his phone off the seat, shoved it into his jacket pocket, and stood next to the Hyundai, making a wide scan of the area. Behind the house was a two-car garage, and further back on the property was a rather large metal shed. Seeing no movement in the windows of the house, he walked over to the garage and peered in the window on the side door. The garage was empty except for a Toro lawn mower.

Cyrus walked slowly back toward the shed and tried the latch on the sliding door. It was locked, so he walked around to a small window on the side of the building and looked inside. He noted nothing of interest: just a small utility tractor, a snow blower, and a workbench with numerous tools hanging from a pegboard. He had turned to head back to the house when out of the corner of his eye he noticed a patch of white reflecting the morning sun from beneath a pile of sapling branches. He walked to the pile of brush and pulled some of it aside, revealing the rear of a car with a chrome Mercedes logo clearly displayed on the trunk.

"Well, I'll be damned," he said softly. He turned toward the house, pondering his next move.

Byron was dozing in the easy chair downstairs when he was startled by the sound of a vehicle pulling into the driveway. He quickly checked to make sure the curtains were closed and all the lights out. "Damn it," he said under his breath. Peering through the curtains, Patterson could see that the vehicle was adorned with the Cane County Sheriff's Department emblem on the door. He watched a man get out of the vehicle and walk first toward the garage, and then up toward the storage shed. Patterson wondered if the visitor would discover the car. When the stranger came into view again, he was standing near the garage, talking into his cell phone. "Shit," said Byron emphatically.

"Hello?"

"Hey, Tom. It's me, Cyrus. I've got something here. I think it's the white Mercedes we're looking for."

"Where are you?" Tom replied excitedly.

"Over at the Barnett place. It's a two-story house on the blacktop . . ."

"Yeah, I know where it is," Tom interrupted. "Tell me what you see there."

Cyrus took about thirty seconds to explain about the open car door and his cursory search of the property.

"Have you seen any movement whatsoever in the house?" Tom asked.

"No, but I really haven't gotten very close yet."

Tom said, "Don't do a thing, Cyrus. You stay right where you are. Don't get close to that house. I'll be there in twenty minutes. I'm just leaving my house now, heading your way."

Cyrus walked carefully over to the Hyundai and focused on the windows of the house. He understood Tom's orders, but he couldn't help but wonder what was going on inside. Could the Barnetts be in serious danger? What if Patterson wasn't here anymore, and the Barnetts were in dire need of medical help? The twenty minutes it'd take for Tom to arrive could mean the difference between life and death. Cyrus had learned in Iraq that time is of the essence in medical emergencies. Yet he held his ground, determined to follow Tom's directive, at least for now.

Mary Barnett had been awake the entire night. She was emotionally drained and physically battered. Patterson had been in the room three different times with a knife on the bed stand, vowing to use it if Mary resisted. Tied to the bed and gagged, she had little recourse but to submit to his sexual assaults. By morning, she lay there exhausted and terrified, fearing when the bedroom door would open again.

Suddenly, she could hear a vehicle pull into the driveway. Intensely focused now, Mary began to struggle, pulling at the restraints around her wrists. Patterson had bound her securely, and she gave up after only a short time. She went silent and began to listen for any sound outside. She heard nothing for several minutes and decided she needed to do something desperate. She figured this might be her only chance of survival. She began trying to dislodge the gag from her mouth by using her shoulder. After several minutes, she was finally able to pull off the end of a strip of the duct tape and loosen some of the cloth in her mouth. Her screams were audible now, and she was determined to make as much commotion as she possibly could to attract the attention of whoever was out there.

Cyrus heard the screams, and he thought he saw movement on the first floor of the house just as the screaming began. He reached into the Hyundai and pulled the Glock from the glove compartment. He slammed the clip into the pistol and started toward the house, taking a wide berth as he did so. He noticed that the latch on the kitchen door was broken, and he slowly pushed the door open. Cyrus paused momentarily. He could now hear the screaming much more distinctly, coming from up the stairs. Suddenly the screaming stopped, followed by muted but audible sobs.

Cyrus called out, "This is the Cane County Sheriff's Department. Come out with your hands in the air, Patterson." Cyrus heard only faint sobs now. Wondering how close Tom was to the scene, Cyrus pondered whether he should wait for Tom or do what his instincts were demanding of him.

Cyrus stood motionless at the base of the stairs, listening to the frantic sobs coming from above. He began to move slowly up the staircase, trying not to make a sound, but the occasional creak of the steps betrayed his presence. Suddenly he heard a door slam shut on one of the bedrooms upstairs, and he quickly moved to the top of the staircase. He brought the Glock up and moved forward along the hallway. Two of the bedroom doors were closed, and he took a position to the side of the first one.

Hearing nothing, Cyrus pushed the door open and peeked inside. He was met by the repugnant smell of death. The body of a man lay in a heap in the corner amid what appeared to be a pool of dried blood. Cyrus surmised that the body had been there for a couple of days. After a quick scan of the room, he backed out into the hallway and moved to the second door. He raised his weapon and pushed the door open. Patterson had taken a position behind the woman on the bed. Her wrists were tied to the bedposts, and Patterson had clamped his left hand firmly over her mouth. His right hand held a knife with a small blade resting against her throat.

Patterson was the first to speak. "Well, well. If it isn't a sheriff wannabe. Where's the real sheriff? At home watching *Law and Order* on TV?" Then he said, "If you want this gal to live, you'll put that gun down."

"I think I'll leave it just where it is, if you don't mind," replied Cyrus, trying to appear in control of his emotions. "This won't end well for you, Patterson. You kill her and you're a dead man. You might as well drop that knife and lie down on the floor spread-eagle."

Just then, Cyrus thought he heard Tom's vehicle on the gravel driveway outside. A few seconds later, the door creaked open downstairs. Cyrus turned his head slightly, still watching Patterson closely, and called out, "Up here, Tom. I've got Patterson." Then he turned back and carefully drew a bead on the killer. "I could take you out right now if I wanted to."

"Not the way that gun is shaking. I figure you'd have just as much chance of putting a bullet in this nice lady's skull."

Cyrus knew Patterson was right. Killing members of Saddam Hussein's Republican Guard was one thing. This situation was quite another. He tried to steady the weapon. Just then he sensed movement behind him and turned, expecting to see Tom. Instead, what Cyrus saw was a glimpse of something swinging at him with considerable force. Before he could duck, a piece of two-by-four hit him squarely on the back of the head and sent him sprawling onto the bedroom floor. His gun fell, clattering across the wood flooring, coming to rest next to the opposite wall.

20

Cyrus opened his eyes and tried to focus. The midday sun shone through the window, illuminating the room's white walls, making him squint and use his hand to cover his face. He made note of the IV that was in his arm. After a moment, Cyrus surveyed his surroundings, recognizing the medical equipment and signature plastic furniture of a hospital room. His was the only bed in the room. He looked down, noting that someone had carefully tucked a blanket under his legs to keep him warm. Then he touched the back of his head and felt a thick bandage secured by tape.

A nurse walked into the room and immediately went to work adjusting his blanket and pillow. Cyrus tried to focus on her face, but he had trouble seeing clearly, and she appeared blurry and in a double image. Noticing that Cyrus was awake, the nurse spoke to him in soft tones. "Hello, Mr. Brandt. How are you feeling?"

Cyrus began to reply, but the dryness of his mouth caused him to cough instead. The nurse handed him a cup of water. After taking a sip, Cyrus shakily handed it back to the nurse and said, "Where am I? What happened to me?"

"You're at St. John's Hospital in Springfield, Mr. Brandt. You had a pretty nasty blow to the back of your head. You've been here for a couple of days now." She handed the water back to Cyrus and said, "Here, try to drink the rest of this. I should go notify the doctor that you're awake. He'll want to speak with you." She turned quickly and walked out the door.

Ten minutes later, Dr. Sam Miller walked into Cyrus's room, greeting him with a warm smile. "Good afternoon, Mr. Brandt. Welcome back to the land of the living. We were a bit worried about you, but I believe you'll be fine, so don't be too concerned about your condition. We will, however, need to keep you here for a while for observation."

"What happened to me?"

"You received a severe blow to the head. I'll leave it to Sheriff Bales to explain the circumstances surrounding your injury, but since you arrived, we've been treating the laceration on the back of your head and carefully monitoring the swelling of your brain. That seems to have abated, which is really good news. But you've suffered a bad concussion, and you'll be experiencing the effects of that for a week or two."

As he spoke, the doctor examined Cyrus, looking at the wound beneath the bandage and shining a small light in Cyrus's eyes. Then he said, "If you need anything at all, just let the nurses know. I'll be in the building for several more hours, so I'll try to check on you at regular intervals." He walked toward the door before turning to say, "There's someone here who has been waiting to talk to you." And then he was gone.

A few seconds later, Annie walked into the room and offered a worried smile as she walked up to Cyrus's bed. She laid a sympathetic hand on his arm and asked, "How are you doing, Deputy?"

"Been better," Cyrus replied as he tried to bring her into clear focus.

"You had us worried, you know?"

"The weird thing is, I still have no idea what happened to me."

"Don't you remember?"

"The last thing I can recall is getting up early, feeding Molly, and driving toward town for breakfast. Molly! Who's looking in on Molly? I've been here two days? Somebody needs to check on her!"

"Relax, Deputy. I already thought of that. I went out to your place to check on her before I came here yesterday, and I happened to run into your neighbor, Leo. He's been watching over Molly. Somehow he had heard about your incident, too. The two of them seem to get along just fine, though I have to say, that Leo is a pretty weird bird if you ask me."

"You probably said that about me, too, when you first met me."

"That's true. I probably did," Annie joked.

"Anyway, I don't remember much after leaving home that day, except that I think I stopped at the Barnett farm for some reason."

"The doc said you would probably have some memory loss due to the severity of the concussion. He also said it'd come back in time. I probably should have Tom tell you the details, but here's what I know."

Annie described what she knew about Tom arriving at the Barnett house and finding Cyrus unconscious in an upstairs bedroom. She also told him about the white Mercedes parked at the back of the property. What she chose not to tell him was what else Tom had found upstairs in that house.

Then she said, "So you don't remember anything about your attacker?"

Cyrus shook his head slowly. "Not really. But I assume that since I found the white Mercedes, it must've been Patterson who did this to me, right?"

"Looks that way, but Tom sure would like to talk to you about this whole incident." Annie's cell phone suddenly came to life, and she reached into her purse to retrieve it.

"Hi, Tom," she said. "I was just about to call you. Your deputy just woke up. That's the good news. The bad news is he doesn't remember much."

She paused to listen to Tom's response, then replied, "No, Tom. I wouldn't drive up here today. If I were you, I'd wait until tomorrow and see if his memory begins to return. You'd be wasting a trip up here today. Let me call you in the morning. I'll let you know how he's doing." After another short pause, she said, "OK, Tom, will do. I'll talk to you tomorrow then. Bye."

Annie turned to Cyrus and said, "Tom sends his best. If you're up to it, and you have something more to tell him, he'll come up tomorrow from Elby to speak with you. He's really frantic about this whole thing. You guys found the Mercedes, which should've helped you get to Patterson, but now he's disappeared without a trace. He could be anywhere. Anyway, according to the doc, you should gradually recall what happened to you prior to being attacked. That'll help get the investigation back on track. In the meantime, just get some rest, and we'll see if things are better in the morning."

Annie began to turn toward the door, but Cyrus stopped her. "So, Annie, are you just hanging around here at the hospital?"

"I've been here since they brought you in," Annie said.

"What about the diner?"

"I've got some good people helping out. Don't worry about that. You've got enough to worry about."

Cyrus paused before asking, "What did Tom say when you told him you were going to stay here at the hospital with me?"

"He didn't say much about it. He's a smart guy, though. I'm sure he imagines something's up between you and me."

"I suppose you're right, and that's what worries me. He is my boss, you know, and your brother. I don't need him thinking you and I are doing something we're not."

"Aw, what the hell? Let him think what he wants. I don't think you should be concerned about anything besides getting back on your feet, Professor."

"I said, don't call me . . . Oh, never mind," he replied, grimacing from the pain in his head.

21

Tom showed up the next morning at ten o'clock. He moved a chair close to the bed, took a seat, and began, "How are you feeling today, deputy?"

Cyrus replied, "Not too bad. They have me on some good drugs."

Annie walked into the room with two cups of coffee and handed one to Tom. She took a seat in a chair by the window.

Tom said, "Listen, Cyrus, I need to know what happened at the Barnetts'. An investigative team from the state police is swarming over the place as we speak, but there are some unanswered questions only you can answer."

"I am remembering a bit more of the incident. It's a bit hazy, but I think it's coming back gradually, in bits and pieces."

"What can you remember?"

Cyrus described how he had noticed the car parked next to the house, and how his curiosity had been piqued by the door that was left ajar. He was now able to remember his discovery of the white Mercedes, and his entry into the house after hearing the cries of Mrs. Barnett.

Cyrus continued, "When I entered the house, the woman's cries suddenly stopped and I was fearful that she was in danger, so I advanced up the stairs. That's when I opened the door to one of the bedrooms and discovered a deceased male. After that, my memory is still foggy, but I seem to remember opening another door and seeing a woman tied to a bed. I don't remember much after that."

"Good. This is all good. Listen, I drove up today suspecting that you wouldn't have total recall yet. But I thought it'd be helpful if I described what I found when I arrived at the scene. Maybe something I say will jog your memory. How's that sound to you?"

"Seems logical."

Tom went on. "After you called me, I drove directly toward your location, but it took me about twenty-five minutes to reach the scene. When I finally got there, it was dead quiet in the house."

"I think I heard you drive in. I seem to remember that when you entered the house, I called out to you. Do you remember that? Wait, now I remember seeing Patterson. He was holding a knife to a woman's neck. That's when you came into the house, right?"

"No. That can't be. When I got to the scene, there was no sign of Patterson. What I did find was the body of Bob Barnett in one bedroom, and you in the next bedroom."

"And the woman? Is she OK?"

"Sorry, Cyrus. Mary Barnett was tied to the bed and dead, with a bullet hole under her left eye."

"Shit!"

"The thing is, Cyrus, it might have been your weapon that killed her."

"Say what? What do you mean?"

"Well, your weapon wasn't recovered. Patterson must have taken it with him. I don't know if he had one to begin with, but he has one now."

"Damn! So now I've provided him with a firearm. That's just great." Cyrus shook his head and paused for a moment, thinking. "I wonder why he didn't kill me too?"

"Don't really know, unless he thought you were already dead. We found a four-foot piece of two-by-four at the scene that could've been what he used on you. Do you remember anything else that happened between the time you saw him holding the knife to Mary's throat and when he knocked you out?"

"Not really. I'll keep trying."

"I know you will. Just let me know as soon as you remember anything, OK?"

"Of course, Tom."

The door flew open, and Dr. Miller walked into the room to stand at the foot of Cyrus's bed. After the obligatory introductions, the doctor said to Cyrus, "Looks like you'll get to go home tomorrow. You shouldn't drive for about a week, though, and I highly suggest you rest at home for a few days until you feel well enough to resume normal activity. I'd also like a local doctor to check your head wound in a couple of days. We'll give you a prescription for pain, but I don't think that'll be much of a problem at this point. Any questions?"

"No, Doc. Thanks."

"I'll see you before we let you go tomorrow. Until then, enjoy your stay in this luxurious resort hotel." Then Dr. Miller turned and exited the room as quickly as he had entered it.

Tom said, "OK, Cyrus, I'm going to head home. I'll check in with you after you get back to town. I think Annie can take good care of you in the meantime." Tom gave Annie a wink and walked out of the room.

"Yup, he suspects something," Cyrus said after he left.

"Yeah, I guess so," Annie replied. She noticed Cyrus staring out into space, furrowing his brow. "What are you thinking, Cy?"

Cyrus was now animated, and he shouted, "Annie, go get Tom! Get him back here right now. Go!"

"But what is it? What . . ."

"Just do it. I need to tell him something important I just remembered."

Annie rushed out the door. Two minutes later, Tom and Annie were back in Cyrus's room.

"What's going on, Cyrus?" Tom asked.

"You remember how I said I heard you come into the house that day?"

"Yeah? So what?"

"I now remember I was standing in the doorway of the bedroom with my weapon raised. It was trained on Patterson, who had a knife to Mrs. Barnett's throat."

"OK, you told me that already."

"Yeah, but that's when I thought I heard you come in the house. Now I realize that wasn't you, because a moment after I called out to you, I was hit from behind with that piece of two-by-four while I had my gun trained on Patterson."

Tom grimaced and said, "Shit, so you're saying . . ."

"Yeah, he has an accomplice," Cyrus interrupted.

"That explains how Patterson left the scene, because we found your vehicle, the Barnetts' vehicle, and the Mercedes still at the scene. He must've left the scene with his accomplice. Well, that answers some of our questions. Unfortunately, that's also going to make this manhunt a lot more complicated."

"How so?" asked Annie.

"We have no description of the accomplice or the vehicle they left the scene in. We don't know if they're five hundred miles away, or nearby at another location. We have no idea where to look." Then he said, as if to himself, "We're back to square fucking one."

22

Annie drove Cyrus back to Elby the following morning. When they arrived at his house and got out of the car, Molly ran up with her tail thrashing from side to side, trying to jump up onto Cyrus and lick his face.

"Whoa there, girl. Take it easy now," said Cyrus as he pushed the animal off of him. He made a quick check of the dog's water and food bowls by the steps and could see that they had been recently attended to. Under his breath, he said to himself, "Thank you, Leo."

Cyrus was still a little unsteady on his feet. He had a bit of a headache, too. But he was glad to be home, and that alone was enough to make him feel better. He carefully pulled himself up the front steps and opened the door, holding it to let Molly into the house. Once everyone had entered, Annie quickly went upstairs to retrieve a blanket and pillow, and then pulled Cyrus over to the couch, trying to get him to lie down.

"Come on, Annie," he said. "I'm fine. Just let me be."

"No, you aren't fine. Here, at least lie down and put your feet up for a while. I'll bring you a cup of tea."

Cyrus reluctantly lowered himself onto the couch and pulled the blanket up over his lap. Molly clambered up next to him and rested her head on Cyrus's leg. He stroked the dog's soft coat, and let his gaze fall upon the fields outside the living room window. It was a beautiful June morning, but he knew July was just around the corner and the weather would soon be hot and humid. As much as he hated Illinois summers, he knew the Illinois corn crop would absolutely love the heat and humidity. Soon the crops would blanket the landscape for as far as the eye could see. As he took note of the corn and soybeans already beginning to emerge in the fields around him, he noticed a vehicle driving down the road toward his house. He recognized it as Liz's Cherokee. Cyrus called to Annie, "Annie, could you bring me that stack of letters sitting next to the microwave, please?"

"Sure," she replied from the kitchen. A few seconds later she walked out of the kitchen with the letters in her hand. "Are these the ones?"

"Yeah. I see the mail gal coming down the road, and I've been meaning to give these letters to her. Molly retrieved them from the field on the other side of the road. They were left there by the twister. The damn thing blew Liz's mail delivery all over kingdom come that day. I tried to help her pick it all up, but I guess there was a lot of it we couldn't find. Here, I'll take them out to her."

"No you don't, buddy. You stay where you are. I'll take them out. You just rest for now. Your tea should be ready about the time I get back." Then she walked out the door and headed for the mailbox by the road.

Liz pulled up and looked surprised to see Annie standing there waiting for her. Liz said, "Well, hi. You're Annie from the diner, right?"

"Yup, I'm just helping Cyrus get situated since he got back from the hospital. I'm sure you've heard about the incident over at the Barnett place."

"Sure did. Everybody in town is talking about it. Hey, Sheriff Bales is your brother, right?"

"Yes, he is."

"So you must know something about this whole thing, right? Does he have any leads on where this guy went?"

"Well, Tom doesn't share too much official business with me, but no, I don't think so. That Patterson guy could be anywhere."

"People around here are pretty uptight about this, but I think that guy is probably far away from here by now. I'm sure there's nothing to worry about."

"I hope you're right," Annie said.

"So how is the patient doing?" Liz asked as she nodded toward the house.

"Oh, I think he'll live. He got a pretty bad concussion, so it'll take a while before he's thinking straight again." Annie handed the letters to Liz. "Evidently Cyrus's dog has been finding these letters in the field over there."

"Thanks, I appreciate it. If the dog finds any more, you can just stick them in the mailbox here, and I'll know where they came from. OK, I better get going. Oh, here's today's mail for Mr. Brandt," Liz said as she gave a handful of letters and magazines to Annie. "Give him my best."

"I'll do that. Thanks," Annie replied as Liz sped off in a cloud of dust, throwing a few pieces of gravel as she accelerated down the road.

When Annie came back into the house, Cyrus asked, "Anything interesting in the mail?"

She replied, "Are you expecting anything, like maybe your membership card from the Genius Physicist Club? Or perhaps this month's edition of the Hermit Lifestyle Weekly?"

"Very funny. No, I'm not expecting anything as exciting as those." Cyrus paused for a moment and said, "You know, I probably shouldn't burden you with this, but I've been waiting to receive the final papers for my divorce. They should've arrived by now. I'm worried that Janice is dragging her feet on this for some reason. I think she and that lawyer are up to something. Why else would I still be waiting on those papers? It's been a couple of weeks since they told me the papers were in the mail. With my luck, they're probably trying to renegotiate the divorce settlement, the bastards. I guess I'm going to have to find a lawyer to get some closure on this. Do you know anybody?"

"You should go see Max Riegel. He's the best lawyer in town. His office is down the street from the diner and a block to the right, on Prairie. He's a gruff old guy, but he knows his stuff."

"Great, thanks. Hopefully I won't need to go see him. Those papers will most likely show up in my mailbox tomorrow. I just want this frigging divorce over and done with."

23

On Monday morning, Cyrus was feeling much better and accepted Annie's offer to come pick him up for a ride into town. She needed to be at the diner by 5:30 a.m., and though this was a bit early for Cyrus, he didn't think he should be driving just yet. Cyrus knew Tom was having a nine o'clock sit-down with Trooper John Corbit and Agent Robert Backus, the chief investigator from the Illinois State Police, who had been put in charge of the case. Tom had requested that Cyrus be there to recount the events of that day at the Barnett house. If Cyrus needed to be up at sunrise to get a ride with Annie, that's what he intended to do. He figured he could just hang out at the diner for a couple of hours, have some breakfast, and try to organize all his recollections of the incident.

By the time he walked toward the Cane County Sheriff's Office, Cyrus was satiated by Annie's breakfast special and wired by about eight cups of coffee. He walked through the front door past Sarah, who gave a nod toward the back room. Cyrus could already hear men's voices speaking in serious tones before he entered the conference room. As he walked in, the three men's faces turned to greet him.

Tom spoke first. "Hey, Cyrus, how are you feeling? You're looking a bit better than the last time I saw you."

"I'm doing much better. Thanks, Tom."

"Cyrus, I'd like to introduce you to the two gentlemen I told you about." Motioning to Corbit, he continued, "This is John Corbit, the state police trooper assigned to our district, and over here is Agent Robert Backus, who's been assigned to head up this case."

"Glad to meet you, gentlemen," Cyrus replied.

Tom continued, "Let's get right to it, shall we? I'm going to let Robert take over at this point, since he's taking the lead on this thing. Robert?"

Robert began slowly, choosing his words carefully. "I would like to make something very clear. Although I've been assigned to lead this investigation, I want you to understand that my job is primarily to help Tom's department get the resources needed to find Patterson. I won't be throwing my weight around here. If this case is to be solved, it'll be solved by the people who have their fingers on the pulse of this community. That's you guys," he said, looking straight at Tom and Cyrus. "These are your people living around here. If we're going to find Patterson, it'll most likely be because of a tip we get from someone living nearby. And that tip will come to you, Tom, or to one of your deputies. Not me. Do we understand each other?"

Tom, Cyrus, and John all nodded in unison as Robert pushed forward. "Now, let's start from the beginning to make sure we're all clear on the details of this case. Cyrus, we're here today to hear from you. We need you to describe, in as great a detail as possible, what you remember about the incident at the Barnett place."

The next hour focused on Cyrus's recounting of that morning, beginning with his curiosity about the open car door in the Barnetts' driveway. The three other men took careful notes and asked probing questions throughout, trying to squeeze every detail from Cyrus's still-sketchy memory. When they were satisfied he had told them everything he could recall, they sat for a moment in thoughtful silence.

Finally, Robert said, "Thoughts, gentlemen?"

John spoke first. "I've been wondering why Patterson came here to this particular area. I suppose perhaps Patterson and Fromm simply drove in no particular direction during their escape, just trying to get as far away as possible as fast as possible. But I find that really hard to accept. Things usually happen for a good reason. We know Patterson is a pretty smart guy. I think we should assume that he had a plan, and that he came here because of that plan."

"I tend to agree," said Robert.

Tom added, "Me too. This wasn't a random choice on his part. I might have accepted the idea of him being here by chance, except for one thing: the accomplice who clobbered Cyrus. That person could very well be someone from this community who was part of the overall escape plan."

Nodding his head affirmatively, Robert added, "A relative? An ex-con he met in prison?"

"A girlfriend?" Cyrus offered.

"Yes, any of those are possibilities," said Robert. "We need to explore all of them. My people can look into the connection between Patterson and other inmates at Pontiac and the other facilities where Patterson has been incarcerated."

John interjected, "And we should also check phone calls and visitation records at the prison to see who, if anybody, Patterson has been talking to lately."

Tom added, "My guys will look into possible relatives in the area. I know of some Pattersons around Elby, and there are probably a few I don't know about further out in the rural areas. Maybe we'll get lucky."

Cyrus had been quiet for a minute, and now he spoke up. "I have another thought. While we look for the reason Patterson came to Cane County, shouldn't we also ask why he ended up at the Barnett place? Was that simply a random choice on his part?"

"Good thought," said Robert. "I suspect there's a good chance that was also a strategic move on his part. At least it wouldn't hurt to assume that at this point."

For another forty-five minutes, the four men finalized a plan to investigate all the questions posed thus far. When they rose to leave, Tom said to Cyrus, "Tomorrow there'll be a funeral for the Barnetts just outside of town at the Methodist church. They were known by most of the people around here and were well-liked. I'll be going to the funeral, but I understand if you'd rather not, since your only encounter with them wasn't a very pleasant one."

Cyrus replied, "You know, Tom, I think I should go. The more we both know about the Barnetts, the closer we may get to Patterson."

"I agree. I was hoping you'd say that. The funeral's at one o'clock. I'll come out and pick you up around twelve-thirty, OK?"

"I hate to make you drive out for me, but I suppose I should avoid driving a bit longer. Thanks, Tom. I'll see you tomorrow."

24

After the meeting, Cyrus strolled down to the diner just as the lunch crowd was descending upon it. He took a seat at the counter, and Annie poured him a cup of coffee.

"Don't let me drink any more of this stuff. If I drink another cup of your coffee, I'll need to strap a collection bag to my leg and catheterize myself to avoid pissing my pants."

"You always say the sweetest things, Dr. Brandt," Annie replied.

"That would be *Deputy* Brandt to you. Do you have anything worth eating back there in the kitchen?"

"Wow, you must be vying for Customer of the Week or something."

"Sorry, Annie, I'll behave myself. I'll take your special, whatever it is. I'm sure it'll be great."

"That's more like it. Coming right up, Deputy."

A few minutes later, Annie set Cyrus's plate down on the counter, saying, "So I guess the funeral is tomorrow. Will you be going?"

"Yeah, I guess so. Tom will come pick me up," he said. Then, leaning in her direction, he continued at a whisper, "Unless you're thinking of becoming my personal chauffeur."

"Boy, that really sounds enticing, but I'd better not. This poor diner has really missed me since I've been babysitting you. I think you're on your own tomorrow, buster, but let me know if you need anything," she said with a playful smile. "I'll see you at the funeral tomorrow, then."

"There is one more thing you could do for me, Annie. Since you brought me to town this morning do you think I could get a ride home this afternoon? I'd really appreciate it."

"Oh, yeah. No problem, Cy. Can you give me an hour or so till the lunch crowd is out of here?"

"Of course. That'll give me a chance to go see if I can locate that lawyer you told me about."

After Cyrus finished his lunch, it didn't take him long to find the law office of Max Riegel. The office was located in a modest stand-alone building that appeared to have been a small single-family home at some point. The small bell hanging on the doorknob jingled as he opened the door, and he was immediately immersed in the pungent odor of musty books and legal papers. Shelves lined the rear wall of the front room and were filled with large black law books and countless binders, most of which appeared to have been untouched for years, based upon the thick coating of dust covering them. On the opposite side of the room sat a large oak desk that supported numerous stacks of papers. Nearby stood a small table with an ancient coffee machine and a few mismatched coffee mugs. A voice from the next room growled through the door, "Be right with you. Make yourself at home."

Cyrus took a seat in front of the desk and craned his neck to look through the door at the man in the adjoining room. The lawyer was leaning awkwardly over a copy machine, gazing into its innards. In his hand was what appeared to be a plastic bottle of toner. Finally, he sighed, set the bottle down on the floor, and walked into the front room. "Sometimes I miss the old mimeograph machines. At least I knew how to fix those damn things," he said as if to himself. Turning to Cyrus, he said cheerfully, "Hi, I'm Max Riegel."

Cyrus stood up. "Cyrus Brandt. Good to meet you, Mr. Riegel."

"You can just call me Max. What brings you to my little piece of paradise?"

"I just moved to the area about seven months ago, and now I find myself in need of some legal advice regarding my divorce settlement. A friend of mine here in Elby told me you're the best lawyer in town."

Max gave out a snort and replied, "Did that friend also tell you I'm the only lawyer in town?"

"No. She failed to offer that bit of information."

"So who's this friend who referred you to my office?"

"I was talking to Annie Branson, and she . . ."

"Ah, Annie," he interrupted. "She sends me a lot of business, bless her little heart. She's doing a good job keeping old Uncle Max in business."

"*Uncle Max*? You're related?"

Max plopped down in his desk chair. "Well, you know how it is in small towns like this. Most of the people here are related in some way. You'd think with all the inbreeding here we would all have IQs of fifty-five by now. Fortunately, we have just enough outsiders like you coming into town to diversify the gene pool."

"Well, I was actually raised right outside of town here, so I'm part of the local gene pool as it turns out. Besides, I don't know if I'll be sticking around here long enough to do any procreating anyway."

"Well, that's a shame. We could use a bit more procreating in this community. So what can I help you with today— your divorce settlement? Why aren't you talking to the lawyer who's been handling your divorce?"

Sheepishly, Cyrus looked down at his lap and said, "Well, that's one of the problems. I didn't retain a lawyer. I should have."

"Yup, bad move on your part. Well, tell me about it."

Cyrus handed the old man an unofficial draft he had previously received from Janice's lawyer, and proceeded to describe the timeline thus far.

"It just seems like it's taking way too long to get the final paperwork. I'm worried maybe they're planning to renegotiate the settlement. Now that I've inherited my folks' place, I'm worried they'll try to get a piece of that."

The lawyer took several minutes to study the initial settlement papers. Finally, he looked up and said, "I've done a lot of divorces in my day. Way more than I wish I had. Divorce is truly one of the great tragedies of modern society. There's nothing like a divorce to turn a reasonably sane and generous person into a greedy son of a bitch. I've seen it happen so many times."

Max paused and looked down at the papers in front of him. "OK, so from what I'm seeing here, your wife and her lawyer really took you to the cleaners—but you already knew that. They must realize that if they start renegotiating the terms of the settlement, everything will be back on the table. If they in fact are doing this, they're taking a big chance by risking what they've already gained in the hopes of squeezing more out of you.

"Now listen, Cyrus, we don't even know that's the case here. For all we know, all the t's are crossed and the i's dotted and the lawyer just forgot to drop the final papers in the office mailbox. You may be all worked up over nothing. Having said that, you could use this to your advantage. You could let them know you now have a lawyer, and you welcome the idea of reopening negotiations. You could probably get back some of the assets you've lost. On the other hand, you'd be putting your inheritance on the table. It's up to you what you want to do."

"I just want this over, the sooner the better."

"I'll tell you what, I'll give your wife's lawyer a call to see what's going on. I'll get back with you in a couple of days, OK?"

"Thanks, Max. I appreciate your help."

"Well, don't thank me yet, but you'll be hearing from me. And you can thank Annie for me for the business next time you see her."

25

The next day at twelve-thirty sharp, Tom pulled into Cyrus's driveway. He got out of the cruiser and waited as Cyrus came out of the house, locked the front door, and walked toward him. In an adjacent field, Tom could see a tractor pulling a wagon-like implement with a large tank mounted on top of it. A couple of long appendages extended out from the implement, spraying something onto the plants that grew in fifteen-inch rows. As he watched, the tractor suddenly came to a stop, and Tom could hear that the driver had turned off the engine. Tom could now hear strange sounds coming from the tractor, and he tried hard to ascertain what they were.

"What is that sound?" he asked as Cyrus approached. Tom cocked his head in the direction of the tractor.

Cyrus paused to listen, and a smile spread across his face. "Isn't it obvious?" he replied teasingly.

"What do you mean?"

"It's the Beer Barrel Polka, of course."

"What the hell are you talking about?"

"Here," said Cyrus. He reached into Tom's cruiser and grabbed the binoculars that were on the front seat.

Tom trained the binoculars on the man he could now see sitting inside the tractor's cab. The man appeared to be playing the clarinet.

"Well, I'll be damned. That *is* the Beer Barrel Polka!

About fifteen minutes later, the two men arrived at the Elby United Methodist Church, where Bob and Mary Barnett's friends and relatives were gathering to offer their final respects. The church stood off the road about fifty yards, and the gravel parking lot was already full of cars. Tom pulled his vehicle over to the side of the road where others were also parking. Cyrus noted that the old church was in dire need of updating, but through the years the congregation had done a credible job of maintaining it in relatively good condition. Tom and Cyrus climbed the cement steps and entered the narthex of the church. Without a word, they sat down in the back row, giving acknowledging nods to people they knew sitting around them.

Cyrus wondered if any of these attendees might be the accomplice in the murder of the Barnetts. He scanned the crowd as if he would notice a furtive glance or odd behavior that might implicate someone. Who was he kidding? Even if Patterson's accomplice was in attendance, it wouldn't matter. All Cyrus could see were the backs of hundreds of heads, all positioned stoically on rigid shoulders in the pews in front of him.

For the next hour, Cyrus listened to prayers, personal reflections, congregational hymns, a sermon, and responsive readings. Following the concluding remarks and the final "amen," the crowd slowly got to its feet and shuffled toward the door, speaking in hushed, reverent tones. Tom and Cyrus were standing outside the church when Annie walked by with a young woman who was still wiping away tears of grief.

"Hi, Tom, Cyrus. Nice service, wasn't it?" she said.

Tom replied, "Yes, it sure was. There're a lot of people here. Bob and Mary were much loved in this community."

Turning toward the young woman, Annie said, "Tom and Cyrus, this is Emily Baxter. She's one of Mary's friends from the church here. Emily, this is my brother Tom and our friend Cyrus Brandt. Tom is the local sheriff."

"We're sorry for your loss, Ms. Baxter," said Cyrus.

"That's Mrs. Baxter, but thank you. Mary was a good friend, and a God-fearing woman. I'll dearly miss her."

"It appears a lot of people around here will," Tom offered.

Emily went on, "I just can't believe this happened. What's wrong with this world? One day Mary is here, the next day, some maniac murders her. It's insane. Yesterday was the day Mary said she'd be back from their trip to Missouri, and we were going to meet this very afternoon to plan the church soup supper. Now she's gone. I just can't believe it." Her words trailed off as she began to weep quietly. Annie put her arm around Emily, and they walked away the parking lot.

Without speaking, Tom and Cyrus walked to the cruiser, and Tom pulled out of the lot heading for town. After a couple of minutes, Tom took a deep breath and let out a sigh. "This guy has fucked up a lot of peoples' lives here in Elby. It's our job to fix this thing, but we don't have jack shit for clues as to where he is or who his accomplice is." Tom continued to shake his head as he drove on.

Minutes passed as they sat silently in thought, staring at the road ahead of them. Suddenly Cyrus looked at Tom and said, "You need to turn the car around and go back to the church right now!"

"Why, what's wrong?"

"Nothing, but just do it, and I'll explain."

Tom found a place to maneuver the car around and headed back toward the church as Cyrus explained, "Mrs. Baxter just said the Barnetts weren't expected back home until yesterday. Isn't that what she said?"

Tom nodded. "Yes, I think that's right."

"We need to ask her if she's certain about their travel plans, because if she's right, we may have been correct in assuming that Patterson didn't just happen upon their house by chance. Someone may have known the Barnetts would be gone until the end of the month, and may have instructed Patterson to hide out at their house in the meantime."

Tom finished his thought, saying, "So, if that's the case, and this accomplice was privy to their travel plans, who might we be talking about here?"

"Church friends like Mrs. Baxter, family, or a neighbor, perhaps?" Cyrus replied.

"That's a large group of suspects, but at this point it's the only lead we have," Tom said as he pulled into the church lot, where Annie and Emily were conversing with an elderly couple.

Annie spotted Tom and Cyrus as they stepped out of the car. She excused herself from the conversation and walked up to Tom, asking, "What's going on?"

"We need to talk to Emily again. Could you bring her over here when she's finished speaking with those folks?"

"Sure, I guess so," Annie said. She turned and walked away, returning a few moments later with Emily in tow.

"Annie said you wanted to talk to me?" Emily asked.

"Yes. We're sorry to bother you, but we have to know if you're certain that Mary told you she would be returning home yesterday."

"Why is that important?" Emily asked.

"We're trying to develop an accurate timeline in this case. When did Mary tell you this?"

"I talked to her the day before she left. That was just over two weeks ago. I remember because we had our first planning meeting for the soup supper that day, and she said they were leaving the next day for a two-week trip to Missouri. So we planned our next meeting accordingly."

"You're certain about that?" Tom pressed.

"Yes, I'm positive. She was to return on the twenty-seventh, and so we set our meeting for the twenty-eighth. That's today, right?"

"Thank you, Mrs. Baxter," Tom said as he abruptly turned and walked toward his car. Cyrus nodded and smiled to Annie and Emily as he turned to follow him. As they got into the vehicle, Tom said, "Are you free right now to go to the office with me? We need to get John and Robert on the horn to bring them up to speed on this."

"I've got no plans other than catching bad guys," Cyrus replied as the car sped toward Elby.

Ten minutes later, Tom and Cyrus were at the sheriff's office. Tom spent the next twenty minutes talking to Agent Backus on the phone, explaining what they now knew about the truncated travel plans of the Barnetts, as well as the possible steps to take forward at this point. As Tom finally hung up the phone, he said to Cyrus, "Robert said we may have to talk to Bob and Mary's church friends, although that may be a long shot. He thinks we should interview their neighbors first. The Barnetts most likely notified one of their neighbors about their trip out of town, hoping the neighbor would keep an eye on the place. He wants us to go out there first thing in the morning to get going on this."

"Isn't he coming out to help with the interviews?"

"No. He wants us to take point on this. He's pretty busy running background checks on people in the area who may have crossed paths with Patterson in the past. He's also trying to determine if Patterson has any relatives in the area. He should have that information to me sometime soon. And now, with what we found out today, his people are going to need to look into the neighbors living around the Barnett home. Even if he doesn't come up with anything suspicious in the background checks, we still could be looking at a situation where a trusted neighbor happened to mention Bob and Mary's travel plans to someone else, who in turn informed Patterson. In short, we all have our work cut out for us. Let's get started by nine in the morning. Do you want me to come out and pick you up?"

"No, Tom. I think I'm up to driving again. I'll meet you here in the morning. I do need a ride back home right now though. Maybe I can get Sarah to drive me out there.," Cyrus said as he rose from his chair.

"No, I'll take you back. No problem. One more thing, Cyrus. How are you coming with that firearm training?"

"I've been goin' after it, Tom. It was a piece of cake. A couple days before my incident at the Barnett place, I was over at the ISP Academy finishing up. The paperwork should be coming through soon."

Tom reached into his desk drawer and pulled out a handgun in a black leather holster. As he placed it on the desk in front of him, he said, "You'll be needing another one of these, I suppose. It's just a .38 caliber, but I assume you've used one of these before."

"Yeah, I have. Thanks, Tom," Cyrus replied as he picked up the weapon.

"And don't forget to sign for it," said Tom as he handed Cyrus the required paperwork. "Here, take these, too," he said as he handed Cyrus a box of shells. "Let's hope we don't need any of this. And I suppose it's too much to ask that you keep it locked in your vehicle, after what's happened."

"The way things are going, Tom, I probably should keep it close by. I have a feeling this thing will be coming in handy."

"Unfortunately, I have that same feeling," the sheriff replied.

26

It was 8:45 a.m. when Cyrus pulled his Hyundai into the lot behind the sheriff's office. As he exited the vehicle, he noticed Tom standing there waiting for him. Cyrus said, "Boy, you must be itchin' to hit the road."

Tom walked toward his own car, saying, "Let's get going. Robert just called me. I think we have a live one."

Tom headed south out of town as he filled Cyrus in on what Robert had told him. "It appears we have a person of interest who lives across the road and down about a quarter mile from the Barnetts' home. Apparently he's done some time down in the facility in Marion. His name's Ed Chambers. I haven't had any interaction with him since I've been around here, but I've heard a few people mention him. He's something of a recluse and rarely comes into town. But here's the interesting thing: Robert's people cross-checked his record with Patterson's, and it seems both of them were incarcerated at Marion for a brief time before Chambers was released. This was about ten years ago. It could mean something. Then again, maybe not. But it seems too coincidental, don't you think?"

"Yeah. These days I'm becoming less and less of a believer in the concept of coincidence," Cyrus replied. "What was Chambers in for?"

"Through the years he's been in trouble for nonviolent crimes for the most part, and when he was in Marion, he was serving a five-year stint for theft."

"Doesn't sound exactly like the murdering type."

"No, but guys like Ed who spend even a little time in prison end up associating with some really bad people. They can have their worldview changed in a hurry. Prisons are less rehabilitation centers than they are breeding grounds for most criminals. We've known that for years."

Tom slowed his cruiser as he approached Chambers's property, then passed the mailbox and turned into the driveway. He drove a ways along the narrow driveway, among the locust trees and honeysuckle bushes, before they spotted the white mobile home. It showed clear signs of neglect, with more patches of rust than it had of white, and it sat next to a large red metal machine shed, which didn't look to be in much better shape. An aging Dodge Ram pickup was parked in front of the mobile home, and beyond the pickup lay a variety of discarded artifacts: pieces of old farm equipment, worn-out lawn furniture, scrap metal, and numerous tree limbs of all shapes and sizes.

The sheriff pulled a small spiral-bound notebook and a pen out of his jacket pocket and jotted down the license plate number of the pickup truck. Then he reached into the glove compartment and retrieved a similar notebook, handing it to Cyrus. "Take good notes while we talk to this guy, OK? Record as much detail as possible. Have you got a pen?"

"Yep. Got it," Cyrus replied as he slipped the notebook into his pocket.

"Also, take note of his demeanor as he responds to questions. The way he acts can tell us a lot. Let me do most of the talking, but feel free to press him on any issue. Let's not get this guy riled up, though. At this point, we want him to think we're simply talking to neighbors of the Barnetts, which I guess we are, right? All we have on this guy is totally circumstantial right now."

Tom and Cyrus got out of the car and cautiously walked toward the front door of the trailer. Tom motioned for Cyrus to stand to the side as he climbed the three steps and knocked on the metal screen door. Fifteen seconds passed, and Tom knocked again before retreating to the bottom of the steps. Cyrus noticed someone peaking through the curtains of a window on the side of the mobile home. He motioned to Tom, who shouted, "Cane County Sheriff's Department. We're here to speak with Ed Chambers."

A man's voice came through the door. "What do ya want?"

"We'd like to talk to you, Mr. Chambers. That's all. Why don't you open up and let us come in?"

"You got a warrant?" was his reply.

"Why? Do you think we should get one? Are you trying to hide something? We just want to talk. That's all."

The man opened the front door a crack and gazed through the screen door. "Can I see your badges? How do I know you are who you say you are?"

"Here, take a gander at this," Tom said as he slapped the badge against the screen. Cyrus also held his badge up where the man could see it.

"I don't like people coming around here. And I especially don't like the law hanging around."

"Well, you know, Mr. Chambers, we don't much like being here either, but we have a job to do. Can we just come in and ask you a few questions?"

The man considered this for a moment and then said, "Hold on. I'll come out there to talk to you. Now back away from the door."

Cyrus and Tom did as he requested, positioning themselves about ten feet apart among the junk strewn about Chambers's front yard.

Cyrus looked around and said, "He isn't going to win any Good Housekeeping awards. That's for sure." Tom ignored him and kept his eyes trained on the door.

Chambers slowly opened the screen door and edged down the steps. He carried a baseball bat, holding it in both hands as if he would need to use it.

Tom quickly put his hand on his sidearm, saying, "Now Mr. Chambers, you need to put that down before you come any closer."

"Why should I? This is my property. I have a right to protect myself on my own property. I think I'll hold onto it if you don't mind, Sheriff," Chambers replied.

"He's a real friendly sort, isn't he?" Cyrus said to Tom under his breath.

Tom's eyes were intent on the man, and he said, "Look, Ed, we can ask you some questions here, or we can require you to come down to the office. Either way, we need to talk to you, and we sure aren't going to do it like this. It'll be a lot more convenient for all of us if we just take care of this here without any problems. When we're done, we'll be on our way." Tom paused, then said, "So if you'll just put the bat down . . ."

Chambers stared straight at Tom for a few moments, then slowly walked over to a large maple tree and leaned the baseball bat against it. Tom took his hand off his weapon and pulled out his notebook and pen. Cyrus did likewise. Chambers motioned for Tom and Cyrus to take a seat at a nearby picnic table.

They all sat down and Chambers said, "So, what do you want?"

Tom began, "Have you heard what went on at your neighbor's place last week?"

"Not really, though I did notice a bunch of state police driving by blaring their damn sirens while I was trying to sleep. When was that, last Wednesday?"

"Yes, it was. So you don't know what happened over there?"

"No. Why would I? I don't get out much."

"Your neighbors, the Barnetts, were brutally murdered. Do you know anything about that?"

"You mean the couple who live up that way?" he asked, pointing through the trees.

"Yup. That house right up the road there."

"Jeez! Those are the Barnetts, you say?"

"Yup. So apparently you don't know them very well."

"Nope. I like to keep to myself."

"Did you know they were out of town for a while, and planning to return this week?"

"Hell, I don't give a shit about what my neighbors do or where they go. It's a free country. They can do whatever they want. It's their own damn business what they do."

"So you were home last week when the state police came to their house. Is that right?"

"Yeah, so what? I was sleeping late, like I usually do, when those damn sirens woke me."

"Was anybody else here with you who can verify that?"

"Does it look like anybody else lives here?" Chambers said as he spat into the dirt next to his boot.

"Do you know a Byron Patterson?" Tom suddenly asked.

"No. Should I? Who is he?"

"He's a person of interest in the murders. You probably knew him at Marion when you were in prison down there."

Chambers was suddenly agitated. "Now wait just a minute. What're you talking about? Are you trying to say I had something to do with the Barnetts' murders just because I served some time? I don't know any Byron Patterson. That place, Marion, has a crap load of inmates. When I was there, I tried not to associate with any of them."

"Well, maybe you didn't, maybe you did. We know you were in the same cell block with Patterson. It seems highly unlikely

92

that you didn't encounter him at some point. So did you or didn't you?"

"There were a lot of guys in that cell block. It'd take a long time to rub shoulders with all of them, and besides, Patterson was only there for a short . . ." Ed stopped mid-sentence, realizing what he had just said.

Tom looked him dead in the eyes and said, "So, you did know Patterson. If I were you, I would be a bit more forthcoming with your answers, Mr. Chambers."

"So I might have talked to him once or twice. No big deal. That doesn't mean anything."

"Well, here's the thing, Ed. You knew Patterson in prison. You live next door to two people who were probably murdered by Patterson. And you have no one to verify your whereabouts at the time of those murders. What would you think if you were us?"

"Sounds pretty circumstantial, if you ask me. Why are you harassing me anyway? He probably committed those murders all by himself. Why do you think I was involved? Do you think there were two of them?"

"If there were two, you sure would be a prime suspect, don't you think? We'll most likely want to speak with you again, so don't plan on leaving the area."

"I got nowhere else to go," Ed replied. With considerable effort, he got up from the picnic table and slowly made his way back toward his front steps. He stopped briefly and turned to mutter, "If you come here again, come with a warrant. I don't much like talking to you two." Then he climbed the steps, one step at a time, and shuffled into his trailer, slamming the door.

Cyrus shoved his notebook and pen into his vest pocket as he said, "Well, Tom, what do you think?"

Tom replied, "I think he knows more than he's telling us. I'm going to the county courthouse this afternoon to see about a warrant. Not sure if we'll get it, but this guy is involved. I just know it."

Cyrus gazed in the direction of the mobile home and said, "Well, Chambers may be involved with Patterson, but he isn't the guy who beaned me at the Barnetts' house."

"How's that?"

"Did you see how much effort it took him to climb those front steps?"

"Yeah, he's not the picture of health," Tom agreed.

"Well, he sure as hell couldn't be the person who came up the stairs at the Barnetts' home and laid me flat with that piece of lumber. It would've taken him all day to get up those steps."

Tom and Cyrus were walking back to the car when Tom stopped suddenly next to Chambers's old Dodge pickup. "What's that look like to you?" he asked Cyrus.

Tom crouched down and picked up what looked to be a cigarette butt on the ground just below the driver's door. Cyrus moved in closer to take a look and said, "Well, that sure isn't a Lucky Strike butt, is it?"

Tom brought it close to his nose and took a sniff. "That's weed, all right." He took a quick look back at the mobile home, where he thought he could see Chambers peeking through the window curtains. Then he walked to his cruiser and reached through the open window into the glove compartment, retrieving a ziplock bag and placing the butt inside.

"This just might be the thing that'll get me that warrant."

27

Cyrus awoke early the next day and got ready to drive into town. As he slipped on his jacket and gazed through the window, he could see that a gentle rain had just begun to fall. He considered how the crops in the surrounding fields would enjoy the much-needed nourishment. As he walked out the door toward the Hyundai, he noticed Molly making her way up the driveway with something hanging from her mouth.

"Christ, is there no end to this?" Cyrus said, taking a large, damp envelope from Molly. He froze as he recognized the return address of his wife's lawyer. Turning back toward the house, he walked quickly up the steps and into the kitchen.

He was about to rip the letter open when he noticed a piece of paper stuck to the back of the envelope. It appeared to be a receipt from a McDonald's restaurant, but the rain had caused the ink to run, rendering it almost unreadable. Cyrus peeled it off the envelope and was reaching to place it in the trash when he noticed a couple of words he actually could make out. They appeared to be part of an address: *Reynolds St., Pontiac.*

"Pontiac. Hmm, that's kind of weird," he whispered to himself. "The Pontiac Correctional Center is where Patterson was being held before he escaped." Then he disgustedly tossed the soggy receipt into the trash. "Jeez, now every little shitty coincidence seems to have some great significance. Get a grip, Brandt!"

As Cyrus was about to open the envelope, his cell phone chirped. Cyrus didn't recognize the number, but he answered anyway.

"Cyrus Brandt."

"Hey, Cyrus, it's Max Riegel. I just wanted to let you know that I got ahold of that lawyer and asked him about the status of the divorce papers you were expecting. He seemed to be as confused as we are about it and wondered why you hadn't responded."

As Cyrus stood holding the damp envelope in his hand, he recognized that Max's call was the second odd coincidence of the morning. He wondered what the rest of the day had in store for him.

"It's funny you called, Max. I'm standing here in my kitchen holding the letter in my hand at this very moment. Haven't opened it yet. Molly retrieved it from the field across the road. It must've been part of the mail delivery the twister sucked out of the mail carrier's vehicle."

"The what?"

"Oh, never mind. I guess you didn't hear about that. It's a long story. Anyway, I have the letter now."

"OK, good. Look it over and if you have any concerns, bring it in and I'll take a look. On second thought, bring it in regardless. I'll give it a once-over just to be sure."

"OK, Max. I'll do that. I'll try to have it to you later today."

Cyrus laid the phone down on the countertop, then opened the envelope. He scanned through the document, skimming the legalese and noting the items that referred to their negotiations weeks before. Everything seemed to be in order, and there was no mention of his recent inheritance or Janice's interest in it.

Cyrus realized he had been holding his breath as he read, and he let out a sigh of relief as he finished the last page. He would be glad to have this behind him. He was angry with his wife over this entire affair, but he recognized that, down deep, he still had some feelings for her. Or were those feelings just a longing for his life as it used to be? Who was he kidding? There was only one direction he could go now, and that was forward.

28

Cyrus parked in a spot right in front of Annie's diner. It was still raining, so he grabbed his umbrella. Pushing the car door open with his foot, he opened the umbrella as he stepped out of his vehicle. He walked into the diner, wiped his feet on the rug, and took a seat at the counter, shaking water off the umbrella and scanning the breakfast crowd to see if he recognized anybody. He received a few friendly nods before turning his attention to the aproned woman standing on the other side of the counter.

"Hey, remember me?" Annie asked as she poured him a cup of coffee.

"Yeah, I remember you. Aren't you the sharpshooter who humiliated me the other day?"

"Yup, that was me all right. I hope you're not holding that against me. Is that why you've been avoiding me?"

"I'm so sorry, Annie. This case is taking over my life. Besides, maybe you should be enlarging your circle of friends beyond just my sorry ass. I'll bet there are lots of eligible billionaires lining up to hang out with you," he joked.

"Yeah, right. Maybe I should just put a sign in the window that says *Billionaire Wanted. Inquire Within.*"

"That just might work. Why don't you do that, and then if you're not too busy interviewing all those applicants, you can get me some eggs over easy with a side of bacon."

"Coming right up," Annie said, smiling as she scribbled on her pad, ripped off the top sheet, and slapped it on the kitchen window shelf for the cook. She turned back to Cyrus and asked, "How are you feeling? Any headaches or other issues?"

"I'm feeling pretty good. Close to a hundred percent, I think," he replied. He took a sip of his coffee, noting that Annie continued to examine him as if she were making her own assessment of his condition. Choosing to ignore her studious gaze, he said, "I was wondering if you'd like to have dinner tonight. I have some news you may find interesting. It involves your uncle Max and my soon-to-be ex-wife."

"Boy, that sounds enticing," she joked. "I suppose I could clear my social calendar for an over-educated lawman with an alimony problem, Dr. Brandt."

"Jesus, when are you going to stop calling me that?" He pretended he was perturbed. Then he went on, "I'll pick you up in front of the diner at seven if that's all right. Where would you like to go?"

"No preference. Actually, pizza sounds good to me."

"Pizza?"

"Yeah, why not?"

"I just thought, with all the great food you serve here, pizza wouldn't be your meal of choice for this evening."

"Well, I guess there's a lot you don't know about me, buster."

"True, but I'm willing to learn."

"If you must know, pizza happens to be one of my favorite foods. Don't judge me."

"OK, then. Pizza it is! And no judging, I promise. I'll see you at seven."

By the time Cyrus had finished his breakfast, the rain had stopped, so he walked over to Max Riegel's office to drop off his divorce papers. After spending a few minutes chatting with Max, he made his way to the sheriff's office. Tom was sitting on the corner of his desk waiting for him.

"Look what I've got," Tom said.

Tom was waving a warrant in front of Cyrus's face. Cyrus said, "Wow, that was pretty fast."

"Yup, the judge signed it last night. It's not hard to get a warrant to search the home of an ex-con who lives down the road from two murder victims who were killed by one of his prison buddies. And the joint butt helped, too."

"Are we going out there this morning?"

"Yes, but I'm waiting for John and Robert. They want to be in on this, which is fine by me. No offense to you, Cyrus, but you haven't been adequately trained to execute a search warrant. Those guys have."

"No offense taken," Cyrus replied.

"Good, but I do want you to come along and help if help is needed, OK?"

"Great. Maybe I'll learn something. Don't worry, I'll try not to shoot anybody."

"I appreciate it," Tom replied with a smile.

As they waited for John and Robert, they studied the reports their office had received from the state police regarding possible relatives or acquaintances of Patterson who showed up in their databases. There was nothing of significance yet, but the state police hadn't quite finished their work, so there was still hope of a lead.

About twenty minutes later, Trooper Corbit and Agent Backus arrived together in an unmarked car. Tom and Cyrus were on the street to meet them as they pulled up.

Tom said, "You guys ready? Let's get out there." He headed for his cruiser, with Cyrus following close behind.

29

The two vehicles pulled off the road into the driveway leading to Chambers's mobile home. They parked near the main road and walked silently down the long path toward the trailer. As they neared the mobile home, they attempted to conceal their approach by staying in the trees. Finally, Tom and Cyrus walked quietly out in the open and up to the front door, while John and Robert proceeded to the rear, taking a position to block Chambers's possible escape.

Tom rapped on the door. "Open up, Chambers. We have our warrant. Let us in, or we'll have to break through this door."

They could hear movement inside, and then they heard Chambers shout, "OK, OK. Just hold your damn horses while I get my shoes on."

Cyrus heard rapid footsteps fading to the rear of the trailer. "I think he's headed out the back," he shouted.

Chambers burst out the rear door just as Robert extended his leg, causing Chambers to trip down the steps and land, groaning, in a heap on the ground.

"Hey, Ed," said Robert. "Did you have a nice trip?"

"Fuck you," Chambers grumbled as he pulled himself up off the ground.

"No need for foul language, Ed. We're just going to have a quick look around. I'm sure an upstanding citizen like yourself has nothing to worry about."

John was frisking Chambers by the time Tom and Cyrus arrived in back to join them.

Tom asked, "What are you running from, Ed?"

Ed spat out saliva as he blurted, "Just leave me the hell alone. I ain't done nothin'."

"Well, we'll just see about that," Tom replied. Then he turned to John and said, "John, why don't you stay here and watch Mr. Personality. If he gives you any trouble, don't be afraid to cuff him."

"We'll be just fine," said John. "We're going to get to know each other better, right, Ed?" Chambers gave him the finger and took a seat on the steps.

Tom turned to Cyrus, pointing his thumb toward the door. "Let's you, me, and Robert take a look inside." Then he disappeared into the trailer.

Cyrus watched as the sheriff and Agent Backus began to scour every inch of the home, moving deftly from room to room checking heating vents, the toilet tank, the clothes dryer, as well as all the storage containers in the kitchen. About halfway through their search, Tom said, "Cyrus, why don't you go see how John is getting on with our friend Ed. I'm hearing some kind of ruckus back there."

Cyrus walked out the back door to find Chambers handcuffed securely to the steel post of a clothesline. Chambers was in the middle of a tirade of profanity, while John stood nearby with his arms crossed and a grin on his face.

"Things OK back here?" Cyrus inquired.

"Oh, we're getting along famously," replied John. "We'll be exchanging Christmas cards, I'm sure."

Chambers halted his string of expletives to direct his ire toward Cyrus. "You call yourself a deputy? You're nothing but a damn cowboy. Why don't you leave law enforcement to the experts? They're incompetent enough without any help from an amateur like you. You guys have nothing on me. The guy you should be worried about is that murderer, whatever his name is."

"Patterson," Cyrus replied quietly. "I think you know him."

"And so what if I do? You ain't got nothing on me."

"Yeah, you said that already."

"Well, it's true. If I was you, I'd be worried about this Patterson guy, not me. If you keep pushing on this thing, he's going to find you, and you'll end up like those Barnetts down the road."

"Is that some kind of threat, Chambers?" Cyrus asked.

"I'm just saying you're in way over your head, Junior Deputy."

"Just shut up, Ed," John finally said.

But Chambers wasn't finished with Cyrus. "And I'd also be worried for that little girlfriend of yours. You never know when Patterson might take a liking to her."

"I said *shut up!*" John repeated more insistently.

Cyrus walked up to Chambers and calmly said, "You know what, Ed? You are one stupid son of a bitch. Maybe you had nothing to do with this after all. Why would a smart guy like Patterson ever hook up with a moron like you?" Then Cyrus abruptly turned to walk back into the mobile home.

Before he took two steps, he heard Tom yell from inside the trailer, "We've got something here." A moment later Tom and Robert walked out with a backpack that had been hidden in a dirty clothes hamper. Tom said, "Ed, you're going to have to do better than that if you want to succeed in this line of work."

Tom unzipped the backpack and out fell several ziplock bags of what appeared to be weed, accompanied by three or four smaller bags of pills.

"Well, look at that," Tom said. "Your customers must love you, Ed. This is one-stop shopping for all your illegal substance needs."

"You're a real smart-ass, you know that?" said Chambers. "You think it's easy for an ex-con like me to go straight? Nobody will give me a damn job. What am I supposed to do? I have to make a living somehow."

"I really feel sorry for you, you moron," said Cyrus. "I'll send you a sympathy card when they stick your sorry ass in jail."

"Shut up, Boy Scout," Chambers responded.

Tom said, "OK, John, take him down to the cars and wait for us there. We got what we needed here, but we should go search that shed over there."

Twenty minutes later, having found nothing incriminating in the shed, Cyrus, Tom, and Robert headed down the driveway toward the cars, where John and Ed were waiting for them.

Before he got into the car with John and Chambers, Robert said quietly, "I'm anxious to get this guy into interrogation. He could split wide open and lead us right to Patterson."

"I think he just might," said Tom. "He has a hard time controlling that mouth of his, and he's not very smart. Plus, we have the drug charge to hold over his head. That's a good combination as far as this investigation is concerned. This could be the break we've been looking for."

They arrived back in town around eleven-thirty. Tom and Cyrus took Chambers to book him over at the jail, while Robert and John went into the back room of the sheriff's office to discuss their next move. When Tom and Cyrus joined them, they all agreed that Robert and Tom would conduct the interrogation of Ed Chambers. First they planned to let him sit in jail overnight, thinking about his options. To bring Robert up to speed, Tom and Cyrus shared their notes and observations about their initial meeting with Chambers. When all were satisfied they were up-to-date on the case, they adjourned.

When John and Robert got back in their car and drove off, Cyrus and Tom stood on the curb outside the office watching the car disappear down the street.

Tom said, "I'll meet you back here in the morning. We can look through some more of the data from the state police research team before Robert and I talk to Chambers."

"Sounds good. I also need to follow up on something Chambers said to me today."

"What's that?" Tom asked.

"I'd rather not say until I make sure it means something. It's a bit personal."

"You really should share it with me, if it has anything to do with the investigation."

"Just give me a day, OK, Tom? It's probably nothing. I'll fill you in tomorrow. I need to talk to somebody first."

30

Cyrus picked Annie up precisely at 7:00 p.m. in front of the diner. They made the short drive to the outskirts of town, where they pulled into the parking lot of the pizza joint and parked near the door. Cyrus was rather quiet, and Annie could tell he had something on his mind.

Finally, she said, "The talk around town is that you guys brought in someone today. I heard it was that loner who lives out by the Barnett place."

"How did that information get out so fast?" Cyrus asked.

"The town has eyes—or rather, ears," she replied.

"Well, we do have a person of interest in custody. I'll tell you that much, but I shouldn't really talk about it. Not even to you. Sorry."

"Well, excuse me, Mr. Hawaii Five-O! I guess you wouldn't want me to spill the beans to any of my criminal friends, right?"

"Oh, come on. We don't really have a solid lead yet anyway. This might amount to nothing."

Annie and Cyrus got out of the car and entered the front door of the place. It was pretty busy, but they managed to find a corner booth. The waitress brought them some water and then, upon request, showed up with a couple of beers. Their pizza order was placed, and the couple finally began to ease comfortably into conversation.

Cyrus said, "Listen, Annie, I was going to talk to you about an envelope Molly found in the field yesterday. It contained my divorce papers, finally. But I have something a bit more important to ask you at the moment."

"What is it? It's not a proposal, is it?" she said as she took a sip of beer, smiling into the glass.

"Sorry, no. That's not it."

"Oh, darn. Foiled again."

"Listen, Annie, have you said anything to anybody about you and me spending time together? I know maybe Tom has his suspicions about us, but have you mentioned anything whatsoever about us hanging out together or anything like that to anyone?"

"No, why would I? It's none of anyone's business."

104

"I know, but sometimes something slips out during casual conversation. Do you think anyone overheard us making social plans at the diner?"

"No, I don't think so. When we did that, we always kept our voices down, and I don't think we would've talked about it if people were sitting nearby. We've been very discreet, although it's not like we're trying to hide anything. There's nothing to hide. Why're you so concerned about this?"

"I don't want to scare you, Annie, but this suspect we brought in? He was quite irate while we were searching his house, and he did a lot of yelling and swearing and so forth. At one point, he mentioned something about my girlfriend. He said that word, *girlfriend*. How would he know about us? I'm trying to figure that out. I haven't said a word to anyone."

"What did the guy say about me?" Annie asked.

"Oh, nothing really. It's not important," Cyrus lied, and then went on. "Do you think Tom has mentioned anything about us to anyone?"

"I doubt it," Annie replied. "He's pretty tight-lipped about family issues, but I suppose we could ask him."

"Yeah, I guess we should, though I don't look forward to bringing it up."

"Come on, Deputy. Get a set of balls, will you? Sooner or later you'll have to face this head-on. We might as well get our little relationship, as platonic as it is, out in the open."

"Yeah, I guess you're right. I'll talk to Tom first thing in the morning."

"I want to be there, OK? I might need to step in if he challenges you to a duel."

"That sounds good to me. I'd like you to be there. Maybe he'll spare my sorry ass if you're there to protect me," Cyrus said as he watched the waitress slide a huge sausage and mushroom pizza onto their table.

31

Cyrus and Annie walked into Sheriff Tom Bales's office first thing Saturday morning. The sheriff was leaning back in his desk chair reading the newspaper. Tom's eyes appeared above the top edge of the paper and he slowly lowered it to his lap.

"I don't know what's going on here," he said, "but I don't think I'm going to like it. What do you two want?"

"Just relax, Tom," said Annie. "Cyrus just wants to ask you something."

"Well, spit it out, Deputy. I want to get to my funnies before I go on patrol."

"OK, so I was just wondering if you'd noticed your sis and I have been spending a little time together," Cyrus said.

"Yeah, I suppose I did, but I was hoping if I ignored it, it'd go away," Tom said, staring up at Cyrus. "You're not going to tell me you guys are eloping or anything, are you? Because if you are, I'm going to have to book you into the county jail for a couple of days till you come to your friggin' senses."

"Ha ha, very funny, Tom. I'm being serious here." Then Cyrus noticed that Tom was, too. Cyrus pushed forward. "Look, Tom. This is related to the investigation."

"How's that?" asked the sheriff, now showing more interest.

"I'll explain, but first tell me if you may have happened to mention anything about Annie and me to a friend or acquaintance, anybody you might've visited with or talked to on the street. Anybody at all."

"No, I haven't mentioned anything to anybody. Why would I? I didn't really know if there was anything happening between you two at all. Is there?"

Annie said, "No. We just like hanging out to complain about you."

"Very funny, Annie," said Tom. "What's this about, Cyrus?"

"Well, when we were watching Chambers outside his mobile home yesterday, he started saying I should watch my back, or Patterson might come after me."

"Yeah, so? Probably just empty threats."

"Then he said something about my girlfriend."

"What did he say?" Tom asked.

"That's not important. What's important is that he mentioned my girlfriend. He used that term, *girlfriend*. How would he know I had a girlfriend? Annie and I haven't talked about it to anybody, and if you haven't said anything, how would he know that?"

Tom looked puzzled now. "Have you guys been out in public together?"

"No, not until last night when we went to get a pizza together."

They all were quiet for a moment, thinking about the possibilities.

Finally, Annie's eyes got very wide, and she said, "Wait a minute. Cy, remember when I first brought you home from the hospital, and you sent me out to meet the mail carrier? I remember she looked rather surprised to see me there."

"Are you talking about Liz Chance?" Tom asked.

"Yeah, that's her name," said Cyrus.

"Of course, that doesn't really mean anything. I'd be surprised too, if I found you out there unexpectedly," said Tom.

Annie went on, "Sure, but I'm just saying, besides a couple of the girls at the diner, she's the only one who could possibly know Cy and I have been together. And I don't think any of my girls could have any connection to Chambers."

Tom thought for a moment and then said, "Here's something else to think about. We were wondering earlier who might know of the Barnetts' travel plans, right? Who would you tell if you were heading out of town?"

Cyrus answered almost before Tom had finished the question. "Your mail carrier, that's who. You'd want them to hold your mail until you returned."

"But it's still highly circumstantial and doesn't really prove anything, does it?" Annie said.

Tom answered, "Nope. Each of these incidents by itself means very little, but when you put them all together, it makes you kind of wonder, doesn't it? What do we know about Liz Chance? Is she from around here?"

"I think she's about your age, Tom. Don't you remember her from high school?" Annie asked.

"Nope." Then Tom said, "Cyrus, I want you to do some snooping around for me. Do it quietly. I don't want to raise any red flags here. Try to find out what you can about Liz Chance.

Where is she from? Is *Chance* her maiden name? That sort of thing. Talk to Sarah about getting you the authorization to look at any records you're interested in at the courthouse. And Cyrus, I expect you to keep me in the loop."

Cyrus and Annie turned to leave and were almost out the door when Tom called to Cyrus. "Cyrus, don't get too caught up in this part of the investigation yet. We need to be on our toes for the Fourth of July festivities this Monday, so I want you around the office early that day, OK?"

"All right, Tom. I'll be here."

Cyrus and Annie paused outside the sheriff's office. Annie said, "What are you going to do now?"

"I'm not sure. I don't think I can get much done at the courthouse today since it's the weekend."

"I have an idea. Things are kind of slow at the diner this morning. Why don't you and I head over to the library to do some research?"

"What do you mean?" Cyrus asked.

"I'm thinking we can get our hands on some old high school yearbooks. Maybe we can find Liz Chance in one of those. Then we could find out a little about her. Maybe even determine who some of her friends were, and start asking around."

"I don't know how much asking around we can do yet, but looking through the old yearbooks is a great idea. I appreciate your help. This could take some time. Are you sure you don't need to be at the diner?"

"They can manage there for now. This could be kind of fun."

"You have a weird idea of fun, if you ask me," Cyrus said as they turned to walk toward the town library.

Cyrus and Annie spent the next three hours perusing dozens of yearbooks from Tri-City Consolidated High School. They didn't know for sure what Liz's surname was in high school, so when they found students with a similar first name, Cyrus took time to scrutinize each face. They were nearing the end of their final stack of yearbooks when Cyrus's cell phone chirped. He took a look at the display and recognized his wife's number.

"Jesus, what now?" Cyrus thought. Turning to Annie, he said, "I guess I'd better take this. I'll be right back." He walked out to the sidewalk in front of the library as he answered the call.

"Yes?"

"Hi, it's me. Just calling to check in with you, you know, just to see how you're doing," Janice said cheerfully.

Cyrus said nothing for several seconds, then replied, "How am I doing? OK, I guess. I'm still walking upright on two feet." He hadn't talked to Janice for several weeks and wasn't sure if he wanted this conversation now, or ever.

"I see you're back out on your folks' place. I bet it's really pretty out there right now."

"Yeah, I suppose so."

"I remember being out there in the spring when the air seemed so fresh and the crops were just peeking out of the ground. I kind of miss that."

"Uh-huh," replied Cyrus cryptically. He wondered why she was calling. In the days before their final breakup, Janice hadn't said more than a dozen words to him, treating him like some kind of pariah. Now she spoke with a different tone, a tone Cyrus remembered from a happier life a long time ago. This made him more than a little suspicious. Finally, he asked, "Janice, is this a social call, or is there something you need from me?"

"Well, I was kind of curious about you. It's been a long time since we spoke. I still worry about you sometimes."

"Really?" Cyrus replied sarcastically.

"Yes, I do. I still remember some of the good times we had together, don't you?"

"Sure I do, but it seems our life together wasn't good enough for you. You found someone else who had more money, more potential, and more charisma evidently."

"It was a difficult time, Cy, remember? You and I could hardly make ends meet. You were depressed; I was lonely. I just couldn't take it any longer."

"You left me when I needed you most. That's what I remember," Cyrus said impatiently. "So what do you want, Janice? What are you calling about?"

The phone was silent for a moment. Then Janice said, "Well, I noticed you were taking some time getting those divorce papers back to my lawyer. I had the feeling maybe you were having second thoughts about the whole thing."

"Second thoughts?" he asked incredulously. "Hey, as you recall, this *whole thing* wasn't my idea in the first place! It was yours!"

"I know. I know." Then she said sweetly, "I was just wondering if maybe this was moving too fast. Maybe we should stop and think about this for a minute."

Cyrus thought for a moment and said, "He left you, didn't he, Janice?" A long silence followed, and Cyrus added, "Tell me the truth." He could hear her sniffling faintly. "That fucking asshole left you and found somebody else, didn't he? Jesus! After all this hell he put us through! I can't believe it!" Cyrus lowered the phone for a moment and stared down the street, looking at nothing in particular. Then he put the phone to his ear and said, "So tell me what happened, Jan."

Janice spoke in fragmented phrases amid the sniffles and occasional pauses to regain her composure. The story was a sad one. Her business-school-dean boyfriend had taken a job in the private sector with an investment firm, and he'd relocated to Cleveland—with a graduate student he'd been bedding on the side for the entire duration of his affair with Janice. He had left very suddenly. One day they had been planning their future, and the next day the bastard had left town with someone younger and more to his liking. Janice was on her own now, and Cyrus knew she wasn't the type of person who would do well on her own.

On the sidewalk in front of the library, Cyrus listened to Janice weep quietly. He could see Annie through the window, examining yearbooks at a large table not far from the circulation desk. He was feeling something now, and those feelings confused him. Were they feelings for Janice? Did he miss her? Or were they just feelings of pity? He wondered if he could hit "reset" and go back to the way things were. It would be possible, he supposed, even with all the baggage they would now carry.

Annie looked up and smiled at him through the window before looking back down at the book in front of her. Cyrus thought about his life since he'd come back home. He thought about Annie, and Tom, and he even thought about Byron Patterson. He thought about the Barnetts. This was his life now.

He couldn't deny it. There were people here who needed him, wanted him, and there was work here that needed to be completed. This was his second chance. His future lay ahead, not behind him.

Finally, Cyrus said, "Janice, I'm not sure what you want me to say, or what you want me to do. The thought of you and me together again, as viable as you think it may be, is simply not in the cards. I'm afraid that ship has sailed." He knew his tired metaphors must be falling flat and cruel on her ears. He could hear her sobs grow more intense. He gazed at Annie through the window and forged ahead. "I wish you the best, Janice. I really do. But I'll have the signed divorce agreement on its way back to you in the mail this week. Goodbye, Janice."

Cyrus stood for a long while, motionless, with his finger still against the screen of the phone. Had he done the right thing? Had he made the right choice? Even though he was consciously entertaining that question, he realized down deep that there was only one choice he really could have made. He turned and walked up the steps into the library.

As he took his seat next to Annie, she asked, "Is everything all right?"

He replied, "Everything's great. Let's finish up here, then catch some lunch. I hear there's a nice diner down the street that serves up a good lunch special on Saturdays."

"Yeah, that joint isn't terrible, I guess," Annie said as she slammed the last yearbook shut and smiled at Cyrus.

32

Monday was Independence Day, a holiday that was great for parties and family get-togethers, but not so great for sheriff's departments around this great country. Sheriffs were the ones who had to deal with calls regarding unruly revelers or the occasional idiot who blew off a couple of fingers while putting on a private fireworks display.

This particular Fourth of July was a fairly uneventful one in Cane County. Nobody lost any fingers, and the only unruliness took place in the Elby town square, where Tom and Cyrus had to end the Independence Day celebration of a half dozen lonely old men who spent the day there drinking out of bottles clad in brown paper sacks. All in all, it was a rather subdued, even boring, Fourth, and Cyrus couldn't help but notice the pall of concern covering the community like an ashen residue left by the double murders the previous month. He knew Elby and the people who lived in the surrounding area would not rest easily until closure was achieved on this case. He knew it, and he could see that Tom knew it, too. The investigation was beginning to weigh heavily on Tom, who had recently been spending more and more of his time either in his office or aimlessly patrolling the rural areas, hoping for some kind of break.

Cyrus couldn't help but feel rather inadequate in his ability to be of any great use to the investigation. Beyond his own patrols out in the countryside talking to the locals, there was little he could do. The murders had occurred about three weeks ago, and they had yet to get a lead in the search for Patterson. Still, Cyrus had high hopes regarding the ongoing interrogation of Ed Chambers. Maybe Tom or Robert would get Chambers to spill some crucial information that would get the investigation moving ahead. That could happen tomorrow, next week, or maybe never. Cyrus couldn't control that.

The only thing Cyrus could do right at the moment was to complete the assignment Tom had given him regarding Liz Chance. Cyrus realized it was probably a dead end, but at least it'd keep him busy. He resolved to complete the task to the best of his ability, regardless of the outcome. If nothing else, he would get some experience with the investigative process. The experience he would gain could pay off the next time Tom assigned him a similar task.

Now Cyrus thought to himself how odd it was that he was taking this law enforcement job so seriously. He had even been entertaining the thought of a possible future for himself in this field. That surprised him as he thought more about it. Just last year he had been an academic who studied the various forces existing in the universe and the ways those forces interacted with matter. Now he was dealing with people who were also subject to forces, but these were forces of social and personal interaction, experienced through the lens of emotion and often fear.

The forces of the universe, as awe-inspiring as they were, were predictable and quantifiable. The forces he dealt with now were unpredictable and complicated—not just theoretical, but real forces impacting real people in real time. The work in which he was involved now seemed vital and necessary. He realized that in spite of the horrendous nature of this case, he was feeling something he hadn't felt in a long time. He was feeling useful, even happy.

33

On Tuesday morning, Cyrus drove to town mentally going through the checklist of things he was determined to accomplish that day. He intended to stop by Max Riegel's office and get the divorce papers in the mail, but his main goal was to look further into the comings and goings of Liz Chance. Something just didn't seem right with her. He couldn't put his finger on it, but she seemed somehow out of place in this town. Cyrus chuckled to himself at that thought, as he realized how out of place he himself must seem to people in Elby. Still, he wondered if she was hiding something. If she was, he was determined to find out what that *something* was.

Cyrus parked along Main Street and entered the diner. He was greeted by a smiling but very busy Annie.

"Hi, Cyrus. Find a seat and I'll grab you some coffee."

"Thanks, Ann."

Annie walked over to his table with a cup of coffee and some silverware, placing it all down in front of him.

She said, "I see you survived the Fourth unscathed."

"Yup, it was pretty tame in town last night. I'm sorry I couldn't hang out with you. That brother of yours is a real taskmaster."

"That's OK, Cy," Annie said. "I can entertain myself. I actually went with some of the girls to see the fireworks over at the county fairgrounds. We had fun."

"That's great. Hey, thanks again for helping me go through those yearbooks on Saturday. Today I'm going to snoop around and see what else I can find out about you-know-who," Cyrus said, furtively looking around to see if anyone was listening.

"Wow, Deputy, you're another Sherlock Holmes, aren't you?" Annie said with a crooked smile.

"That's right, wise ass," Cyrus responded. "And you better watch out, because I might just take an interest in *your* sordid past. Who knows what kind of dirt I might be able to dig up?"

"I bet you can tell I'm really worried," she deadpanned. "So, did you come in here just to threaten me, or are you going to order something?"

"The usual, I guess."

"Eggs and bacon coming right up," Annie said as she turned and walked away.

Cyrus entered Max Riegel's office about twenty minutes later. The front office was vacant, but he could hear Max's voice in the back room. "Goddamned piece of shit! And I thought mimeograph machines were bad! Right now I'd take one of those over you, you sorry piece of horse dung!"

Cyrus poked his head through the door and said, "Isn't technology a wonderful thing?"

Max spun around, startled and then embarrassed. "Oh, I'm sorry about my French, Cyrus. This damn machine will be the death of me. It seems to work fine for weeks, and then when I have a deadline to meet, it decides to go on the fritz. I swear it does it on purpose."

"Yeah, I know what you mean. It's kind of like a bad marriage."

"Well, if you say so," said Max. "I suppose that's why you stopped in today."

"Yup, sure is. Have you had a chance to look that stuff over?"

"Yes, I have, Cyrus. It seems to be in order, and nothing has been amended from the earlier draft you gave me. Do you want to sign it?"

"Yes, let's get it in the mail and off my plate for good."

Max handed Cyrus a pen and stood by as he signed the divorce agreement. "That should do it," said Max. "I'll get it out in the mail later this morning."

Cyrus made his way to the county building downtown. It housed many of the government and municipal agencies of Cane County as well as the office that handled billing for water, gas, and electricity. That's where Cyrus was headed today. He walked in the door and stood at a long counter. The young woman on the other side of the counter finally tore herself away from her cell phone and said, "May I help you?"

"Yes, I'm Deputy Brandt from the Cane County Sheriff's Office. I'd like to make an inquiry regarding one of your customers."

The young woman excused herself and soon returned with another woman, this one much more professionally dressed. She asked, "May I help you?"

"Yes, I'm from the Cane County Sheriff's Department, conducting an investigation. We need to access your files for some information regarding one of your customers."

She said, "Please follow me. Let's go back to my office and I'll see if I can help you."

Cyrus walked past the young woman with the cell phone and followed the other woman, whom he presumed to be the supervisor, into a rather small and spartan office.

"My name is Janet Spaulding, and you are . . . ?"

"Deputy Cyrus Brandt, ma'am. Here are my credentials."

Spaulding looked carefully at these, and finally said, "We don't like to disclose that kind of information. I don't think I've seen you before. Are you new to the department?"

"Yes, I just joined two or three weeks ago."

"I hope you don't mind if I call the sheriff's office just to verify."

"No, not at all."

Spaulding made the call, and after talking to Sarah at the office, she ended the call and looked up at Cyrus. "OK, everything seems to be in order. What can we look up for you?"

"I'd like some information on a customer of yours named Liz Chance."

"OK, let me take a look." She pecked at a computer keyboard and finally said, "All right, here we go. Elizabeth Chance. She lives at 424 East Bannon Street here in Elby."

Cyrus was writing in his notebook as she spoke. Without looking up, he asked, "Do you have a record of when she established that account?"

Spaulding studied the screen and then said, "It looks like she opened it seven years ago this month. The location is a real nice area over on the east side. There's a lot of new construction over there."

"So it's possible her account was established on a new home?"

"I'm not sure, but it could be."

"And hers is the only name on the account?"

"Yes, sir."

"OK, thank you very much, Ms. Spaulding. You've been very helpful."

It didn't take long for Cyrus to get back to the Hyundai and head east to the edge of town where Liz lived. He hadn't been in this neighborhood before, and as he drove down the wide, curbed streets weaving among newly cropped bluegrass lawns, he wondered how a mail carrier, one apparently living alone, could afford to live in such an opulent neighborhood.

He soon spotted Liz's house. "424 East Bannon. There it is," Cyrus announced to himself. "Nice digs, indeed." He was careful not to stop, but instead he drove slowly past so as not to arouse suspicion. The house was indeed a fairly new construction. It was a nice two-story with an elegant front porch, surrounded by beautiful grass and landscaping that he assumed was being maintained by a professional lawn service.

He was just about out of the neighborhood when his phone sounded. Cyrus noticed that the call was from the sheriff's office, so he pulled off to the side of the road and answered. "Hello, this is Cy."

"Hi, Cyrus. This is Sarah. I just got a call from Janet Spaulding at the county building."

"Regarding?"

"Well, she called back after you left her office, and she's trying to get ahold of you. She left her number and said you should call her."

Cyrus wrote down the number in his notebook and, after ending Sarah's call, immediately dialed Spaulding. She answered on the second ring.

"Janet Spaulding."

"Hi, Ms. Spaulding. This is Deputy Brandt. Did you want to speak to me?"

"Yes. After you left, I discovered something I'd missed when I first looked at Liz Chance's account information."

"What's that?"

Janet continued, "Well, her account also includes another property. It's out in the rural area, east of town."

"What kind of property is it? A farm? Another house?"

"I can't really tell from our information, but it does currently have electric service, though it's not using much power at present."

"Do you know when that part of her account was activated?" Cyrus asked.

"It looks like she took over the power responsibilities for that property the year before she started her account on Bannon Street. The address for this property is 1167 Clover Street. Your navigation app should be able to find it. I believe it's out on County Road 28."

Cyrus was writing this down as he said, "Thanks for the update, Ms. Spaulding." Then Cy disconnected and sat for a while thinking about what he had just learned. He was now discovering more questions than answers, but he wouldn't find those answers sitting here. He put the Hyundai in gear and headed east out of town toward the address Spaulding had given him.

Ten minutes later, the sexy woman speaking from his phone's navigation app told him he had reached his destination. He rolled slowly by the farmstead and came to a stop opposite the mailbox. The name on the mailbox said *Mr. and Mrs. Frank Brennan*. The old farmhouse loomed large in the middle of an expansive yard. The house appeared to Cyrus to show little evidence of habitation. The weedy lawn had grown long, and there were no vehicles of any type that he could see. The farmstead reminded him of his own, a once-proud working farm now standing idle. He wondered if he was at the correct address. He double-checked his phone app and the address in his notebook. This was the correct location, all right.

Cyrus turned into the driveway and drove up to the house. He could see no movement of any sort. The house was totally dark inside, and as he looked around the farmyard, he could see no pets or livestock. He decided to take a few pictures of the house and nearby buildings, and then he turned the SUV around and headed out of the driveway and back to town.

34

Tom took another swig of his beer and set it back on the bar in front of him. "So, she has a nice new home on the east side and owns all or part of a farm out on County Road 28. While it's true this is kind of interesting, given that she's just a local mail carrier, it doesn't mean a whole lot, does it? What else you got?"

Annie and Cyrus sat on either side of him, listening as he spoke into his brew. Then they were all silent as they nursed their cold drafts in concert.

Cyrus said, "Well, a couple of things in particular. First of all, Annie and I looked through a lot of high school yearbooks a couple of days ago, and found no trace of her. Then I checked the utilities office downtown. According to their records, she opened her utilities account for the farm about eight years ago, and opened another one a year later for her new home. So unless she was living in the area on someone else's dime before that point, I guess we can place her arrival here in Elby at around eight years ago. And here's the second thing that has me confused. Her name wasn't on the mailbox out at the farm. The name on it was *Mr. and Mrs. Frank Brennan*. What do you make of that?"

Annie's eyes lit up as she said, "Frank Brennan? Are you talking about the Brennan farm? His wife's name was, let me see . . ." Annie hesitated for a moment.

"Doris. I think it was Doris," Tom said.

"Yes, Doris. That's it," she confirmed.

Cyrus said, "So what's the big deal about these Brennans? Are they famous or something?"

"Well, not exactly famous," said Annie.

Tom was just finishing another sip of his beer when he interrupted Annie with an explanation. "No, I wouldn't say famous. Maybe tragic would be a better word for it. As I recall, it was about nine or ten years ago, when I was still a deputy for Sheriff Gaines. Frank and Doris Brennan were well on in years, and poor old Frank was dealing with cancer that was slowly killing him. Sheriff Gaines got a call from one of their neighbors who had stopped in to see how they were getting on. What that neighbor found was a very grisly scene there in the farmhouse.

"Apparently Doris couldn't bear the thought of her husband suffering so much, so she took his twelve-gauge Winchester, shot the old codger, and then stuck the business end of the gun in her own mouth. I was with Sheriff Gaines when we entered the house and saw the carnage. I'll never forget what we saw that day. That's something you never want to see, or remember."

"I can't imagine," said Cyrus solemnly.

"No, you can't," replied Tom.

They sat in silence for a while as they sipped on their beers. It seemed inappropriate to speak about this for a moment, and the beers gave them an excuse to avoid saying anything insensitive.

Finally, Cyrus said, "What happened then?"

"What do you mean, *then?*" asked Tom.

"What I mean is, what happened to the farm?"

Tom thought for a moment. "I can't really say. I guess someone eventually purchased it. Apparently Liz Chance bought it, or at least she bought the homestead. I haven't been by that place in years."

Tom, Cyrus, and Annie each took another swig of beer before Annie said, "Tom, do you remember when Mom used to talk about Doris Brennan?"

"Can't say as I do. What did she say?" he asked.

"I just remembered something about them being in high school together, and Doris creating quite a stir because she got pregnant and had to drop out of school. Do you remember anything about that?"

"Not really. Do you remember what happened to her, regarding the baby, I mean?"

"No," Annie said, "but now that I think about it, I don't remember any Brennan children showing up at their funeral."

"Now that you mention it, neither do I," Tom replied as the wheels in his head began to turn. "I remember going to that funeral, and I don't recall any immediate family members whatsoever being there. So what do you suppose happened to the kid? Maybe the baby didn't survive."

Cyrus had been listening intently to their discussion when he finally said, "Tom, if you don't mind, I'm going to look into this further. I'm going to start by checking the newspaper obit from the time of the funeral to see if there's any mention of a son or daughter. Then I'll drive out that way tomorrow and talk to some of the Brennans' neighbors. They might give us more information about their personal history. I'll let you know what I find out."

Tom grunted his approval as he swallowed the remnants of his beer and placed his glass back on the bar.

35

Cyrus was on the road early the next morning. He went into town to see if he could find the Brennan obituaries from the archives of the local newspaper, and then drove out toward the old Brennan homestead. As he moved through the countryside, he noticed how much the corn and soybeans had grown in the last month since he began driving these country roads looking for the white Mercedes. The landscape had given up its dark brown pigment to a vibrant, fresh green, now moving this way and that at the pleasure of the Illinois summer breeze.

Cyrus stopped at three different farms near the Brennan place before he found anyone to talk to. He pulled into the driveway of an old two-story clapboard house where an elderly woman was tending her flower garden. Cyrus noted that the mailbox simply said *Wagner.* As he stopped next to the flower bed, the old woman pulled herself to her feet and watched as Cyrus exited the Hyundai.

"Good morning," Cyrus offered cheerfully. "Your roses there are looking very nice."

"Thanks. I sometimes wonder why I spend so much time on them. They're pretty finicky little buggers. But it gives me something to do, I guess," she said as Cyrus pulled out his badge and extended it toward her.

"I'm Cyrus Brandt, from the Cane County Sheriff's Department. I was wondering if I could ask you a couple of questions regarding the Brennan farm down the road there," Cyrus said as he gestured eastward.

"I'll help if I can. What would you like to know?"

"Well, first of all, did you know the Brennans?"

"As a matter of fact, I did. I was a sophomore in high school when Doris and Frank were seniors. I rode the bus with Frank every morning since it went past both our places. I really liked Frank. I kind of had a crush on him at that time."

"So then you're well aware of the circumstances surrounding their deaths."

"Yes. It was so sad," the woman recounted.

"I understand Doris got pregnant while she was in high school. Do you know anything about that?"

The old woman looked at Cyrus warily and said, "Why are you digging up stuff like that? Can't you just let those poor souls rest in peace?" Then she turned to continue her work on the roses.

"Ma'am, I don't mean any disrespect for the Brennans, but we're currently conducting an investigation and this information could be a great help to us."

The woman turned back to Cyrus and said, "Yes, it's true. Doris and Frank got into trouble their senior year. When that happened, Doris dropped out of school and moved in with Frank and his parents for the duration of the pregnancy. They eventually got married and stayed on the farm after Frank's parents died. That's the long and short of it."

Cyrus was busy taking notes in his little notebook. Then he looked up, saying, "I noticed that no sons or daughters were mentioned in the obituary in the newspaper. How do you explain that?"

"After the pregnancy was out in the open, I didn't have much contact with Doris or Frank anymore. My parents didn't want me associating with them. But in those days, girls who got pregnant were even more prone to giving up their babies for adoption than girls nowadays. That's what Doris and Frank did."

"That makes me wonder if maybe the woman who currently owns the Brennan place might be Doris and Frank's daughter from that pregnancy. What do you think?"

"I don't rightly know. She could be. I haven't had the opportunity to meet her. I think Doris named the little girl Elizabeth, if I remember correctly. Don't know if that name stayed with the child or not."

"Elizabeth, huh?" Cyrus replied as he put his notebook back in his vest pocket. He extended his hand to the old woman, saying, "Thanks so much for your help. I really appreciate the information. I won't bother you any further."

"It wasn't a bother at all. Your visit helped bring back some painful memories but also some nice ones about Frank and Doris. I really miss them. If you find out the new owner is in fact their daughter, I'd appreciate it if you'd let me know. I might just stop by and speak with her. She might want to hear some of my recollections of Frank and Doris."

"I'm sure she would." Cyrus turned and walked toward the SUV.

"And also let me know if you find out anything about the boy."

Cyrus stopped in his tracks. *"The boy?"*

"Yes, Doris had twins. Didn't I mention that? I think she named the boy Brian or something like that."

"Could it have been *Byron?*" Cyrus queried.

"Yeah, that was it. Byron."

Cyrus was on his cell phone as soon as he had peeled out of the old woman's driveway. After several rings to Tom's phone, he picked up,

"What is it, Cy?"

"Can you meet me at the office?"

"Yeah, sure. Robert and I just finished our interrogation of Chambers. We're still at the jail, but I can be back at the office in fifteen minutes."

"Great, and bring Robert along. He'll want to hear this."

"OK. See you then."

Then Cyrus said, "Oh, wait, Tom. I need to get something at my house before I meet you. It could be important. Let's meet in thirty minutes, OK? That should give me enough time."

As Cyrus hung up, he turned his vehicle southward on the next road and raced toward home. There were just too many coincidences here regarding Liz Chance, he thought. She had to be deeply involved in this Patterson case. He had one final bit of evidence that he thought could implicate her, and it was in his kitchen at the bottom of his wastebasket.

Cyrus slid to a halt in his driveway, sending dust and gravel in every direction. Ignoring Molly's wagging tail, Cyrus hurried to his front door and into the kitchen. It took him about thirty seconds to locate the receipt he had found days ago stuck to the letter from his wife's attorney. He was now glad he hadn't had time to take out his trash for several days. "Sometimes it's good to be a sloppy housekeeper," he thought to himself.

Cyrus laid the receipt on the counter and tried to flatten it out, being careful not to tear it. He studied the piece of paper, trying to make out the ink that had been smeared with moisture.

He could still read the address of the McDonald's in Pontiac, and now he looked for the date. As his eyes became better focused on the printing, he finally found it. "Bingo!" he shouted. Then he carefully put the receipt in his jacket pocket and ran down the steps, slamming the door loudly behind him.

36

Robert and Tom were sitting at the table in the back room of the sheriff's office when Cyrus walked in. Tom was intently examining the file on the Brennan murder/suicide case, and Robert was going over his notes from the Chambers interrogation.

Cyrus said, "Hey, boys, are you ready for me to make your day?"

"What's going on, Cyrus?" Tom wanted Cy to get right to the point.

Cyrus took a seat and pulled out his notebook in case he needed to confirm a detail or two. "I'm as suspicious as anyone when it comes to coincidences," he began, "but at some point, you simply have to relent and begin looking for connections."

"What are you talking about, Cyrus?" Tom was getting impatient.

"OK, just hear me out. I found the Brennan obituary in the paper from nine years ago. There was no mention of any children. My next stop was at a farm down the road from the Brennan place, where I spoke with an elderly lady tending her garden. I noticed the mailbox said *Wagner*. Didn't catch her first name. Anyway, she claimed to have known Frank and Doris when they were in high school.

"Annie was right about the fact that Doris got pregnant when she was in high school. Apparently Doris dropped out of school and moved in with Frank and his parents. But the question was: What happened to the baby from that pregnancy? No children were mentioned in the obit, as I said.

"According to Mrs. Wagner, they put the kid up for adoption soon after birth. They'd even given her the name *Elizabeth*. That's the first coincidence. This made me naturally suspect that Liz Chance, who now owns the Brennan place, might be the child from that pregnancy. Maybe she showed up after their deaths to claim her inheritance. Maybe she had contacted them prior to their deaths. Who knows? Anyway, I wondered if Mrs. Wagner might know if Liz is the daughter of Frank and Doris. She didn't know, but here's the kicker: She said Frank and Doris didn't just have one child from that pregnancy, they had twins!

126

Apparently there was a boy, whom they named . . . wait for it . . . *Byron*. Coincidence number two."

Cyrus paused to let that fact sink in. Tom whispered, "No shit!" as he looked over to Robert, who was staring back at him.

"And here's one more thing," Cyrus said as he pulled a scrap of paper out of his pocket and set it on the table. "This could be just another coincidence, or it could lead us somewhere. My dog Molly found this across the road from my house. She's been retrieving pieces of mail that the twister sucked out of Liz's vehicle and distributed all over the field. Liz and I picked up what we could find out in the field that day, but since then, Molly has been finding more and bringing it to me. This receipt was stuck to a letter that was addressed to me, oddly enough."

"So what?" Tom replied.

"Well, if you look closely, you'll see it's a receipt from the McDonald's in Pontiac, Illinois, near the correctional center where Byron was being held before his escape. The date on the receipt is June 8th, the day before Patterson escaped. Now it could mean nothing, but considering this probably came from Liz's vehicle, it could have significance, don't you think? I'm thinking we should check to see if Byron had any visitors on or around the date you see on that receipt. If we can put Liz at the correctional center around that time, I think all these facts are more than just coincidences."

Robert and Tom were both nodding their heads in agreement. Robert said, "We need to request a warrant for Liz's property, but first I want to do some more digging into her background. I'd be interested in talking to her adoptive parents, if they're still alive. That could give us some insight into this woman, and the timeline leading up to her ownership of the Brennan farm.

"Cyrus, why don't you drive up to the Pontiac Correctional Center to see if you can take a look at their visitors' log. Maybe you'll be lucky enough to spot Liz on a video surveillance file."

Tom interrupted, saying, "Robert, there's one more thing we need to look at."

"What's that?"

"I've been looking at this file from the Brennan deaths. Sheriff Gaines had scribbled some notes on the inside of the file jacket. It appears he wasn't so sure Doris committed murder and suicide. In light of what we know now, I think I should have a visit with Sheriff Gaines about the Brennan deaths. Maybe there are grounds to open this case again. Liz has suddenly become a person of interest, it seems."

"I agree," Robert said. "It looks like this may be the break we've been looking for. But for now, keep this all under your hats. Patterson and Chance aren't looking to make themselves visible at present, so let's just let them lay low till we're ready to roll on this."

Robert added, "Cyrus, you need to know we've been talking to Chambers for days now, and he hasn't been very forthcoming with information about Patterson. Either Ed is smarter than we thought, or he's just as dumb as we previously assumed and has nothing to tell us. I suspect the latter."

Tom added, "We got him on possession and possible distribution of controlled substances, at least. So he should find himself back in a jail cell real soon."

"Yes, but don't forget the reason we started looking at Liz Chance in the first place. It was because Ed Chambers made a reference to Annie when we were searching his trailer," Cyrus pointed out. "The only way he could've known about her was if Liz told him. Unless Ed was just talking out his ass and making shit up, he's connected somehow."

"Point taken," Robert conceded.

37

Later that afternoon, Tom met the now-retired Sheriff Gaines outside the Cane Count Sheriff's Office. "Afternoon, Bill. Thanks for stopping in on such short notice. Come on in."

Gaines walked through the front door and was greeted affectionately by Sarah. "It's good to see you, Sheriff," she said. "I've missed you."

"I imagine you have. It can't be easy working for this green whippersnapper who replaced me," Gaines joked.

"Hey, I'm standing right here, you know," Tom shot back.

"Yeah, we know," said Sarah, smiling. "Nah, he's all right, Bill. He doesn't have your sense of humor, but he does most things the way you used to. You were a good teacher."

"Now there's something we can all agree on," said Tom. "Come on back, Bill. I have something to talk to you about." Tom led the old sheriff back to the conference table, where the Brennan file still was strewn about the tabletop.

As they sat down, Tom said, "Bill, this is the file on the Brennan murder/suicide from nine years ago. We've come upon a possible connection between the Patterson investigation and this one." He paused and slid part of the file over to Bill. "I noticed here some notes you took regarding this case. It appears you weren't totally convinced that Doris did this. Is that true?"

"That's right. She and Frank were so connected, so devoted to one another. All of their acquaintances said as much. The other thing that came to our attention was Doris's aversion to firearms. She never wanted them in the house and would never go close to one. She had a deep fear of them. I just didn't feel she could use one on Frank and then on herself. It wasn't in her nature to do that. But you and I both know people can do most anything under the right circumstances, and with the emotional pressure of Frank's illness, she could have just snapped."

"That's true," said Tom.

"There were a couple of other things, too. We lifted a print from the murder weapon that we couldn't match with anyone involved in the incident. We ran it through the database but found no matches. It was a dead end. So with no evidence beyond my suspicious nature, the case appeared to be pretty clear-cut."

"I assume we still have a record of that print in the database, right?"

"Yeah, it should still be there somewhere. And here's one more thing I want to show you." Gaines pointed at a small notation at the bottom of the file cover. Tom squinted as he tried to read the ex-sheriff's handwriting. Gaines read it for him. "It says *remission for three months*. I spoke with Frank's doctor after his death. The GP said Frank's cancer had been in remission for the three months prior to his death. I never could understand why Doris, a woman who was devoted to her husband and a woman who abhorred firearms, would kill her husband if his health was improving, or at least stabilizing. It made no sense. Does that make sense to you?"

***

Agent Backus was back at the regional office in Springfield the next morning, speaking on the phone with his connection at the Department of Children and Family Services. Robert jotted down some information on a sticky note on his desk. The note said *Jim and Gail Chance*. Below the name was an address in Kankakee, Illinois, and a phone number. Robert thanked the woman on the other end of the line and pledged his undying gratitude before he hung up. It was nice to know the right people, he thought, and Robert realized he was fortunate to have built a network of connections in many of the departments around Springfield. This wasn't the first time he had called upon DCFS for information, and he knew it wouldn't be the last.

By lunchtime he had contacted Gail Chance and arranged a meeting with her and her husband that afternoon. He was on the road by one o'clock to make the two-and-a-half-hour drive to Kankakee. It was around three forty-five when he pulled into the Chances' driveway on the west side of town.

An attractive elderly woman greeted him at the door and led him to a well-appointed living room, where he took a seat on a comfortable leather sofa.

Jim Chance stood as Robert came into the living room, then sat once again in his recliner. Jim was a man of about eighty years, but well-preserved and showing no apparent lack of mental acuity.

Mrs. Chance spoke first. "Mr. Backus, how can we help you? I understand this has something to do with Elizabeth?"

"Yes, it does, Mrs. Chance. Unfortunately, I can't tell you much about it since we're in the middle of an investigation. I can tell you it involves her biological parents. Beyond that, it's confidential, you know. She's just a person of interest who may be able to help us solve a case. It'd be a help to know a little more about her, if you don't mind telling us."

"What would you like to know?" she asked.

"Well, OK, let's start with this. When did Liz first come to live with you?"

"It was just about ten years after we were married," Gail said. "Elizabeth was five when we adopted her. She had been with a foster family for a couple of years before that, but they were apparently having some trouble with her. These poor kids tend to get thrown back into the system whenever their foster parents feel like it. It's really sad."

"Was she a problem for you two, if you don't mind me asking?"

Gail continued, "We had our ups and downs getting used to one another. But that was to be expected, I suppose. She was kind of a daredevil, liked to take chances she shouldn't have. But overall, we were a pretty happy family for several years, until . . ."

Jim carried on for her. "Until she reached her teens, and all hell broke loose. Actually, it wasn't as bad as all that. Many kids go through a wild phase as teenagers. I wasn't the model child when I was a kid either, I suppose."

"What kinds of mischief did she get involved in?" Robert pushed onward.

Gail said, "Oh, mainly acting out aggressive behavior. Hitting and pushing, mostly. By the time she grew out of that, she had graduated from high school, and we didn't see her much after that."

"Really? That's kind of odd, isn't it? Was she still in town?"

"Yes," said Gail. "She had a nice secretarial job at the post office here in Kankakee and was doing well enough on her own. She just never seemed to be interested in visiting us, even on holidays. That was disappointing to us, but we did see her occasionally, and so we tried to be satisfied with that."

"Did you know she was born a twin?" Robert asked.

"Not at first, but we learned that later when she started looking into her background," Jim said.

"When was that?"

"I think it was about ten or twelve years ago. I can't remember," said Gail. "Jim, you're better at remembering that sort of thing. When was that?"

Jim said, "I think that's about right. It was eleven years ago this past summer, I believe. That's when she was let go from her job at the post office."

"What happened there?" Robert asked.

"Not sure," Jim replied, "but she'd been working there for many years, and then she had some kind of altercation with another worker. She never told us all the details, but then again, we weren't seeing her much at that time. But I do remember it was just after she was fired from her job when she stopped by here to tell us she'd found out she had a twin brother and was trying to locate him. I don't know if she ever found him."

"But we know she did finally locate her biological parents," said Gail.

"Did she tell you that? Do you remember when that was?" Robert had been anxious to get to this part of the story.

"Jim?" Gail turned to her husband.

"It was around the time of our fiftieth wedding anniversary party. She told us she couldn't come to the party because she was going to see her *real parents*, as she called them. So, let's see, that had to be exactly ten years ago this past May."

Robert was writing on a notepad when he said, "Mr. Chance, I have to ask if you're completely sure about that. You're saying she went to visit her biological parents ten years ago this past May?"

Gail said, "If he said it was ten years ago, you can believe it. Jim sometimes can't remember what day of the week to take the trash can to the street, but he can remember the day of the week when he saw the first Star Wars movie."

"That was a Thursday," said Jim.

"See what I mean?" she said to Robert.

Robert asked, "Did Liz, or rather Elizabeth, tell you her biological parents died nine years ago?"

Jim answered, "No, we hadn't heard that, but I must tell you we haven't seen her since then."

"You haven't seen her for ten years?" Robert asked incredulously.

"No," Jim answered, "though we heard from friends of hers that Elizabeth had been regularly visiting the Brennan's. Those are her biological parents, you know."

"Yes, I know," said Robert.

"Anyway, she hasn't contacted us for all those years. One of her acquaintances recently told us she now lives downstate in some small town, can't remember the name. Elizabeth is a very complicated person," Mrs. Chance said, as if defending her daughter.

"It seems that way, doesn't it?" Robert replied.

***

When Cyrus arrived in Pontiac, he took the exit off the interstate that led to the McDonald's where the receipt indicated that Liz had stopped to eat. It was time for lunch anyway, so he ordered some food at the drive-up window. Then he pulled to the side of the lot and sat in his car eating his grilled chicken combo.

He thought about Liz Chance and her connection to Byron Patterson. The date on the receipt was June 8th, which was the day before Byron's escape. If he could determine that she had visited Byron on the eighth, the day before his escape, that would not only show the two of them were reunited, but could also indicate she was probably involved in his escape in some way or other.

Cyrus pulled into the parking lot of the Pontiac Correctional Center about thirty minutes later. Before he left Elby, Cyrus had called ahead to make an appointment with a Mr. Matthew Borles. When Cyrus entered the building, Borles was waiting for him in the lobby.

Noting Mr. Borles's name tag, Cyrus extended his hand, saying, "Mr. Borles, I'm Cyrus Brandt from the Cane County

133

Sheriff's Department. I appreciate your meeting with me on such short notice."

"No problem whatsoever," replied Borles as he shook Cyrus's hand. "Just follow me to my office, and I'll try to be of some help."

Cyrus followed him through a workroom full of small cubicles where men and women were intent on their computer screens. Borles led him into a small office that offered at least a modicum of privacy. He sat down, without inviting Cyrus to sit, and immediately turned to his computer.

"I've done some preliminary work based on the information you gave me when you called. It appears Patterson did in fact have a visitor on June 8th, a woman by the name of Liz Brennan. Our records show she had visited him several times in the last few months. In fact, she was the only person who visited him."

"That's exactly the info we were hoping to get," said Cyrus. "Do you have video of her? I assume you have video surveillance in the visitation area, correct?"

"Yes, we do. Here, let me bring that up, and we'll take a look," Borles said as he pecked at the keyboard. "She signed in at 1:15 p.m., so let me find the video from that time."

Borles fast-forwarded through the video, and it didn't take long to spot Liz Chance walking into the visitation room. Cyrus watched intently as she sat down on the opposite side of the private window from Byron Patterson. Cyrus now knew all his suspicions about Liz had been validated, and this was the break they had been looking for.

Cyrus said, "That's her alright. This is what I came to see, Mr. Borles. That's all we require at this point. Thank you very much. At some point down the road, we may need a copy of that video, however."

"That won't be a problem at all. In fact, I'll make a digital copy of that segment right now and send it to your email."

"That would be great," Cy replied as he leaned down to jot his email address on a pad on the desk in front of him.

The drive from Pontiac back to Elby was a long one. Cyrus was anxious to meet with Robert and Tom to compare notes and plan their next step. He assumed they would have no problem getting a search warrant for Liz's property now, in light of the evidence he had acquired today from Borles. If Liz was hiding Patterson, he wouldn't stay hidden for long. Cyrus was sure it was just a matter of time until Patterson was back behind bars.

38

"What do you mean we didn't get the warrant?" Cyrus exclaimed when Tom broke the news the next morning. "Did the judge consider all our evidence?"

"Yes, he did, but he considers it all circumstantial evidence that doesn't add up to anything concrete. He's right, you know," Tom said with resignation. "We've got a local woman who turns out to be the sister of the escapee. That doesn't make her guilty of anything. And while it is true she may be a person of interest in the Brennan murder/suicide case, there's no hard evidence there either. And the unidentified fingerprint from the Brennans' shotgun doesn't mean anything even if it turns out to be Liz's. Since she was reportedly visiting the Brennans, maybe she just moved the shotgun from one place to another one day. Who knows?"

"Jesus," Cyrus blurted out in frustration. "I just can't believe it!"

"Well, believe it," replied Tom.

At that moment, the door to the sheriff's office opened and Agent Backus walked in. "I got your message, Tom, regarding the warrant. I thought I'd come right over since I was in the neighborhood."

Cyrus was still leaning against a desk, shaking his head. Robert said, "Aw, come on, don't take it so hard. This happens all the time. The question now is, What's our next step?"

"We could at least question Liz about her involvement with Patterson, couldn't we?" asked Cyrus.

"Yes, we'd certainly be within our rights to bring in Liz for questioning. We could do that," said Tom, "but that would alert her to the fact that we know about their connection to one another. Liz and Patterson might just bolt to who-knows-where."

"Yeah, that's right," agreed Robert. "But I'm not sure we have another option at this point. In fact, now that I think about it, maybe that's exactly what we want her to do. If she makes a run for it, that will certainly implicate her in either the Brennan murders or the Patterson investigation. We just need to make sure we're there when she makes her move."

Tom looked up from his notes and said, "The more I look at this case, the more I'm convinced Liz is as guilty as a cat with a mouthful of feathers. We do have some information regarding Liz Chance that we didn't have nine years ago. In particular, I'm talking about what Robert found out from Jim and Gail Chance: the fact that Liz had visited the Brennans prior to their deaths. It seems very odd that she was at their farm developing a relationship with them, but she was nowhere to be seen at the time of the funerals. What was she afraid of back then? What was she hiding? Her involvement seems very fishy if you ask me. And we know Frank's cancer was in remission at the time of his death. Why would Doris commit murder and suicide if he was in remission? It makes no sense."

Tom paused for a moment and then said, "We could begin questioning Liz under the pretense that we're interested only in what she knows about the Brennan murders, and not show our hand regarding our knowledge of her relationship with Patterson. At that point, if we don't get anything from her that would help support a search warrant request, we could confront her with our discovery about her and Patterson. That should really shake her up."

"It's worth a shot," said Robert. "I like it."

"I'll try to get her in here tomorrow afternoon for questioning," said Tom. "How's this all sound to you, Cyrus?"

Cyrus was shaking his head dejectedly. "I really thought we had this thing in the bag. If we'd gotten a warrant, we could've searched her two properties and probably nabbed this guy. Now we have to go through all this bullshit and let Patterson hide out there right under our noses." He turned to walk out of the office, muttering, "This is just great. I guess I'll just sit on the street corner like a mushroom and wait for Patterson to turn himself in."

Chuckling, Tom said, "Hey, Cy, no one ever claimed law enforcement was a very efficient game. We're closer than ever on this case. Let's dwell on that, shall we?" Cyrus barely heard Tom's last few words as he disappeared out the door.

Cyrus walked down Main Street, going nowhere in particular. He wondered if Patterson had already fled the area. Where could he go, though? Liz was his lifeline, the most likely ally for him in concealing his whereabouts. If Byron was left to his own devices, he would most likely be spotted soon as he tried to travel cross-country looking for his next hiding place, wherever that might be. No, his best strategy right now would be to lay low, letting Liz cover for him. It was up to the Cane County Sheriff's Department to find him, but Cyrus knew it'd be tougher than he'd anticipated.

Cyrus was feeling frustrated, but he realized his own impatient expectations in bringing this case to an end were unfounded. He wasn't used to the workings of a criminal investigation, and he knew it. He was in a whole different world than he was accustomed to. Tom and Robert hadn't been troubled by the roadblock they had just encountered. They were used to things not always going their way. Their experience had shown them they simply had to seek another way around the roadblocks. Cyrus was slowly beginning to understand the dynamics of law enforcement. Things didn't always happen in a linear fashion. In fact, they rarely did. The patience required in playing a waiting game seemed to be a prerequisite to this type of work. Cyrus would need to learn that patience if he was to succeed in law enforcement.

Academia was never like this. Achieving one's goals as a university faculty member and physicist had been much less messy than what he was now experiencing. The academic life was a clearly definable order of events, both in one's day-to-day functioning and also in one's long-term career. He had always been able to rely on the fact that his classes would meet at a prescribed time and in a predictable interval of occurrence. The long-term life of an academic was no less predictable, with its eternally repeating pattern of semester after semester after semester. As years of this pattern passed by, the academic had yet other professional patterns laid out before him: the push toward tenure, and finally, upon receiving tenure, the ongoing teaching and research activities that continued until one's retirement party. This life pattern of the academic was pretty much universal for all people who enjoyed this rather rarefied existence.

Unfortunately, Cyrus's academic life hadn't followed these patterns as smoothly as he had hoped, and now he found himself working in a field that was far removed from anything academic. He was working a job that required him to embrace the complexities of human behavior, especially the more unsavory kinds of human behavior, and he wasn't yet certain he was cut out for this line of work. In the beginning, he'd thought this new experience would be fun and exciting—and to be sure, it had proved to be just that at first. Now, however, he was realizing just how difficult this job was. He also realized how very much he had to learn if he was to be effective doing it.

As Cyrus crossed the street and ambled in the opposite direction, he continued to reflect on the life he had left behind and the new life that had replaced it. Had he done the right thing in coming back to Elby? Had this shift in his life really been of his own choosing? Destiny was a concept Cyrus had never put much stock in. He'd always believed people could effect change in their lives by making the correct decisions and following through with them. Life should be lived, he thought, in a rational way. Before coming here, he had truly lived a life of rational thought. Physics was based on rational thought and the scientific process. The forces of the universe happened in consistent and predictable ways, and the scientist could make future decisions based upon a rational consideration of these forces. But now he felt as though his embrace of reason had been overtaken by irrational reactions to feelings and emotions.

Still, coming back here felt like it had been the right thing to do. Working with Tom and Robert in this investigation, as frustrating as it was, felt right. He found himself drawn closer and closer to Annie, and that felt right, too. Was this destiny at work? He didn't know, but he remembered something his mother used to say: *people always end up where they're meant to be.* Was she talking about destiny, or was she talking about the way a person's personality and capabilities directed them to a certain place in the world? Or was that all the same thing?

Cyrus was still thinking about this when he heard a knocking on a window next to the sidewalk. He stopped walking and realized he was standing in front of Annie's diner. He could see Annie on the other side of the windowpane smiling at him. Her bright smile cleared away the fog of anxiety shrouding him, and he suddenly felt like he had returned comfortably to his new world. Annie gestured toward the door, and Cyrus responded by walking in.

"Have you had any breakfast yet, Professor?" she asked.

"I'm going to pretend you didn't call me that, and the answer to your question is *no*," he replied as he took a seat at the counter.

Annie brought him a cup of coffee and a menu, placing them both on the counter in front of him. "The special is pretty awesome today. It's biscuits and gravy. You want some?"

"That sounds delicious, Annie," Cyrus replied as he raised the coffee cup to his lips.

She was gone and back before he had taken another sip. She set the steaming plate on the counter. The sight and aroma of the delectable feast brought an approving grin to Cyrus's face, prompting Annie to say, "I told you it was awesome, didn't I?"

Cyrus was too busy digging in to reply. Finally, he paused for a breath. "Listen, Annie. Tomorrow is Friday night, and I understand the new Brad Pitt movie is showing at the Savoy. We could get something to eat before that, then head to the movie. It'd be fun. I need to do something to get my mind off this case."

"That would be great! I'll see if I can get out of here a bit early," she said gleefully. Then Annie added, "There's one thing, though."

"What's that?"

"I'd love to go out and eat, but instead of going to that stuffy old movie theater, I'd just as soon go to your place after dinner and watch an old DVD or something."

"OK, but you need to know that Matt McConaughey is in that movie with Brad Pitt. And he's got those great abs, you know. I'll bet those abs look especially great on the big screen."

"You seem to have a kind of weird fixation with Matthew McConaughey's abs," she teased. "Hmm. Let me think about this for a second. Matt McConaughey's abs and Brad Pitt together on the big screen, huh? Wow, that's a tough choice," she said. "How about if we go out to eat and watch a movie at your place as I suggested. The entire time, I'll just imagine that under your shirt, you have Matt McConaughey's abs. Is that a good compromise?"

"Yeah, I guess so," Cyrus muttered hesitantly, knowing in reality his torso paled by comparison to Matt McConaughey's exquisite midsection. "I hope you have a good imagination."

39

At four o'clock the next day, Liz Chance was sitting at the conference table in the back room of the sheriff's office. Tom, Cyrus, and Robert all sat on the other side of the table. Earlier, Tom had waited for Liz at the post office until she had finished her route. She had agreed to come in for questioning, even though Tom was vague about the reason. He had told her this was a serious matter and it'd be best if she came in voluntarily. She had reluctantly agreed to come, and had followed Tom back to his office in her Cherokee. She now sat with her hands in her lap, staring worriedly at the three very serious men who were arranging their files and notes in front of them on the table.

Robert was the first to speak. "Ms. Chance, my name is Robert Backus I'm a crime scene investigator with the Illinois State Police. I think you know Tom and Cyrus here." Liz nodded stiffly as Robert went on. "Do you have any idea why we asked you here today?"

"No. Should I?"

Ignoring her question, Robert said, "Is it true you own a property on the east side of Elby, a fairly new house on Bannon Street?"

"Yes. Well, not exactly new. I moved in about eight years ago."

"And you also own a farm out on County Road 28. Is that true?"

"Yes. Is there any law against that?"

Again, Robert ignored the question. "How did you acquire that property?"

"What property?"

"The farm. I'm interested in how you acquired ownership of that farm."

"Is that any of your damn business?" Liz was becoming indignant. "Look, what is this about? So I bought some property. Big deal! People do that all the time, don't they?"

Robert interjected, "So you're saying you purchased that property?"

Liz looked down into her lap and said, "Well, I didn't exactly purchase it."

141

"Elaborate, please," pushed Robert.

"I inherited it," Liz said.

"Oh, really?" Tom said dramatically, as he joined the proceedings. "You know what, Liz? I knew the people who used to own that farm. Their names were Doris and Frank Brennan."

"I know what their names were," Liz shot back.

"Oh, you do, do you?" asked Tom, feigning ignorance of Liz's relationship to the Brennans. "Just how did you know the Brennans?"

"They were my parents," Liz offered quietly.

Robert replied, "Yeah, we knew that already, Liz."

Liz was shaking her head, wondering why she had agreed to subject herself to this little game they were playing. "Look, I think I'm going to leave now. I don't need to take this bullshit!"

Robert continued, "You can leave if you want, but that might result in a search or maybe an arrest warrant that could make your life a lot more difficult."

"Let's just get this shit over with. What is this about? Or are you just having fun harassing me?"

Robert said, "No, Liz. This isn't our idea of fun. We're actually looking into the deaths of the Brennans, the people who were apparently your biological parents, the people who left you their farm, the people whose funeral you didn't even bother to attend. Why is that, Liz?"

"Why is what?"

"Why didn't you attend their funeral?"

"Hell, I didn't even know they existed until after they died and some lawyer called me saying they'd named me as the heir to their farm." She had regained her composure, along with her indignation.

"That's really not true, is it, Liz?" Tom asked. "We know you visited the Brennans at least once prior to their deaths, and quite possibly multiple times. Isn't that right?" He waited for her answer.

Cyrus continued to hold his silence. He knew he was out of his league here. He knew Tom and Robert must have done this type of interrogation many times, and he decided this was his chance to observe and learn.

After an uncomfortable pause, Liz said, "OK, so maybe I met with them a couple of times. So what?"

Robert was in attack mode now. "Why did you just lie to us about that, Liz?" Liz fell silent, and Robert probed on. "Look, Liz, the three of us are sitting here looking at a woman who inherited a sizeable property from her biological parents whom she hadn't known until just before their deaths, and who met a tragic and rather suspicious end. We're looking at a woman who had motive, and a woman who had opportunity. And we're also looking at a woman who is not being truthful with us. How do you think that looks to the three of us sitting at this table?"

Liz shot back, "I don't give a flying fuck how it looks. I didn't kill anybody! Why would I kill my real parents?" Liz began to sniffle, and Tom slid a box of tissues across the table to her. She took one out of the box and wiped her nose. "I was aware they had written me into their will. I knew that, OK? But if there's one thing important to me it's family, and I would never have hurt them. Never. My family is everything to me!"

"Is that why you haven't spoken to your adoptive parents for years?" Robert said sarcastically.

In a subdued voice, Liz slowly said, "They aren't my real parents. Not my real family. Doris and Frank were. I wouldn't have hurt them."

"Then why is it you were not at the funeral?" Robert asked again.

"I'll tell you why, and it's God's truth, I swear it," she answered.

"Well, we already know how you treat the truth, don't we?"

Liz ignored the jab and explained, "I didn't come to the funeral because I didn't even know they had died until several weeks later. How would I know? I didn't know anyone around here who would've contacted me. I hadn't been visiting them that regularly, and nobody around here even knew I existed. At the time of their deaths, I wasn't even in the state."

"Is that so?" asked Tom. "Where were you?"

"I was in Columbia, Missouri, interviewing for a job."

"And what kind of job was that?"

"There was an opening at the Columbia post office, and I thought I had enough experience to possibly get hired there. I had just lost my job in Kankakee, and I was looking . . . ."

"Yeah, we know all about that," interrupted Robert impatiently. "Do you have any proof you were in Missouri at the time of their deaths?"

Liz thought for a moment and said, "That was quite a while ago, but I'll bet I could find some evidence I was there. I might still have the letter they sent me to verify my appointment. I still have my job search file somewhere at my house."

"We'll need to see that, Liz," said Tom, jotting some notes in his notebook. "We also need to know where the interview was conducted. We need a location and any names you can remember."

"I'll see if I can find that information."

"I'm sure you will," said Robert dryly. Then, without another word, Robert opened his laptop computer, turned it toward Liz, and hit the play button.

Without showing any emotion, Liz watched the video clip of herself visiting Patterson at the Pontiac prison. When it was over, she stoically looked up at Robert and said, "So what?"

"So what? That's all you have to say?" Robert asked. "This video shows you knew Byron Patterson. Not only that, but this video was taken the day before his escape. I find that very interesting."

"So I knew Patterson. That doesn't mean I helped him escape or anything." She knew she was in trouble now. How could she possibly talk her way out of this one?

Robert forged ahead. "And here's the kicker, Liz. Although we haven't verified this with Patterson's records at DCFS, we have it on good authority that you and he may be brother and sister, twins in fact."

"Shit," she said under her breath. Then she thought for a few seconds and said, "OK, look, so let's say he is my brother. That would explain why I was visiting him at the prison, right? Why wouldn't a sister visit her brother in prison? He's family. This doesn't mean anything. It doesn't mean I'm a criminal or even a bad person. You have no proof I had anything to do with my parents' deaths or my brother's escape, right? Sure, I'm involved here, but only because I'm related to all these people. That's it. You ain't got shit on me, do you?"

144

Liz was showing more confidence now. She rose from her chair, saying, "I'm done talking to you people. Any more talking will be done through a lawyer."

As she turned to leave, Robert said, "Oh, I'm sure we'll be talking to you again real soon, Liz. I suspect the next time we talk we'll bring an arrest warrant along with us."

Liz slammed the door as she stalked out of the building. The three men sat in silence for a moment. Robert was writing some final notes on a piece of paper. Then he said, "Tom, you know what we need to do, right?"

Tom replied, "Yup. I'll keep an eye on her tonight, and tail her if she goes anywhere. If she's going to make a run for it, it'll likely happen soon. I'll let you guys know if and when it happens, so be ready." Tom abruptly got up and left the office, heading for his vehicle.

After Tom left, Robert said to Cyrus, "Well, Deputy, you wanted things to start happening in this investigation. You should be careful what you wish for, because we may find ourselves in a shitstorm real soon. Liz is pretty riled up. I suspect she'll make a move, and it'll happen in the next few days if my instincts serve me well."

40

Cyrus drove to town and picked up Annie precisely at six o'clock in front of the diner. Annie jumped onto the seat of the pickup with a radiant smile. "Where are you taking me to eat, moneybags?" she asked.

"I made reservations at that steakhouse down the street. I hope that's OK with you."

"Sounds great to me. But why don't we just leave the pickup here, and walk down there. It's not very far away, and it's a beautiful evening," she said as she looked up through the window into a sky that was just beginning to show the dimming signs of a summer sunset.

Annie curled her arm around Cyrus's as they ambled down the sidewalk toward the restaurant. A warm wind was blowing just enough to muss Annie's hair, but she didn't care. It felt good to walk with Cyrus through this town that she had always called home.

"How do you like being back in Elby?" she asked Cyrus.

"I like it well enough, I guess. It's pretty peaceful here, aside from the occasional double murders," he replied, giving Annie a little nudge in the ribs.

"I'm counting on you guys to solve those murders so we can return to our peaceful ways."

"We're trying, but this law enforcement business is turning out to be a bit more complicated than I expected."

"Do you want to tell me about it?" Annie offered.

"Not really, Annie. I probably shouldn't be talking about it anyway. In fact, what I would really like to do is make a point of *not* talking about it tonight. Let's just pretend Byron Patterson and Liz Chance and the Barnetts and the Brennans never existed. Just for tonight, can we do that? What do you say?"

"Sounds good to me."

Cyrus and Annie walked the rest of the way to the restaurant in silence. Upon entering, they were led to a nice table in the back, where they spent the next couple of hours enjoying the conversation, the meal, and the bottle of Cabernet Cyrus ordered. After dinner, they walked in the moonlight back to Cyrus's pickup and drove to his house on the old farmstead.

Outside of town the cicadas were in fine form, and both Annie and Cyrus enjoyed the beetle chorus rising from the verdant surroundings. They had become accustomed to that cacophonic chatter. It was as much a part of their lives as the ubiquitous corn and soybean fields. They drove most of the way without speaking a word. Annie laid her head back on the seat and thought how perfect this all felt. She had been taking care of herself since her husband's death, she now was surprised to admit how much she enjoyed being taken care of by someone else. It felt good to ride through the countryside next to Cyrus, and she was just a little sad when the trip came to an end in his driveway.

Molly emerged from her small dwelling by the garage and lumbered over to greet them. "Hey, Molly. How are you, sweetie?" Annie asked cheerfully. Molly's tail was wagging double-time as she walked by Annie's side to the back door. "Can she come in with us, Cy?" Annie asked.

"I suppose so," he said with a smile. "OK, just for a little while then, Molly. Then out you go."

Within fifteen minutes, the three of them were sitting on the couch watching an old Clint Eastwood movie and sharing a large bowl of popcorn. Annie just stared at the screen, letting the storyline carry her to a place far, far away. Cyrus, on the other hand, wasn't paying attention to the screen at all. He was thinking about the way Annie had so unhesitatingly put her arm around his as they walked to the restaurant earlier in the evening. And he thought about the expression of contentment on her face as they drove through the countryside on their way to his farmstead.

It was suddenly clear to Cyrus that she didn't consider him to be just a good friend, but much more. He now realized that despite the lip service Annie had given to the notion of taking things slowly, she had completely given herself over to the idea of them as a couple. And why wouldn't she? Cyrus hadn't really discouraged it. This tight wire act they had been playing had now become serious. And perhaps irreversible.

It wasn't that he didn't want her. Of course he did. Who wouldn't? She was smart, beautiful, funny. He truly enjoyed being with her. Was that love? Hell if he knew. He had given up trying to figure that out. But he knew something that she didn't.

It was something they had never talked about. Annie assumed that Cyrus was here to stay, and Cyrus had been afraid to tell her otherwise. Despite his past professional woes, he had begun to think more about returning to academia. He suspected that if an attractive position at another college came his way, he might jump at it. After all, he was a trained physicist. That's how he defined himself. That was his life's work. And he knew the longer he stayed away from his profession, the tougher it'd be to get back into it. That's just the way it worked.

Annie now presented a complication. If he allowed his relationship with her to blossom further, what would happen if he skipped town for a teaching or research job somewhere? Would she come with him? Highly unlikely. Not with her diner to take care of. Annie would be devastated. The certainty of that fact descended on him with unbearable weight. Annie would be crushed, and it would be his fault. He glanced over at Annie, who was resting her head on his shoulder, and closed his eyes tightly against the guilt and shame he imagined waiting for him just over the horizon.

At one o'clock in the morning, Cyrus was startled awake by his cell phone vibrating in his pocket. Looking at the phone, he noticed it was Tom calling. Annie and Molly were sleeping soundly beside him, and the TV screen was now dark. The half-filled popcorn bowl still sat on his lap, and he carefully put it aside as he got up and retreated into the kitchen to answer the phone.

"Yeah, Tom? What's up?" Cyrus said in a whisper.

"Hey, Cyrus, listen. I've been sitting around the corner from Liz's home all night. About five minutes ago, her garage door opened and she took off like a bat out of hell in her Cherokee. I'm following her now, and it appears she's heading toward her place in the country, the Brennan place. I think she's making her move. If that's where she's going, we should be there in about ten minutes. Can you get out there right away?"

"Yes. I'm on my way, Tom."

"Make sure you kill your lights as you get close, and park down the road. You'll most likely see my vehicle there. Bring your weapon."

"Got it." Cyrus put the phone back in his pocket and ripped a page off the notepad on the counter. On it he wrote: *Liz is on the move. Going to help Tom. Stay put. I'll be back soon I hope. C.* He laid the note on the coffee table in front of Annie and the dog, and covered Annie gently with the throw from the nearby chair. Molly looked sleepily up at him as he did so, but then laid her head back down and closed her eyes.

Cyrus watched the two of them sleep for a few seconds. Seeing them there together on his couch in such a peaceful state made him feel oddly content. He hadn't felt that way in quite some time. He took a mental picture of them for future reference, then walked back into the kitchen, strapped on his gun, left the house, and drove the Hyundai out onto the road.

41

About fifteen minutes later Cyrus pulled up behind Tom's cruiser, which was parked about a quarter of a mile down the road from Liz's farm. Both vehicles were hidden from view by a grove of old fruit trees in the pasture next to the house. Cyrus got out of his SUV and walked up to Tom's window.

"What's going on?" Cyrus asked.

"Not much yet," Tom responded. "I've just been waiting on you before we take a closer look. Come on!" Tom quietly got out of the car and led the way to a position just up the road. They had no sooner crouched down in the ditch next to the fence line when the side door of the house flew open. The yard light clearly illuminated the area at the side of the house, and through his binoculars Tom could see a man walk out with a suitcase in one hand and a cardboard box in the other. The man placed both items in the back seat of Liz's SUV.

"Is that Patterson? Can you tell from here?" asked Tom as he handed the binoculars to Cyrus.

Cyrus took a long look through the binoculars and said, "That's him all right. I could never forget that ugly mug. He just went back in the house!"

"This isn't good, Cyrus," Tom said. "It looks like he's ready to take off. If he gets in that Cherokee and gets out on the open road, we'll have a tough time apprehending him. It'd be much better to confront him up at the house. We need to move now!"

The two men moved quickly and quietly along the ditch to the driveway. Tom said, "Cyrus, I'm going to make a beeline to the side of that porch so when Patterson comes out again, I can get the drop on him. Go around the rear of the house to make sure he doesn't head out that way if things go wrong and he spots me. Let's do it!"

Tom raced toward the porch, angling toward the corner of the house to avoid direct sight lines out the side windows. Cyrus stealthily crossed the driveway to the ditch on the other side and continued in the darkness along the road to the end of the property line, where he cut back through a windbreak of white pines that concealed his approach. He took a position next to a back door that led out to the garage and waited there with his weapon at the ready. It wasn't long until he heard Tom shouting, "Down on the ground, Patterson. Now!"

Cyrus began to sprint to Tom's location, but before he got there he heard a commotion, followed by Tom yelling "Damn it!" and a door slamming. As Cyrus rounded the corner, he could see some luggage pieces strewn about Tom, who was getting up off the ground. Tom shouted, "Get on back there, Cy. Make sure the rear of the place is covered. I'm going in after him." Then Tom scaled the steps and shoved through the side door with his handgun pointing the way.

Cyrus returned to his earlier position near the back door and waited. Growing impatient, he tried the screen door. It was unlocked. Next he tried to open the inside door and was surprised to find it too was unlocked. He considered entering but he hesitated, wondering what Tom would have him do.

He didn't have to wonder long before he heard a gunshot from inside the house. Cyrus ripped the screen door open and quickly entered the house. He found himself in some kind of mudroom or pantry. He carefully moved through the room to a door leading to a hallway. He could see the hallway turned abruptly to the right, but he couldn't see where it led. Cautiously he walked down the hallway, staying close to the interior wall.

Then Cyrus heard a groan from somewhere in the house. The gunshot he had heard must have hit its target. Whether the target had been Tom or Patterson wasn't relevant now. Either way, it was time for Cyrus to move. He ran around the corner and burst into a kitchen area where Tom lay bleeding on the floor, holding his right shoulder. Blood was flowing freely through his fingers, but Tom appeared to be conscious and aware of his surroundings.

Tom saw Cyrus standing across the room from him and started looking frantically around for his weapon, which had fallen from his grip when he took the hit. Cyrus scanned the room to assess the potential danger. Then he holstered his gun, raced over to Tom, and retrieved a dishcloth that was hanging on a nearby cabinet door handle. Kneeling next to Tom, Cyrus pressed the cloth firmly onto the wound. As calmly as possible, Cyrus said, "Try not to move, Tom. Let's keep pressure on this wound, and I'll get you out of here before you know it."

"Get up and move away from him, or I'll shoot you where you stand." Patterson had appeared from another doorway and was pointing a gun directly at Cyrus. Cyrus recognized the weapon as his Glock, which Patterson had taken from him at the Barnett home. It was the weapon Byron had used to kill Mary Barnett, and it was trained on Cyrus now with similar intent.

Cyrus pleaded, "I need to keep pressure on his wound, or he'll bleed to . . ."

Patterson interrupted him. "I don't give a rat's ass. Do I look like I care? Now get up and stand over there." Patterson gestured away from the sheriff. Cyrus did as he commanded, with his wrist pressing against his holstered weapon.

"Oh, no you don't, Deputy," warned Patterson. "Take that gun out with your thumb and index finger and lay it on the floor in front of you. You try anything and you'll eat a bullet."

Cyrus knew he meant it, and complied. Then he said, "Look, I'm unarmed now. Let me help the sheriff. I can help slow the bleeding."

"Stay where you are, asshole," Byron replied. "He can die for all I care." He called into the next room, "Lizzie, come on out here. I need you to help me."

Liz stepped into the kitchen from an adjacent room. Patterson said, "Liz, go pick up that gun and train it on the sheriff there. He shouldn't cause any more trouble, but if he does, shoot him." He motioned for Cyrus to step back as Liz carefully picked up Cy's gun and pointed it awkwardly at the injured officer. Patterson scanned the floor until he located the sheriff's weapon and kicked it to the opposite side of the kitchen.

Cyrus said, more to himself than anyone else, "Well, it looks like we were right about you all along, Liz."

"Shut up, Brandt," shouted Patterson.

"What are we going to do now?" asked Liz, looking at her brother.

"There's only one thing we can do, Lizzie. If we're going to get a head start out of this shithole county, we can't leave these two here alive, can we? I shouldn't have let you stop me the first time from killing this deputy."

"Say what?" asked Cyrus. He now realized why he had made it out of the Barnett house alive.

"I said, shut the fuck up, cowboy!" Patterson shouted.

Without thinking, Cyrus said under his breath, "Don't call me that." As soon as the words came out of his mouth he froze, trying not to meet Patterson's eyes.

"I can call you anything the hell I want," said Patterson. "Hey, I know what I'll call you. I think I'll call you *dead*." He stepped closer to Cyrus, pointing the Glock directly at his face, and slowly began to squeeze the trigger.

"No!" shouted Liz. "There's been enough killing. I won't stand for any more." She was a different woman than Cyrus had observed just a moment ago. She was now challenging Byron, a brutal and unrepentant murderer. She was confronting him without fear, as only a sister could. Byron didn't even look her way. Instead, he smiled and took another step closer to Cyrus, letting his finger squeeze just a bit harder on the trigger.

"I said *NO!*" Liz screamed, now pointing her weapon at Patterson. "Put the gun down!"

"You're not going to shoot me, Lizzie," Patterson said. He had barely finished speaking when Liz discharged the weapon, aiming about a foot to the right of his head and sending a bullet through the window above the kitchen sink. Cyrus winced, expecting Byron to fire the Glock into his forehead at that very moment. Fortunately, Patterson's weapon remained silent, and his grip on the gun relaxed as he slowly took a step backward.

"I said *put the gun down*." Liz enunciated each syllable. "I am so tired of covering for you, Byron. My life was going just fine till you came back to town." Byron brought the gun down and turned toward Liz. She went on, "Now I've got the law on my ass, accusing me of everything from aiding and abetting to the murders of my own parents. I'm helping you because you're my brother, but I certainly didn't kill anybody."

Cyrus said quietly, "You know, Liz, we'd like to believe you, but look who's holding a gun right now. Your claims don't seem to hold much water."

Patterson pointed his finger at Cyrus and said, "Look, you damn cowboy, this is between Liz and me. You stay out of it."

Liz continued, "I told you guys I was out of the state at the time of their deaths, and I can prove it if you let me. I liked the Brennans. I really did. Even Byron here will tell you they were very nice people. Why would I want to murder my own flesh and blood?"

Cyrus was looking at Tom, wondering how much longer he could last. He realized that he would need to keep Liz talking if he were to gain any advantage. Suddenly the words Liz had just uttered registered with him. He said, "Are you saying Byron met the Brennans before their deaths?"

"Of course. I wanted him to meet his biological parents before they passed. Our father wasn't in the best of health," Liz said.

"Could he have gone to see them while you were interviewing for that job in Missouri?" Cyrus asked.

"Why would he?" she asked, curious as to why he asked such a question.

"I think you know why, Liz," replied Cyrus.

"Enough of this!" Byron said. "We need to get out of here, Liz, and we can't leave any witnesses. You know that, right?"

Liz still held the gun in front of her, pointing it first at Cyrus, then at Patterson. "Just shut up, Byron!" She turned back to Cyrus. "What do you mean?"

"We discovered something when we re-examined the file on the Brennans' deaths. Frank's cancer was in remission at the time of his murder. Now why would Doris, who hated guns in the first place, decide to end her beloved husband's life if his cancer was in remission? It makes no sense."

Liz looked at Byron for a long while before she said slowly, "Byron, tell me you didn't do this. They were your parents, too."

"They weren't my parents any more than they were yours, Liz. They gave us up for adoption when we were babies. We didn't owe them a damn thing. They were going to die soon anyway. I was just trying to help you out. You had just lost your job and had no way to pay your bills, remember? This inheritance was your ticket to a better life. It was *our* ticket to a better life."

Cyrus waited a moment to let that all sink in. Then he said calmly, "What are you going to do, Liz? Tom here is in a bad way. Are you going to let him die? Are you going to let Byron kill the sheriff and me, too?"

Liz thought for a second and then said, "Byron, I'm going to give you a head start. Take my Cherokee and go. I don't care where you go, just go. You're my brother, the only blood relative I have left. I'll give you this last favor, but you're not going to kill any more people today if I can help it. If you turn that gun on the sheriff or Mr. Brandt, you'll have to turn it on me, too. You decide." Liz continued to aim her weapon at Patterson, and he could see she meant every word she had spoken.

"Shit," said Patterson. "But you need to give me about an hour head start, OK? At least give me that, will you?"

"I'll give you an hour. No more. Now get going." Liz turned to Cyrus, saying, "And if you think I won't shoot you, you should think again. No matter what Byron did, he's still my brother, and I'll shoot anyone who threatens to harm him."

As Byron walked toward the door, he raised the Glock to Cyrus's head. For a brief moment, Cyrus thought he was a dead man. But Patterson merely said "Bang," mimicking a gunshot, and walked on. "It looks like she saved your ass again, Brandt." Then he stomped out the door, got in the SUV, and threw gravel as he peeled out of the driveway.

Liz watched Byron's taillights disappear down the road. Then she turned to Cyrus and said, "Now, we wait."

"No, we can't wait, Liz. While we wait, Tom's going to die. Please let me call an ambulance. Now!" Cyrus pleaded.

She pointed the weapon at Cyrus and said, "We'll give Byron an hour head start. I promised him I'd do that, and that's exactly what I'll do."

"If you do that, you'll be responsible for Tom's death. Do you want that on your conscience? You claim not to have killed anyone. I tend to believe you. But if we don't help him, you'll be the one to answer for his death."

Liz hesitated and looked at her watch. Then she said, "OK, put your cell phone on the kitchen counter. Then you can attend to him."

Cyrus quickly found his phone, threw it on the counter, and knelt down next to Tom. His bleeding seemed to have slowed a bit, which Cyrus took as a good sign. Cyrus pressed the dishcloth firmly against Tom's shoulder. The sheriff was still conscious, but he couldn't really speak. Cyrus knew he was going into shock. He checked Tom's pulse.

"His pulse seems slow to me, Liz. Now I'm no doctor, but I had some experience in Iraq with gunshot wounds, and I don't think we can wait an hour to get him out of here."

"We'll wait, as I promised," Liz said with finality.

Minute after minute passed, and after about twenty minutes, Cyrus was becoming desperate. Tom had fallen unconscious, and his pulse was weakening. Cyrus could no longer just sit and wait while Tom's life faded away in front of his eyes. He finally said, "Liz, I'm walking over to that cell phone, and I'm going to call for an ambulance. You can shoot me if you want, but I don't think you really want to do that."

Liz pointed the gun straight at his face and said, "You're only going to do what I tell you to do. I'm still calling the shots here." She looked over at the sheriff. He didn't look good. She knew Cyrus was right, and the sheriff wouldn't make it much longer. Reluctantly Liz said, "OK, I'll let you call for an ambulance, but only an ambulance. If you alert the law, I swear you'll regret it."

"OK, it's a deal. Just an ambulance." Cyrus reached for his phone and called 911.

When he had finished the call, he slipped the phone into his pocket and said, "You do realize that the 911 dispatch will also notify the law, don't you? When the ambulance gets here, you'll have to surrender that weapon."

"Damn it! Byron will just have to do with that much lead time, I guess."

"Listen, Liz, you don't owe him anything. I know he's your brother, but he's also a cold-blooded killer who has messed up your life."

Liz knew he was right and solemnly nodded her head.

156

42

Fifteen minutes later, an ambulance pulled into the driveway with lights flashing, creating a surreal light show upon the farmhouse, trees, and outbuildings. Cyrus was waiting on the steps, and he helped to quickly haul the gurney into the kitchen. Tom was no longer conscious, but at least he was still alive. Cyrus knew if the bullet had hit anything vital, Tom would be dead by now. Fortunately, the sheriff had been very lucky.

As Tom was being prepared for transport, Cyrus walked up to Liz, who had placed the weapon on the countertop, and said, "Sorry, Liz, but I need to take you into custody. You'll have to turn around and put your hands behind your back." She did as she was instructed, and Cyrus placed his handcuffs on her wrists. Then he led her outside, sat her down on the steps, and called Sarah on his cell phone.

"Sarah, sorry to wake you, but listen very carefully. I need you to call Robert Backus and Agent Corbit right away and get them out here to the old Brennan place. You know where it is, right?"

"Yeah, Cy. On County Road 28. What's going on?"

"Tell them we found Patterson, but we lost him just as fast. He got away. Unfortunately, Tom was shot in the process."

"Oh, my God, how is he? Is he OK?"

"Yes, Sarah, I think he'll be fine. He lost some blood, but he's a tough old bird. The ambulance is here and they're just about to transport him to the medical center. I'll wait here for Robert and John. Tell them to hurry. Patterson is on the run, and we need to go after him."

"OK, Cyrus. I'll also call Tom's wife, Angie. She'll wanna get over to the medical center with the girls. I'll call Annie, too, to let her know."

Cyrus replied, "No, I'll call Annie. You just make the other calls."

As soon as Cyrus ended the call he dialed Annie's number. There was no answer, and he assumed she had turned her phone off before they began watching the movie. He would try again later, he decided, and he turned to watch the ambulance pulling out onto the road on its way to the medical center.

Cyrus turned to Liz and said, "We're going to find Byron. There's no doubt about that. A man can't hide forever. It's just a matter of time before he slips up and ends up back where he belongs, in prison."

"Yeah, so what?" asked Liz derisively.

"I'm thinking maybe you could help us find him."

"Why would I do that?"

"You and I both know what Byron is capable of. The longer he's on the loose, the more people he may hurt or even kill. If you don't help us, the carnage he leaves will be on you. And besides, you're in a shitload of trouble right now. If you help us find him, that might help your cause."

"I have no idea where he is or where he might go," Liz muttered.

"I find that hard to believe, Liz. Listen, time is of the essence here. It'll be more and more difficult to find him the longer this goes on."

"I told you I have no idea. I don't. I don't exactly follow all his friends on Facebook. He's probably got connections with ex-cons all over the place. Or maybe he's on his own, without a clue right now as to where he can go. I can't help you, Deputy."

Cyrus was not ready to believe her. He was just about to probe further for any information she might offer when his phone vibrated. It was Robert calling.

"Yeah, Robert. Are you on your way?"

"Yes, Cyrus, but I'm coming from Springfield. It'll take me a while. John is closer. He should be there very soon. Just hang tight. Sarah told me Patterson's on the run again. We need to get an APB out to our people so they can locate him. What's he driving?"

"He took off in Liz's Jeep Cherokee. It's a late model—I'd say a year or two old. Silver. I don't know the plate number and Liz isn't being very forthcoming with that information."

"We can get that. It's not a problem," replied Robert. "OK, we'll get that description out and hopefully someone will spot him. It won't be easy in the dark, but maybe we'll get lucky. Now, tell me exactly when he left the scene."

"About an hour ago."

"And you just notified us now?" Cyrus could hear the concern in Robert's voice.

"Liz was holding us at gunpoint to give Byron a head start. There was nothing I could do. I've got her in custody now, though."

"With an hour head start, it'll be tough finding him. He could be driving rural roads, or for all we know, he could be hiding right under our noses again. What a frigging mess. How was Tom when you last saw him? Is he going to make it?"

"When they got him in the ambulance, he was breathing steadily but he wasn't conscious. He took a bullet in his right shoulder, but I don't think it was life-threatening. However, he did lose a lot of blood."

"OK, Cy. I'll be there as soon as I can. See you then."

John arrived about twenty minutes later, followed by another vehicle with Tom's two other deputies. John and Cyrus reviewed the details of the incident while the other officers were busy taking photographs and searching the house for anything Patterson might have left behind.

Just as they were finishing up, Robert arrived at the scene and took a final look at the interior of the house to make sure the officers hadn't missed anything. When he was satisfied, he said, "That's it for now. Let's head back to town. I want to get a written statement from you, Cyrus. I especially need you to document exactly what you told us about Patterson implicating himself in the Brennan killings. Do you think Liz will corroborate what he said?"

Cyrus replied, "Yes, I think she will. She's not such a bad apple, Robert. I don't think she has killed anybody, or could. In fact, she's saved my life twice already. She knows her brother is no good. Still, he's her brother, and she feels oddly compelled to protect him. That's quite a moral dilemma when the person you're protecting keeps killing people."

"Yeah, I suppose so," Robert said. "OK, let's get going."

As they were heading out the kitchen door, John paused and gazed at a patch of Tom's blood left on the linoleum. He said, "This needs to end soon, or a lot of other people are going to suffer. Tom is a really good law enforcement officer, and a very good friend. We could have lost him tonight. You did good work tonight, Cyrus. Thanks for taking care of Tom."

Cyrus could see John was trying hard to control his emotions. He knew John had worked closely with Tom for many years; they were colleagues in the best sense of the word.

"Don't worry, John. Tom will be back on his feet before you know it. It takes more than that to take down a Mr. Basketball from Tri-City Consolidated High School."

Cyrus got the result he wanted as John cracked a faint smile and said, "That's for damn sure. Go Tigers!"

43

The five law enforcement vehicles headed back to Elby and parked behind the Cane County Sheriff's Office. After John directed the two deputies to drive Liz over to the jail, he followed Robert and Cyrus through the back door. Inside, they found a worried receptionist blocking their path.

Cyrus said, "Hey, Sarah, thanks for coming in so early on a Saturday. Any news?"

Sarah spoke in a quick, excited cadence. "Yes, I just got off the phone with a nurse over at the hospital. She said Tom is stable. He just got out of surgery, and I guess it went well. That's a relief. I'll keep checking on him. Cyrus, did you get ahold of Annie?"

Cyrus had tried calling her on the way to town, but she still hadn't picked up. "I've tried a few times, and she won't answer. It's almost five-thirty," he said as he looked at his watch. "I'm sure she'll be awake soon, and she'll notice I've been calling. But keep trying her for me, would you, Sarah?"

"Sure."

John, Cyrus, and Robert all took their seats at the table in the back of the office and began to review the incident. Every detail was potentially important, and they made every effort to be accurate and complete as they transferred the information from their notes to the official case file. Robert had been through this procedure many times in his career. He knew one small detail could break a case wide open, and he wasn't going to overlook anything. He guided Cyrus through his written statement, and then together they scheduled a time for later in the morning to conduct a thorough questioning of Liz.

Cyrus's phone suddenly vibrated with a text message. He glanced at the phone and noticed it was from Annie.

Cyrus read the text and then jumped to his feet. "Shit! Shit, shit! We've got to go! NOW!"

"What is it?" asked Robert.

"It's a text message from Annie's phone. Here, look at this." Cyrus tossed the phone onto the table as he grabbed his jacket.

Robert picked up the cell phone and read the text: *Hey, Cowboy. Left a little message for you on your coffee table. Have a nice day. Byron.*

Robert looked up at Cyrus and said, "He was at your house?" Then his brow furrowed. "And what the hell is Byron doing with Annie's cell phone?"

They were all on their feet in an instant, heading for the back door.

From her desk in the front office, Sarah called out at the clamor. "What's going on?" But there was no reply other than car engines coming to life, as three vehicles peeled out of the parking lot toward Cyrus's farmstead.

Cyrus slammed down hard on his brakes, and the Hyundai slid to a stop next to his house. John and Robert were right behind him. In an instant they were out with weapons drawn, standing behind the protection of their vehicles as they scanned the area around them.

It seemed eerily quiet to Cyrus. Where was Molly? Why wasn't she raising a ruckus? Jesus, he thought, three men with guns drawn outside the house, and that damn dog had apparently found something better to do. And where was Annie?

Robert said, "John, take the back. Cyrus, you keep a watch on those windows. I'm going in there."

Cyrus spoke as Robert began to move. "Robert, be careful. Annie's in there."

Surprised, Robert asked, "Why is Annie in there? It's six o'clock in the morning, for crying out loud."

"It doesn't matter now, but she's in there. We need to help her."

When John had made it to the back door, Robert and Cyrus approached the house. Robert entered first, and after about sixty seconds he returned and said, "It's clear down here. I'm going upstairs. I want you to stay right here, Cyrus."

As Robert inched his way up the steps, Cyrus waited anxiously just outside the kitchen door. A few endless minutes later, John and Robert came to the door and motioned for Cyrus to come in.

Robert spoke. "Cyrus, you're not going to like what you see in here."

"Is it Annie?" Cyrus cried out.

"No, no, no. Annie isn't here. You have a dog?" John asked.

"Yeah. Her name is Molly. Did you find her?"

"Sorry, Cy. I think she's dead," said Robert.

"Oh, no! Poor Molly. Where is she? I want to see her," Cyrus said as he pushed his way between the two men and walked into the living room.

Molly lay on the carpet next to the couch in a pool of blood. Cyrus could see the wound in her neck where a stream of blood still appeared sticky on her beautiful golden fur.

Cyrus knelt, and for a long moment he stroked the top of Molly's head without saying a word. Then he uttered, "That fucking, fucking bastard! I'm going to kill that son of a bitch if it's the last thing I do."

"We'll get him, Cy," said Robert. "We'll do it together, OK?"

"Hey, take a look at this," John said. He was bent over, looking at something on the coffee table.

The three men scrutinized the handwritten note that had been set conspicuously on the table.

"It's hard to make out. Can you read it, Cyrus?" asked Robert.

Cyrus began to read slowly and haltingly: *Look what I found, Cowboy. I thought I'd come by and leave a message via your little pooch, but then I found something even better. I found a cute little insurance policy. I'm getting out of this hellhole of a county, and don't think of following me. If you cops follow me, or even get close to me, I'm putting a bullet in this pretty girl's head.*

Cyrus stood up straight, saying, "He's got Annie! What are we going to do?"

"OK, calm down, Cyrus," Robert said calmly. "The good news is that because Byron stopped here, he hasn't yet traveled as far as we thought. Also, it doesn't make sense that he would hurt Annie. He needs her, like he said, for *life insurance*. Let's take a close look around and see if we can find anything of interest."

"But shouldn't you call off the manhunt for Patterson? If one of your people gets too close to him, he might kill Annie," Cyrus insisted.

Robert turned now to look at Cyrus and said, "Cyrus, come in the kitchen with me and have a seat. John, you continue looking around, OK?"

Robert and Cyrus took a seat at the kitchen table. Cyrus asked, "Why are we wasting time sitting here? What's this about?"

"Look, Cyrus, it appears you're having a personal relationship with Annie, correct?"

"I guess you could say that," Cyrus admitted.

"Do you have a weapon on you?" Robert asked.

"Yeah, why?"

"Is it your own weapon?"

"No, Tom gave it to me after Patterson took my handgun at the Barnett place. What are you getting at?"

"Would you please put the weapon on the table for me?" Robert said as calmly as he could.

Cyrus was agitated now. "What's this about? Are you accusing me of something?"

"No, not at all. Just do as I say, please, Cyrus," Robert said, being careful not to raise his voice.

Cyrus slowly but reluctantly did as Robert had asked. Robert then said, "Please take out your badge and place it next to the weapon."

Cyrus pulled out his credentials and slid them onto the tabletop, all the time staring straight ahead at Robert.

Robert looked intently at Cyrus and said, "I want you to listen very carefully to what I have to say, Cyrus. We're not going to call off the manhunt. We need to find Patterson. He's a danger to everyone around him." Cyrus opened his mouth to protest, but Robert quickly went on. "We have a specific protocol for searches like this. We won't take unnecessary risks when a hostage is involved. Our guys are trained to do this, so you have to trust that they know what they're doing."

Cyrus was listening carefully to Robert's every word. "And here's the thing, Cyrus. You have to realize there's a good chance a guy like Patterson will kill his hostage regardless of what we do. He's killed before. He knows we know he's killed before. So what would keep him from killing again?

"I don't say this to scare you, because I know you have a personal investment in Annie's well-being. I'm just giving you the truth as I believe it to be. On the other hand, I've been in manhunts like this in the past, and many have had positive outcomes, with the hostage recovered unharmed. So think positively and let us do our job. OK, Cyrus?"

Cyrus nodded slowly and looked at his weapon, realizing that Robert had more to say. Right on cue, Robert continued. "I'm going to take your weapon and your badge because we need to take you off this case."

"There's no way you can do that. Too much has happened for me to just walk away from this," Cyrus protested.

"Well, that's exactly what you're going to do: walk away. You cannot be involved in this investigation if you're in a relationship with the hostage. It's just not feasible. We can't trust you to do the rational thing in a high-pressure situation. Hell, you can't trust *yourself* to do the rational thing."

Cyrus knew deep down that Robert was right. All Cyrus wanted to do at this moment was put his gun to Patterson's forehead and pull the trigger. He wasn't exactly thinking straight, and he knew it.

"So I'm sorry to say that for now we're ending your service with the Cane County Sheriff's Department. When Tom recovers and gets back to work, he can reinstate you if he so chooses. In the meantime, I promise to keep you updated on this case, OK, Cyrus? I promise I will. And you can call me anytime for an update. I owe you that much."

Cyrus remained silent, staring emotionless into Robert's eyes. Finally, Cyrus said, "Is that it?"

"Yes, Cyrus. That's it. Can we do anything for you before we head out? Do you want some help with Molly?"

Cyrus seemed distracted now as he gazed out a nearby window. He said dryly, "No, Robert. I'll take care of my Mo girl by myself." He walked into the living room and sat down on the floor next to the dead animal.

44

The morning sun had risen far enough that a mid-morning heat fell like a tarp over Cyrus's farm. Light was blaring through the east windows into the house. It looked like it'd be a hot one today. Cyrus could tell already. He had been sitting next to Molly for two hours, and he only now felt like he had the emotional and physical energy to complete the task ahead of him.

He slowly rose to his feet and reached for the blanket draped over the back of the couch. He reverently wrapped it around Molly, gently lifted her in his arms, and walked slowly out of the house.

The air smelled of dirt and honeysuckle and clover. Cyrus could swear he even smelled the corn and soybeans that blanketed the land around his house. His eyes took in the vibrant spectacle of green surrounding the farmstead. Every shade of green imaginable was now apparent to him in the trees, shrubs, flowers, and crops adorning his world. And the sounds he heard. How awesome were these sounds? How could he not have noticed them before? It seemed he could hear each leaf brushing against its neighbor at the whim of the eolian gusts which were forming waves in the crops around him.

Cyrus stood and took this all in as he cradled Molly in his arms. He felt as if he were experiencing his surroundings for the first time. His memory of the last few days seemed to vanish, and all he could comprehend now was the task which lay immediately ahead.

He walked between the farm buildings toward the back of the property, then followed the fence row that bordered a large field of soybeans. He continued through yet another field and came to a stop in a place where four fields intersected. A large mulberry tree loomed over him, teeming with berries. It had already dropped a good portion of its bounty onto the ground where he stood.

As a child, Cyrus had often walked to this spot to pick the berries, enjoying their tart sweetness. Invariably he would return home with his hands, clothes, and shoes stained from the mulberry juice. He remembered how upset his mother would be when he came home in this condition. In recent years, his mother had complained similarly about Molly, her young Labrador, who often came back from wandering the fields with mulberry stains on her feet and legs. The dog must have enjoyed spending time under this tree as much as Cyrus had years before.

Cyrus gently laid Molly on the ground, and then walked all the way back to the farmstead to retrieve a shovel. Returning to Molly, Cyrus began to dig until he had dug a grave big enough for the large animal. Then, without hesitation, he carefully laid Molly, blanket and all, in the hole and began filling it with soil again. When he had finished, he turned and walked slowly with his shovel back home.

45

Robert sat alone at the conference table at the rear of the sheriff's office. He had read through the Patterson case file three times in the last hour, and had repeatedly reconstructed the timeline of events since the felon's escape from Pontiac. He tried to envision every detail as it had unfolded, and tried to imagine Patterson's thinking at each juncture. Where was he going? What was his plan? What would be his next move?

Robert reached for his cell phone and dialed one of his assistants in the Springfield office. "Hi, Sam. Robert here. Any update on the location of Annie Branson's cell phone?"

"No, Robert, not yet. You realize, don't you, that you called me with that same question about fifteen minutes ago?"

"I'm sorry. Has it been just fifteen minutes?"

"Yeah, Robert. Fifteen minutes. I've got the same answer for you. The phone's still powered off, so we can't get a location, but when and if it's turned back on, you'll definitely be the first one I call."

"OK. Thanks, Sam. I'll try not to bother you again, at least for a while." Then Robert clicked off and set his phone down on the table. He wasn't sure Patterson knew his location could be traced through the cell phone, but Patterson was a smart guy. He probably was well aware of the danger. Most likely that's why the phone was powered down. Still, there was a chance Patterson would make the mistake of using the phone. And if he did, they would find him.

It was barely a minute later when Sam called him back. Robert answered after the first buzz.

"Did he power up the phone?" he asked excitedly.

"No, Robert, but we just got the report back about Patterson's background. I have a list of foster parents from his youth. There are a bunch of them. We also have verification about his birth parents, but I guess that's old news. I'm faxing all this to your location right now."

"Great, thanks," Robert replied as he disconnected. He walked over to the fax machine as it began to chatter. Three pages printed and settled into the deposit tray. Robert began to examine the names and locations, wondering if Patterson might hide out at any of these places. Patterson most likely hadn't had any contact with these people for decades. But then again, anything was possible. Robert set the papers on the table with the rest of the file and sat down again. He knew he would have to talk to each of these contacts, but he had the feeling this would lead nowhere and get him no closer to Patterson.

As Robert sat there alone at the table, he kept asking himself if he had missed something. All the evidence was there at his fingertips, yet he couldn't anticipate Patterson's next move. It was frustrating to say the least.

Robert had been involved in law enforcement all his life. Even before he had gone through his training and received his first assignment with the state police, he had observed his father, a well-respected policeman—and later detective—in midtown Chicago. Robert knew how cases like this could become personal. He had often seen his father totally immersed in a case that would wear on him for weeks, draining him both emotionally and physically. This wasn't a task one could undertake from nine to five and then simply forget until the next day. No, engagement in a murder case was more like having an unseen companion who was with you 24/7, constantly whispering in your ear, taunting you about your inability to unscramble the clues right in front of your nose.

Robert was in the throes of this kind of engagement right now. He knew his immediate future working on this case would be fraught with anxiety, impatience, self-doubt, and self-deprecation. He recognized that this was all part of the process. The anxiety and impatience were to be expected, but the self-doubt and self-deprecation were due to his own insecurity, fed by the notion that he wasn't really good enough for this job. He always felt this way as he tried to find the subtle relationships in a complicated case—relationships that might indicate causality or help him anticipate any future occurrence. Worry that he would miss some important detail always weighed heavily on his mind, for he knew even a minor error on his part might result in someone's injury or death when a violent criminal was on the loose.

He sat now with his elbows on the table and his head resting on his clenched hands, letting his mind process the myriad of facts he had just scrutinized. He realized he would regularly be sitting here in the days ahead, mulling again and again over the annotations in this file, until hopefully there would be some kind of break in the case. Right now that hope was dependent on successfully locating that cell phone or positively IDing the suspect fleeing the area. Until that happened, Robert was resigned to sitting here alone with his thoughts.

***

Angie Bales sat next to Tom's hospital bed holding his hand as she watched him sleep. Their daughters, Rachel and Megan, sat nearby in silence with worried looks on their young faces. John Corbit sat there with them.

Tom had been sedated since the surgery and was expected to awaken at any time. John was still on duty and he knew he should be on the road searching for Tom's assailant, but he would remain right here until he knew his friend was out of the woods.

John had known Tom for over ten years, dating back to when Tom was a deputy working under Sheriff Gaines. At that time, John had recently joined the Illinois State Police and had been assigned to an area that included Cane County. Tom and John had instantly hit it off, sharing many of the same interests as well as the same intense commitment to serving the people in their jurisdiction. Over the years, as John and Tom each married and had children, their families had also become close friends. They had often socialized, each family taking a keen interest in the life of the other. Tom Bales was indeed one of the important people in John's life, and he considered him family.

It was no wonder John was shaken by Tom's injury, for he knew how close his good friend had come to death. An inch or two to the left and Tom would've been dead before he even hit the floor of that farmhouse. Fortunately, Tom would survive this. John had no doubt of that. But John also knew a gunshot wound wasn't something you simply recovered from and forgot about. The residual effects of a wound like this could be life-changing even with a successful recovery. The stories of the cowboys of the West who suffered gunshot wound after gunshot wound with no ill effects were falsehoods. John knew an injury from a bullet was so traumatic to the human body that one's life expectancy could be significantly reduced. So now, as John waited for his friend to come to, he wondered how this incident would affect Tom's future. He also wondered how he would find the words to tell Tom that his sister had been taken by Patterson, who was now on the run.

***

Liz sat in a holding cell at the county building in Elby. She wondered how she had let her life take such a turn for the worse. How could she have been so stupid as to get involved in this entire mess? She had tried to keep a distance from Byron's criminal activities, refusing to let her brother hide out at either of her places. That's why she had told him about the Barnett place. Of course that had turned out to be a disaster, and Liz had had no recourse but to hide him at her farm after all. That had been another huge mistake.

She knew Byron was violent. She knew he'd been in and out of prison for all kinds of violent crimes. She knew of his tendency to strike out first and think later. He had always done that. Like her life, his had been difficult. She didn't know the details of his early years, but she was aware he had bounced from one set of foster parents to another until he went out on his own. Though he'd only hinted to her about it, she suspected he had experienced considerable abuse at some of those foster homes. He was damaged, and she knew it. Still, how could she not help him? She, too, had had her share of hardships in life, and it hadn't been easy to take control of her life. She could only imagine how difficult it had been for Byron. She believed the only choice open to her was to help him the best she could. Yes, he was a violent criminal, but he was still her brother.

Liz knew the price for making that choice had been a high one. She had aided and abetted an escaped convict and jeopardized a criminal investigation, not to mention the fact that she had held Brandt and Bales hostage at gunpoint while Byron escaped. She knew her previous life was over. She would most likely serve time. She would never be able to work in the postal service again. While she would still have her property, what would she do? She would be a pariah in her own community.

171

She'd gotten what she deserved, Liz thought. She sat, lips tensely closed, eyes fixed, as she let out a conclusive sigh. She was ready to accept whatever the future offered her, and she knew it wouldn't be good.

46

Patterson drove into the parking lot of a truck stop and parked between two other vehicles. He looked over his shoulder to check on Annie, who was tied in the rear seat, gagged and partly covered with a blanket. She wasn't moving. In the past, Patterson had found the drug Ketamine to be very useful in situations like this. It dissolved easily in water, was tasteless, and induced unconsciousness in a matter of minutes. He'd had no problem getting Annie to drink the concoction when he offered her some bottled water. Now she was sleeping like a baby and most likely wouldn't awaken for quite a while.

Byron pulled the blanket off her, powered up her phone, and took her picture. He covered her back up and began watching trucks as they turned off southbound Route 51 toward the truck stop. He watched with interest as a large rig carrying a piece of a giant wind turbine turned off the highway and headed toward the parking lot. The rig pulled around the back of the truck stop where there was more room to maneuver, and finally came to a stop. Byron observed as the driver climbed nimbly down from the cab and made for the restaurant door.

Patterson did not move as he watched the driver enter the building. Then he picked up Annie's phone and sent her picture to Cyrus's number via text messaging. Next, Patterson got out of the Cherokee and began walking casually toward the rig in the rear of the lot. He stopped for a moment and made a phone call. Then he disappeared behind the trailer of the rig and duct-taped the phone securely to a hidden portion of the cargo. He walked slowly back to the Cherokee, backed it out of its spot, and drove out of the truck stop parking lot. He was headed north on a back road in the direction he'd just come from.

47

Cyrus drove to town Monday morning. It had been two days since Patterson had taken Annie, and he wasn't about to wait for Robert to call with an update. He planned on checking in with Robert himself. He also planned on leaving the Hyundai at Tom's office since it was the property of the sheriff's department where Cyrus was no longer employed.

He pulled into the parking area behind the office and walked around the building to the front. As he came in the door, Sarah looked up. With a sympathetic expression she asked, "How are you doing, Cyrus?"

"If I was doing any better, I'd have to pinch myself," he replied sarcastically, maintaining a serious countenance. "Is Robert back there?"

"Yes, go on back," Sarah replied, warily watching him as he walked past her.

Cyrus found Robert in the back room scrutinizing the file that lay strewn about the table.

"I'm here for an update, Agent Backus," Cyrus said without offering any pleasantries.

"I'm sorry to say there isn't one, Cy. But I'll let you know as soon . . ."

"Yeah, I know. You told me that," Cyrus interrupted tersely. "By the way, here are the keys to the Hyundai. It belongs to the sheriff's department, and since I'm no longer a part of it . . . well, anyway, here you go." He tossed the keys onto the table.

"That isn't necessary, Cyrus, but thanks." Then Robert said, "Look, Cyrus, I'm really sorry about this whole thing. I wish I could keep you involved. I know how hard it must be to play this waiting game, but you have to understand my situation."

"Yeah, Robert, I do. I really do. I'm just going crazy feeling so helpless."

"I know the feeling. Here, Cyrus. Take these keys back. How were you planning on getting home?" Robert asked as he offered the keys back to Cyrus.

"Uh, I hadn't really thought much about that." Then Cyrus acquiesced, accepting the keys and saying, "OK, thanks. If you need it back, let me know." Without another word, Cyrus walked back through the office and left.

Sarah turned to Robert. "Is he going to be all right, do you think?"

"I hope so. That guy lost his dog, his woman, *and* his job all in the same day. What would suck more than that?"

Just then, Robert's phone buzzed. It was Sam.

"Yeah, Sam. What's up?" Robert asked.

"Annie's phone just powered up. We're trying to get a location now. Hold on a sec."

Robert leaned out the front door of the office and shouted to Cyrus, who was walking toward the diner. "Cyrus, come back! I think we've got something!"

Seconds later Sam was back on the line, saying, "Robert, we have a location. Down in the Carbondale area. It'll take us a while to be more exact. I'll get back to you." Then he was gone.

Cyrus was standing outside on the sidewalk, staring at his phone. Suddenly he turned and walked into the office, saying, "You've got to take a look at this." He handed his phone to Robert.

On the phone was a text message in the form of a photo of Annie. Robert and Cyrus were both trying to get a closer look at the screen as Robert asked, "What's she doing? Is she sleeping?"

"It looks to me like she's in the back seat of a vehicle. Is that the Jeep Cherokee? It does look like she's sleeping. That's odd, isn't it?"

"Yeah, sure is. She seems to be in good shape, though," Robert said. Then he added, "Cyrus, we just got a location on Annie's phone. It's down in the Carbondale area. This picture indicates that Patterson is still in the vehicle, so he must still be on the move. I'm going to head down that way. The state police are on high alert. They should spot him soon. I want to be there when we find him."

"What about Annie?" Cyrus reminded him. "Your guys can't do anything stupid."

"Don't worry, Cyrus. We'll take every precaution. I'll keep you posted."

Robert began to ready himself for his drive, and Cyrus walked out the door, still staring at the photo on his phone. Cyrus headed toward the diner, but he'd only made it about twenty yards before his phone chimed. Annie's name was on the screen.

"What the . . . ?" he said as he pushed to answer. "Annie?" he asked hopefully into the phone.

"Did you enjoy that pic I sent you?" It was Patterson.

"You fucking bastard, what did you do to her?" Cyrus shouted into the phone.

"Cool your jets, cowboy. She's just taking a little nap, that's all. She's a pretty high-strung little filly, cowboy. You ought to know that. I just gave her a little something to calm her down a bit. Sometimes when you're trying to break a spirited little filly like that, a little sedative makes it easier to get on and ride, if you know what I mean."

"Listen, fuckwad, if anything happens to her, I'm going to kill you. I'll find you and kill you! You hear me?" Cyrus was losing control and he knew it. He realized he'd better calm down and find out as much as he could about Patterson's location and Annie's condition.

"Just calm down there. She's resting real quiet-like right now. We're just having a nice time driving down the road, enjoying the sights, making memories. She makes a real nice traveling partner. Not very talkative at the moment, though." Patterson rambled on. "I told you I'd take good care of the little lady as long as you guys stay off my tail. If that doesn't happen, there's no telling what I'll do. She could end up just like that mangy mutt of yours."

Cyrus was livid again. "You are the lowest of the low. You won't get away with this, you shithead!"

"Oh, but I think I will, as long as I have this pretty little piece of ass right here in my back seat. We might just keep on driving till we find a nice secluded spot to settle down, raise a mess of kids, have the perfect life. She won't even remember who you are, cowboy."

"You're a dead man, Patterson."

"Quite the contrary," Byron said, now dead serious. "If you come anywhere close to me, it'll be the last thing you do. You're way out of your league here, cowboy." Then he abruptly disconnected.

"Damn it!" said Cyrus to himself. He knew he had let his emotions take over, and he had lost perhaps his one and only chance to learn some valuable information about Patterson's location and his plans regarding Annie. He wondered if he should call Robert right away to tell him about his conversation with Patterson. He decided to pause and just think for a moment.

He turned the corner and walked down the sidewalk with no particular destination in mind, reviewing the phone call over and over in his mind. What was he missing? He couldn't stand the thought of Annie in the hands of Patterson. He had to do something, and he had to do it soon. He turned yet another corner and found himself in front of Max Riegel's office. He gazed through the large front window of the office and saw Max sitting at his desk all alone. Cyrus walked in and sat down in the chair opposite Max.

Neither man said a word. This had been one of the worst weeks of both their lives. Cyrus had lost his job, his dog, and Annie. Max had seen his nephew shot and his niece kidnapped.

Max finally spoke. "How are you doing, Cyrus?"

"About as well as you, I suppose."

"Anything new regarding the manhunt?"

"Actually, yes, Max, and I could use another brain to help me sort this out."

"What do you mean?"

Cyrus explained to Max what had transpired in the last twenty minutes, including the call he had received from Patterson. Then he leaned over the desk to show Max the picture of Annie lying gagged on Patterson's rear seat. Cyrus said, "The thing I've been pondering is why Patterson sent me that picture, and why he called me."

Max stared at the picture and said, "Well, Cyrus, I've worked with a lot of criminals in my day. A lot of them have been dumb as a box of rocks. But there are some who really surprise you with their ability to deceive, misdirect, misrepresent, lie, cheat, and manipulate in ways you could never imagine. You've been after this Patterson guy for about a month now, and no one has managed to even get close to him. My feeling is this guy is a highly intelligent person who does most things for a reason. He may have psychotic urges that get him into trouble, but he often has the creative wherewithal to elude capture."

"If that's the case, then he didn't just call me to piss me off, did he?"

"I doubt it," answered Max.

Cyrus thought through his conversation with Patterson one more time and finally said, "It's weird that Patterson gave us definite indications he was traveling, don't you think?"

Max was examining the picture of Annie. "Yes. This picture clearly shows the back seat of a vehicle."

"And he mentioned several times in our conversation that he was traveling. He said stuff like Annie was a nice traveling partner, and how he was just going to keep driving until he found a secluded spot, or something like that."

"Hmm. Why would he do that, unless he wants you to keep looking for him on the roads? Do you have any idea where he is?"

"Robert said the phone was traced to the Carbondale area. He's apparently heading south, I guess."

"Well," said Max. "That could be true, and then again, maybe it's just a deception."

Cyrus left Max's office without mentioning that Patterson had admitted to drugging Annie. He didn't want to worry Max further. In fact, Cyrus didn't even want to think about it himself. He knew Annie could probably defend herself pretty well—she was no pushover—but what might Patterson do to her while she was sedated? He couldn't bear to consider it now, so he shifted his thoughts elsewhere. He decided he had better update Robert regarding the phone call from Patterson. He punched in the number and Robert answered. "Hi, Cyrus, can I help you?"

"No, but I might have something that helps you."

"What's that, Cy?"

Cyrus explained, in great detail, the call from Patterson. Then he told Robert about the discussion he'd just had with Max and their theory about Patterson trying to mislead them.

Robert said, "Well, you may be giving Patterson a lot more credit than you should."

"Yeah, I realize that," replied Cyrus.

"We got a better fix on the location of that phone. We traced it to a truck stop off of Highway 51 just north of Carbondale, but before we got there, it started moving south. We're zeroing in on it right now, so I should have news soon. Patterson must not be as smart as you think. Apparently he forgot to turn off the phone after he called you. I knew he'd make a mistake."

"Or else he wants you to follow him," Cyrus speculated.

"Why would he want that?"

"Don't know. I'm just thinking that he's been ahead of us this whole way. He may be just that clever."

"Could be, but this phone location in Carbondale is the best lead we have right now, so we're going to pursue it."

"I suppose that's all you can do."

"Now, Cyrus, do you remember anything else about that call, like his pattern of speech, particular phrases he repeated, maybe some extraneous sounds?"

Cyrus paused and then said, "Well, the only thing I can think of is he kept making cowboy references. He called me a cowboy several times and referred to Annie as a filly." Cyrus couldn't bear to utter the words Byron had said about riding her.

"The term *cowboy* could just be a generalized name he attaches to anybody," Robert said. "It also could be something he learned in prison."

"What do you mean?"

"Well, in prison inmate slang, the word *cowboy* is a pejorative term that inmates sometimes use for a young, inexperienced prison guard, someone they hope to manipulate for their benefit. Patterson probably knew you had just become a deputy. He could have intended it as an insult."

"Well, it may have been an insult, but it isn't exactly inaccurate." Then Cyrus added, "He also told me I'm way out of my league. I guess that's consistent with my *cowboy* status."

"I suppose so . . . or rather, that's probably what he was insinuating."

48

Robert pulled into a rest area near the Illinois state line. Three other state police vehicles were parked next to a large rig carrying a section of a wind turbine. As he walked up to the other troopers, he got a sick feeling in the pit of his stomach. They were standing near the semitrailer talking casually with one another. It was obvious that Patterson and Annie were nowhere close to this location. As Robert approached, one of the troopers held out a ziplock bag containing a cell phone with a strip of gray duct tape attached to it.

The trooper said blandly, "Is this what you're looking for?"

"Not exactly," replied Robert with a dejected sigh. "Did the driver see anything?"

"Not a thing," the trooper answered.

"So now we know why Patterson didn't turn the phone off. Damn it!" Robert turned and walked around the parking area, deep in thought. What was Patterson's next move? Where could he be? Was Cyrus's theory correct after all? It appeared so. Patterson had been playing them all along.

Robert grabbed his own phone and called his office to report the bad news.

49

The next morning, as he sat on his front steps, Cyrus couldn't stop contemplating what Patterson's strategy might be. Patterson had made such an effort to focus them downstate toward Carbondale, and he'd been successful in convincing everyone he was on the run. Why would he do that unless it was all a deception on his part? Cyrus hadn't heard from Robert yet, so he had a feeling they'd struck out down south. He would check with Robert later to make sure.

And something else gnawed at him: this *cowboy* moniker Patterson had given him. It seemed like he'd heard someone else use that term recently. Who could it have been? Maybe Annie? She always liked to call him names. No, it wasn't her. He seemed to remember someone using it in a derisive way, just as Patterson had. He struggled to remember. Who was it?

Then his mind side-slipped a bit to the fact that Patterson was drugging Annie. He had known Patterson was a violent criminal, but he hadn't heard of him being involved with drugs before this. But who was he kidding? Everybody had access to drugs these days, especially ex-cons. His thoughts then moved on to Ed Chambers, and the opioids and weed they'd found in the backpack at his home. Cyrus's mind was skimming over a variety of facts and coincidences, trying to allow things to fall into place. Then, suddenly, it came to him.

"That's it!" he spoke out loud. That's who had called him a cowboy. It was Ed Chambers, during the search of his trailer.

Cyrus thought through his next move, and then jumped up and found his phone. He dialed the office at the county building where the evidence lockers were located. He had been there only once with Tom. What was the guy's name who ran that office? Jim? Joe? That was it, Joe! Cyrus hoped Joe hadn't yet heard that Cyrus was no longer a member of the sheriff's department.

Joe answered the phone. "Evidence room."

"Hey, Joe, how's it going? This is Cyrus Brandt from the Cane County Sheriff's Office. I met you when I was down there a few weeks ago with Sheriff Bales. Remember me?" Cyrus held his breath.

"How is the sheriff doing? I heard you guys got into quite a scrape outside of town."

"I think he'll pull through just fine, Joe. It'll take more than that to slow him down."

"What did you say your name was again?"

"Cyrus Brandt."

There was slight pause before Joe said, "Cyrus Brandt. Oh, yeah, I think I remember you. You're the guy someone told me was a physician or something."

"Well, no. Actually I used to teach physics. That's probably what they told you."

"Oh, yeah, that's it. What can I do for you, Deputy?"

"Well, remember that Ed Chambers guy we brought in? We need an update on the contents of his backpack. Has the lab analyzed that stuff yet?"

"Hold on, let me check." A few seconds later, Joe came back on the line and said, "OK, here we go. They found a lot of opioid drugs, all in small bags apparently ready for sale, and a bunch of weed. Also, something else. It says here they found a small bag of Ketamine tablets."

"What's Ketamine?" Cyrus asked.

"It's a common date-rape drug. It's easy to get, and there's quite a market for it on the street, I'm sorry to say."

"Is it dangerous?"

"It can be, depending on the dose. It can be fatal."

Cyrus didn't even bother to sign off. His phone was off and in his pocket before Joe had moved a muscle on the other end of the line. Cyrus's mind was processing this new information. The fact that Patterson and Chambers both called him *cowboy* didn't mean much if the term was common among prison inmates. They both had, of course, served time. But the fact that Chambers was distributing Ketamine, and Patterson was probably sedating Annie with it at this very moment? That meant something.

Suddenly Cyrus put it all together. The revelation was so sudden and strong that it physically jolted him, causing him to take a step back. He now had a really strong suspicion about where Patterson and Annie might be. It was the perfect place for Byron to hide out, Cyrus thought. No one would think of looking for him there. No one except, of course, Cyrus Brandt.

182

50

Cyrus kept imagining the hell Annie must be going through. He couldn't stand thinking about her in the hands of that monster. As Cyrus thought back to Patterson's background file, he remembered reading that Byron had been imprisoned before on multiple occasions, and many of those convictions had been for sexual violence. Patterson now held Annie as his helpless captive. What would he do to her? Cyrus realized that he couldn't wait for Robert, or even John, to help him. He had to act immediately, for Annie's sake.

Cyrus considered his options. He no longer possessed a handgun. Patterson had his Glock, and Robert had taken possession of the .38 caliber Tom had given him. He walked down to the basement to look in the cabinet where his dad used to store a rifle and a couple of shotguns. He didn't know if his mom had gotten rid of them, but he hoped not. Sure enough, they were still in the cabinet.

Cyrus realized that he might be confronting Patterson in rather close quarters, so he focused his attention on the shotguns. One was a nice Remington pump-action that his father had used for pheasant hunting. The other was a single-shot 16-gauge that Cyrus had hunted with as a kid. Cyrus figured he would only have an opportunity for one shot anyway, so he reached for the 16-gauge. He found an old box of shells and shoved four into his pocket. He was heading upstairs when his cell phone rang. The caller was Robert Backus.

"Hi, Robert," Cyrus said without emotion.

"Hi, Cyrus. I wanted to let you know that Patterson got away again. That cell-phone business was apparently all a deception to take us on a wild-goose chase."

"Yeah, I know."

"What do you mean, you know?" Robert sounded confused.

"I know where he is. I'm going after him," Cyrus replied.

"Oh, no you're not! Tell me what you're talking about. Where do you think he is?" Robert shouted through the phone.

"I don't have time for this, Robert. I'm going after the motherfucker," Cyrus said calmly.

"No, wait! I'll be back in about . . ."

Cyrus ended the call while Robert was in mid-sentence. He tossed his phone onto the kitchen counter, where he could hear it vibrating as he headed upstairs to his bedroom. He didn't have time to talk to Robert or anybody else right now. There was a man who needed to be killed, and he intended to take care of that.

Cyrus knelt down before a large trunk, threw open the lid, and peered inside. He hadn't opened this trunk since he had moved back to Illinois. In fact, he hadn't really examined its contents since the day he came home from Iraq. He searched through its contents until he found what he was looking for: an eight-inch knife cradled in a military-issue leather sheath. Cyrus placed the sheath next to his ankle and secured the straps tightly around it.

He gently slipped the knife out of its sheath and felt the weight of it in his hand. This knife had once taken the life of an Iraqi soldier. That soldier had probably had a mother who longed for him to be home, just as Cyrus's mother had wished him home and safe. The man quite possibly had left a wife or girlfriend behind. Yet Cyrus had killed him without a second thought. The soldier had been on top of a roof, pinning down Cyrus's unit on the street below. Cyrus had sneaked into the building and come up behind the soldier with his knife, thrusting it all the way to the hilt into the man's back. Then he had let the man drop and watched in macabre fascination while he bled out.

Cyrus had never thought of himself as a potential killer of men. Even after going through training and being deployed to the war in the Middle East, he had wondered if he could actually aim his weapon and fire at a human being, let alone stab a man to death. He'd never thought he could do it, but that day he'd found out he could. In the name of country, and in the name of survival, Cyrus had discovered he had the ability to commit the most despicable acts imaginable. Of course, he did those things to help protect the men who fought beside him. This killing was considered the honorable thing to do, necessary in order to preserve the American way of life.

Now he stood holding that eight-inch killing device, and he knew if he let his instincts take control, he could easily use that knife to kill again. All he needed was the motivation to be a killer and he felt he had it; the will to kill. This time it wouldn't be for his comrades or for his country, but for Annie. He would also do it for himself, to satisfy a driving need for revenge—revenge for the things he imagined Patterson was doing to Annie at this very moment.

Cyrus put the knife back in its sheath, grabbed the shotgun, and moved quickly down the steps and out the door toward his pickup. As he strode across the driveway, he looked up and stopped suddenly just short of the truck. Leo was leaning against the front fender of Cyrus's pickup, his arms crossed and a straw hat pulled down over his sun-tarnished face.

"Going hunting, Cyrus?" Leo asked blandly.

"In a manner of speaking, I guess. What can I do for you, Leo?" Cyrus glanced toward the road and saw Leo's tractor parked with the right tires on the grassy shoulder.

"Oh, nothing really. I just stopped by to tell you how sorry I am about poor Molly. I'm really gonna miss her, Cyrus."

"Yeah. Thanks, Leo. Me too. But I'm in kind of a hurry, Leo," Cyrus added as he reached for the pickup's door handle.

"Hmm," Leo said as he paused to take off his hat and wipe his brow with his forearm. "I heard from the sheriff's wife's hairdresser's cousin that you aren't working for the sheriff's department presently."

"You heard right," replied Cyrus bluntly.

"Then I'm kind of wondering where you'd be going in such a damn hurry with that shotgun. Looks like you're going to war."

Cyrus just stared at him, waiting for him to say his piece and move away from the truck.

Leo went on. "You see, Cyrus, I know what a man looks like when he's going to war."

"You do, do you?" asked Cyrus cynically.

"Yeah, I do. I seen a lot of that in 'Nam."

"You were in Vietnam?" Cyrus hadn't known that about Leo. He thought of Leo as just an eccentric farmer who played the clarinet and led a polka band.

"Yep. I seen a lot of guys with that same look in their eyes. A lot of them never came back alive. I'd rather not see that happen to you, Cyrus. What's going on?"

"There's something I've got to do. Now please move away from my truck so I can get going."

"You know, Cyrus, Albert Camus once said that life is the sum of all your choices. Are you sure you want to be defined by the choices you're making today?"

"You know as well as I do that sometimes hard choices need to be made. You guys in Vietnam learned that the hard way, right?" Cyrus stared intently at Leo, who was staring right back at him.

"That may be true, but we really didn't have a choice. It was our job. It was our duty."

Cyrus looked at the ground in front of him and then said, "Well, there you have it. Duty. I have to do my duty now, too."

"As long as you're absolutely clear about this."

"Very clear, Leo. Now let me go."

Leo studied Cyrus's face for a long moment. Then he pushed himself away from the pickup and walked up to Cyrus. He had no idea what Cyrus was getting into, but he sensed that this might be the last time he'd see his neighbor alive. He extended his hand, and Cyrus grasped it firmly in his.

Leo said softly, "Mark Twain once said, *The two most important days in your life are the day you are born and the day you find out why.* Perhaps today is the day you find out why. Good luck, my friend." Then he turned and walked toward the road where his tractor sat waiting for him.

Cyrus pulled the pickup door open and slid onto the hot vinyl seat. He slammed the truck into gear and sped down the driveway, turning without stopping onto the road, driving east.

51

John sat at the diner slowly drinking a cup of coffee. Annie's staff had gallantly maintained the restaurant's usual business hours. However, the mood in the place was somber. People were mostly speaking in soft, reverent voices, as if the diner were the site of a funeral rather than breakfast. The disappointing news from the Carbondale fiasco had spread quickly among the people in town who were emotionally invested in this manhunt, which included all law enforcement officers and anyone connected to them. It also included Annie Branson's large circle of customers and friends, several of whom were now sitting quietly in the diner.

John knew the press would have a field day with the news. The papers had for the last few weeks already been making a big thing about the inability of law enforcement to find Patterson, and now Annie's abduction further enhanced the story line. This recent setback would fuel the flames of the negative press coverage and the numerous claims of incompetence. John couldn't really blame the press for this. After all, over the course of the last month or so, the community had suffered through three murders, a seriously injured sheriff, and a kidnapping. As it stood now, the law was no closer to ending this manhunt than when they found that first body, deposited by the twister along the side of the road.

John believed something had to happen soon. Their manhunt had now made the national news, and Patterson's photo had been broadcast on every major television network, as well as in all the papers. The whole country was on the lookout for him. Patterson couldn't possibly avoid detection much longer. It was just a matter of time before someone spotted him, and John hoped that time would be soon.

John's phone buzzed and he answered, saying, "Hey, Robert, are you back in town yet?"

"No. I'm still about an hour out," Robert said. "Listen, John, you need to get out to Cyrus's place. I just talked to him. He said he thought he knew where Patterson was, and he was going after him."

"You've got to be kidding me! I hope you told him that was a really bad idea."

"I didn't have the chance. He hung up on me, and now I can't reach him. You need to get out there and hopefully stop him before he does something stupid. Call me back right away when you find him."

"OK, Robert. I'm on my way."

John was in his car in a matter of seconds, driving as fast as he dared, with his siren blaring.

Robert was about thirty minutes from Elby when John called him back. Robert juggled the phone clumsily as he rushed to answer it while still keeping his eyes on the road.

"Did you find him?" Robert blurted.

"No, Robert," John replied. "His truck is gone, and the house was unlocked. I found his phone on the kitchen counter."

"Damn!" exclaimed Robert.

"I found something else interesting, as well."

"What's that?"

"I took a look in the basement and spotted an open box of 16-gauge shells on the floor near an old gun rack. There was no 16-gauge shotgun on the rack."

"This isn't looking good," Robert lamented.

"What do you want me to do?" John asked.

"Call in some help. Call in any of your men in the area, and contact Tom's other deputies. You need to get out there and start patrolling the area. I have the feeling Cyrus wasn't planning on going very far. If we put some troopers out there on the area roads, maybe we'll get lucky."

"OK, Robert. I'm on it."

52

Cyrus drove slowly past the driveway leading to Ed Chambers's mobile home. He tried to get a look at the trailer from his vantage point on the road, but the driveway wound through the trees in a way that blocked his sight line.

The lot surrounding the mobile home was about two acres in size, and covered in old deciduous trees that extended from a cornfield in the back of the property all the way to the ditch that paralleled the road in front. Cyrus pulled over to the side of the road at a point where a fence line indicated the boundary of Chambers's property. Then he walked cautiously through the trees until he could see the mobile home, which was situated in a large clearing near the back of the property.

Cyrus was grateful that the trees would provide good cover during his approach to the home, but he knew his final approach would be in the clearing, without any cover whatsoever. He thought for a moment that it'd be wiser to wait for darkness to move in, but he immediately tossed that thought aside as he remembered Annie was in that trailer. He needed to get in there as soon as he possibly could.

Cyrus retreated to where his truck was parked and reached in to grab the shotgun from the passenger seat. With the weapon in hand, he headed up the fence line toward the rear boundary of the property. He crept cautiously along the edge of the cornfield, stopping periodically to listen for anything unusual. He finally spotted the rear of the mobile home and slowed his gait. He came to a halt and crouched down low, hidden by a tangle of honeysuckle. Then he watched the home for signs of movement.

After about thirty minutes, Cyrus hadn't seen any movement at all, and he began to wonder if his theory was correct. The midday sun was blazing down on the trailer and the clearing around it, and he could hear the window air conditioner running. That told him someone was in there. In comparison to the brightness of the area surrounding the mobile home, the inside of the trailer looked dark and empty. Cyrus knew it'd be difficult to detect movement inside that trailer even if someone was in there. He needed a plan, but he wasn't sure how to proceed.

He decided to continue along the back of the property and get a look at the mobile home from yet another vantage point. He needed to determine the best angle for his approach, an angle that offered the least chance of detection. Obscured by the trees between himself and the mobile home, Cyrus walked stealthily along the fence line.

He came to a sudden halt next to an opening in the fence that separated Ed Chambers's property from the field. Cyrus noted two hinges on the corner post on one side of the opening, vestiges of a gate that had once blocked entry or exit between the properties. Now it was simply an opening about ten feet wide. Cyrus noted two ruts in the ground that had been created through the years by farm equipment passing through the opening. He momentarily turned away from the mobile home and gazed across the field. Fresh indentations in the earth indicated a vehicle had been through here recently. Very recently. It was mid-July, and the corn in the field had already attained a height well over Cyrus's head. He could see something had driven through the opening into the field, knocking down the cornstalks in its path. Cyrus peered down the path but could only see that it wasn't straight. He tried to look over the top of the field but was unable to see anything but a sea of green.

Cyrus's curiosity got the best of him, and he decided to venture into the cornfield along the newly forged trail. After about one hundred yards, he rounded a curve in the path and stopped abruptly. Before him sat a vehicle. It was Liz Chance's Jeep Cherokee.

Cyrus peered inside the SUV. On the back seat lay a blanket, but he saw nothing else of interest. He now knew his suspicions had been correct. He was fairly certain that Patterson had left the vehicle here to conceal it and was now hiding in Chambers's mobile home. Annie must be there, too.

Cyrus's resolve stiffened as he walked quickly out of the field. He wasn't sure how he would do it, but he had to gain entrance to that trailer to save Annie. Then he reminded himself of his second objective: to kill the monster who was holding her captive.

53

Byron sat on the old, stained sofa in Ed Chambers's mobile home, watching TV and eating a breakfast bar he'd found in a kitchen cabinet. He looked around and observed the items that had been thrown about the trailer by the officers who had searched Ed's place a couple of weeks ago. Feeling bored, he considered straightening the place up a bit, but then he thought what the hell, why should he? He wouldn't be here long.

He had been here once before, just after his arrival in Elby, to enlist Ed's help and procure some drugs. Patterson had never considered Chambers to be any kind of friend. Hell, the only "friends" Patterson had ever had time for were people he could manipulate for his benefit. Chambers was just such a person, a no-good ex-con drug dealer of limited intelligence and even less creativity. Patterson knew Ed would soon be back in the penal system, but even with as little respect as Byron had for him, he knew Ed was uncommonly loyal and wouldn't reveal any knowledge of Byron's whereabouts. The brotherhood of ex-cons was a strong one, and Byron counted on Ed to keep his damn mouth shut.

Byron now tried to plan his next move. He knew he probably had some more time to think about this, since he had been successful in leading his pursuers to a dead end down near Carbondale. How much time he had, though, was uncertain. A few days? A week? Maybe more. He knew he would have to make a run for it soon, and he needed to find a different vehicle. Every law enforcement officer in the surrounding area was looking for that Cherokee. Ed's old Ram pickup was parked out front, but even if Patterson could find the keys to the pickup, the law would already have a description of that truck from when they arrested Ed. He needed to find another way out of here, but he had no idea how to do it. Not yet. But he knew he would figure it out. He always did.

There was one thing he knew for certain: Annie wouldn't be with him when he left. She was no longer useful to him. He really wasn't sure if she'd ever been useful in the first place. He doubted taking her hostage had caused any pullback of the manhunt. It had probably just made the state police more intent on finding him. No, he knew himself well enough to realize that he'd kidnapped her for two reasons: one, to use her for sex, and two, to make Sheriff Bales and Cyrus Brandt suffer. When he was done with her, she would be more of a liability than an asset, and he would have little reason to keep her alive. He would kill her like he'd killed the rest of them, and leave her in this trailer. She wouldn't be found for weeks. By then, he would be long gone. But until then, he figured he could make good use of her. She'd be a real nice diversion. And when he finally left this place, he thought, he might even regret killing her. Just a little bit.

***

As Byron Patterson was musing about his options, State Policeman Jeff Akers pulled up slowly behind Cyrus's old Ford F-150. He noted the license plate number and carefully copied it onto his notepad. Then he picked up his cell phone. He found the name he was looking for in his contacts and pushed the call button.

"John Corbit," was the answer.

"John, it's Jeff Akers. I'm sitting behind a parked F-150 that appears to be the one we're looking for. The plate number is IL G501854. Is that Cyrus Brandt's truck?"

"Yes, it is! Where are you?"

"I'm over near the location of that double murder."

"The Barnett home?"

"Yeah, but I'm a bit up the road from there to the north, just past a driveway that leads into a wooded area. The name *Chambers* is on the mailbox."

"Shit! OK, Jeff, here's what you need to do. Call dispatch and have them send every available officer to your location. Also, have them send an EMT unit. Got it? This thing isn't going to end without someone needing medical attention."

"Got it."

John then called Robert, who answered on the first ring. "Robert, it's John. We found Cyrus. He's at Ed Chambers's place. I'm on my way." He abruptly ended the call and slammed his foot down hard on the accelerator as he sped down Highway 38, looking for the first county road going south.

54

Cold. It was cold. Annie could sense she was shivering. That's all she could comprehend at the moment, the shivering. She opened her eyes slightly, but she could only see dull colors and vague shapes as she tried to focus. She tried to remember where she was, but her memory was as vague as her vision. What had happened to her? Was she in her apartment above the diner? No. Something felt wrong here. This didn't smell like her place. It smelled dank and musty. And it was cold.

She tried to move, but something restrained her. She could only move her hands so far, and then something refused to let them move further. She could now tell she was lying on her stomach with her arms splayed out. They were tightly secured by some kind of rope or strap, secured to something that she couldn't make out yet. She felt goose bumps on her back, her bare back. She suddenly had the frightening realization that she might be naked. Her entire body felt equally chilled. She pulled more violently at the straps on her wrists, and now felt similar restraints securing her ankles, which were splayed out like her arms. She cried out, but the scream she was expecting was converted into a muted moan by the rag stuffed in her mouth.

She was beginning to see more clearly now, and she could see she was lying on a bed with a sodden sheet under her. She squinted as she began to identify some pieces of furniture in the room. A small desk. A chair. A dresser of some kind. She also noticed a small window aglow with rays from the afternoon sun. Or was it the morning sun? She had no way of knowing.

"Please, let me go back to sleep," she thought. "This must be a nightmare." But as she heard a door open and saw a shirtless Patterson step into her field of vision, she knew this wasn't just a bad dream. Annie tried desperately to focus on his face but had difficulty turning her head far enough to see him clearly.

"Well, well, well. Look who's awake," Byron said. "I was hoping you'd wake up soon. I wouldn't want you to miss all the fun. I hope you enjoy this as much as the Barnett bitch did. She and I had a lot of fun together."

Annie could hear the man unzip his pants and drop them on the floor. She began to thrash about the bed violently, pulling

193

hard at the unyielding restraints, only to have him push brutally down on her back. Annie was stiff now, braced against Patterson's weight that pinned her down on the mattress.

55

Cyrus stood behind the cover of the trees and made one last check of his shotgun and knife. When he got inside that trailer, things would happen fast, and he knew luck would have as much to do with his success as skill with his weaponry. He would be in very close quarters, and he wasn't sure when or if either the shotgun or the knife would be useful. He would need to be ready for anything.

He took one last look around his surroundings and then, crouching low, moved toward the mobile home. When he reached the trailer, he pulled himself upright next to a window. He slowly edged over and looked through the windowpane. He could see Patterson, clad only in his underwear, standing next to a bed. On that bed was Annie, lying prone and naked. She was lying still, but he could see that her eyes were open, red, and moist. Her limbs were secured to the four corners of the bed, and suddenly she began to pull defiantly at the bindings, frantically challenging their resistance. Cyrus watched as Patterson came down hard with his knee on Annie's back to impede her struggling.

"That fucking bastard," Cyrus said under his breath. His mind was now racing with rage, and he had to calm himself for a moment lest he charge into that trailer firing at nothing in particular.

As he stepped back to the side of the window, he stumbled slightly and his shotgun barrel scraped along the metal siding. "Damn it," he thought as he leaned back against the side of the structure, clutching his weapon close to his body.

It was just a small scraping sound. Hardly anything to take notice of under normal circumstances. But Cyrus knew it was enough. Patterson turned to peer out the window and Cyrus froze, pressing himself as close as he could against the side of the trailer. He remained motionless until he heard the sound of an interior door opening and quickly closing.

Cyrus cautiously glanced through the corner of the window and saw that Annie was now alone in the room. Cyrus crouched low and moved along the trailer to a position under the next window. He could hear voices. Was someone else in there? No, he surmised, it was just the TV. Suddenly the voices stopped. Patterson must have turned the TV off. Cyrus ever so slowly raised his head enough to position his eyes above the bottom of the window. He could see Patterson standing above him, staring through the window and scrutinizing the area around the trailer. At that moment, Patterson caught sight of Cyrus and turned abruptly to run back toward the bedroom.

Cyrus crashed the shotgun through the window and fired. The sounds of the shattering glass and the accompanying shotgun blast resonated throughout the trailer. Cyrus paused to look, hoping to see Patterson lying injured or, better yet, dead. Instead he heard the man running in the direction of the bedroom where Annie was tied up. Apparently Patterson had avoided injury by dropping to the floor, and all Cyrus had accomplished was to create a spread pattern of pheasant shot on the opposite wall.

Cyrus ejected the spent shell and shoved a new one in the chamber. Then he ran to the front door and used the gun butt to break his way into the trailer. He remained in the entryway, trying to recall the home's layout. Looking through the kitchen and living room, he could see the door that led to the rear bedroom. Patterson and Annie were behind that door, and Cyrus had a bad feeling about the situation. Patterson had the advantage now. He waited where he was for what seemed an eternity, trying to figure out what to do. He knew there was no door out of that bedroom except the one he was staring at now. His only hope was to let Patterson make the next move.

Patterson grabbed the Glock from the top of the dresser. Then, picking up his pants, he reached into the pocket for his knife and walked over to the bed where Annie lay. She looked weak from hunger and appeared to be barely conscious. Because of her condition, Patterson knew she would be easy to control. He used his knife to cut the bindings that held her on the bed. She remained motionless as she lay there untied.

"Get up, bitch," Patterson ordered.

Annie tried to lift herself up, but her arms were too weak to support her weight. Patterson pulled her roughly to the side of the bed, slipping his left arm under her left armpit and across her chest, then pulling her to a standing position in front of him. He

196

was annoyed that she couldn't stand without support, and he was having difficulty keeping her upright as he walked toward the door.

He stood in front of the door and shouted, "I'm coming out with the woman."

The door creaked open and Patterson, still clad only in his underwear, stepped out into the hallway holding the naked and limp woman in front of him. With the Glock against Annie's temple, Patterson looked through the trailer and saw Cyrus pointing the shotgun directly at him.

Patterson said, "Well, if it isn't the boyfriend. Are you trying to be some kind of hero? You should've taken my advice and stayed the hell away from me. As I told you, you're way out of your league."

"And you're a dead man, Patterson," said Cyrus calmly.

"Oh, I doubt that very much. It seems I'm holding all the cards, cowboy. You need to drop that shotgun right there in front of you, or you'll see your girlfriend's brains splattered all over this trailer."

Cyrus held his ground, wondering what to do. He said, "I don't think I can do that. If you shoot her, Byron, you'll have this shotgun to answer to." Cyrus knew he was speaking with much more confidence than he had a right to. The thought of Patterson shooting Annie was too awful to contemplate. He would do anything to prevent that. But he knew if he dropped his weapon, Patterson would simply kill him—and then probably kill her, too.

"Drop it or she's dead, cowboy," Patterson shouted. Then he laid the gun next to Annie's head, barrel pointed to the ceiling, and discharged it. Cyrus winced and recoiled sharply, but Annie paid it little notice. He now realized what bad shape she was in. He needed to get her out of here and to a hospital.

Patterson edged through the hallway toward Cyrus. Annie was perspiring profusely, and Patterson was having difficulty holding onto her naked body as he moved forward. Suddenly he lost his grip, and she fell limply to the floor. Cyrus saw his chance. He aimed slightly high and to the left of Patterson to avoid hitting Annie, and fired. Most of the shot scattered into the hallway wall and ceiling, but a few pellets struck Patterson and penetrated the skin of his upper right arm. Patterson stumbled and fell forward over Annie's limp body. As he did so, he dropped the handgun and lost sight of it as it clattered to the floor under a nearby chair.

While Cyrus fumbled to get another shell out of his pocket, Patterson quickly assessed the extent of his injuries and noted they were not serious. Although he was in considerable pain, his right arm was still fully operational. Cyrus now had the new shell in his hand and was shoving it in the chamber when Patterson charged.

The collision was a violent one, and Cyrus's shotgun was knocked out of his hands and out of reach. The two men were now engaged in brutal combat on the floor. Patterson outweighed Cyrus by a good thirty pounds and was also his superior in terms of brute strength. Patterson began throwing punch after punch to Cyrus's midsection and head as Cyrus, pinned beneath him on the linoleum, attempted to shield himself from the onslaught. Although Patterson was the stronger of the two, Cyrus proved to be the quicker, and he eventually freed himself from Patterson's control, somehow managing to position himself on the opposite side of the kitchen table.

Cyrus tried to catch his breath, but the table offered scant protection from the raging killer. Patterson threw it aside with remarkable ease and continued toward Cyrus. As Patterson approached, Cyrus kicked with all his might and found his target in the big man's groin, sending him down hard, groaning and swearing. Cyrus tried to get past him to retrieve his shotgun, but Byron reached out and grabbed his foot, causing him to fall noisily to the floor. Knowing the shotgun was no longer an option, Cyrus reached for his knife and pulled it out of its sheath, but it was too late. Patterson was on top of him again, dropping his knee on Cyrus's arm and sending the knife across the floor. Before Cyrus could react, Patterson back-handed him hard in the face, stunning him for a moment.

By the time Cyrus could focus again, Patterson had the knife in his hand. As Cyrus watched, Patterson jabbed the blade into his left arm, cutting deeply into the flesh. The pain was excruciating, and Cyrus cried out in agony, realizing for the first time that Patterson had been right. Cyrus was indeed out of his league here. Patterson now had him on the floor. One of his arms was incapacitated, numb and bleeding, and the other was pinned under Patterson's knee. The killer loomed over him with the blade of the knife an inch from his throat, poised to plunge it into Cyrus's neck.

Cyrus knew there was nothing he could do. He would most likely die now. The irony of dying by his own knife was not lost on him. He had used this knife to take a life once, and now it was only fair that the knife should take his. He was ready, and as he stared up at Patterson, a cynical smile took shape on the killer's face as he moved to shove the blade home. Cyrus closed his eyes and waited for the end.

"Stop!" It was Annie, summoning all the strength she could muster to be heard.

Patterson looked up at Annie while still holding the knife to Cyrus's throat.

"Put the knife down or I'll shoot," she threatened faintly as she held the Glock in front of her, aiming shakily at Patterson. Annie hadn't had the strength to get to her feet after she'd crawled over to the gun, and she was now on her knees trying to keep the weapon steadily aimed at Patterson.

Patterson said flippantly, "Listen, bitch, you're not going to shoot anybody. Have you ever even shot one of those before? Look at you. You're a fucking mess. You can barely hold that gun. Just put it down before you hurt yourself."

Annie slowly lowered the Glock to her side. She looked without expression at Patterson and Cyrus. Patterson said, "That's more like it. Now I'll tell you what's going to happen here. I'm going to ram this knife into your boyfriend's throat, and while he's laying here bleeding all over the fucking kitchen, I'm going to take you into the bedroom and fuck you raw. And if you're a good girl and act like you enjoy it, I might just let you live. Then I'm going to take this cowboy's vehicle and get the hell out of this fucking county. How's all that sound to you?"

Byron turned back to finish the job he had started, but Cyrus was still staring at Annie's face, which had taken on an eerily stony expression. He watched her as she said quietly, "This one's for Mary Barnett." As the weapon came up steady and true, Patterson said, "What's that, bitch?" But Cyrus could see Annie's lips moving again, and he knew exactly what she was saying: *peanut butter.*

The recoil threw Annie backward and she landed hard on her back, the gun still in her hand. Patterson fell against an end table, shattering it into a dozen pieces of particle board and plastic. He lay there in a twisted heap with Cyrus's knife on the floor beside him. Annie's aim had been true, and the bullet had struck dead center in the middle of Patterson's abdomen.

He was panting heavily, struggling to remain conscious, when Cyrus noticed Annie trying to get to her feet. Cyrus pulled himself over to the wall, propped himself up, and clutched his bleeding arm as he watched her shuffle unsteadily toward Patterson. She staggered up to her tormenter, towering over him in defiant nakedness, to watch him suffer for a moment.

"Annie? It's over. Let's get out of here," Cyrus said as she looked down contemptuously at Byron. "He can't hurt anybody anymore."

Annie didn't move, as if she hadn't heard him. She waited until Patterson finally looked up at her with a glassy-eyed gaze. Then she said, "And this one's for the rest of us, you bastard." Calmly she raised the Glock to within six inches of Patterson's forehead and squeezed the trigger.

56

Cyrus was just waking up when Dr. Miller walked into his hospital room. The young doctor said, "I first want to say I think you need to find a different job, because this one doesn't seem to be working out for you."

"Yeah, I suppose you're right," Cyrus replied, grimacing at the pain in his arm.

Acknowledging his pain, Dr. Miller said, "The surgery went well, Cyrus. There may be some lasting nerve damage, but hopefully not much. You're going to be sore for a while, though. We'll get you any painkillers you need."

As he examined Cyrus's arm, he went on. "We'll probably keep you here another day or two to keep an eye on your arm, change the dressing, stuff like that." He checked Cyrus's pulse, shined a light at his pupils, and asked, "Beside the soreness in the arm, how are you feeling?"

"Not bad, Doc. When can I see Annie?"

"Soon, Cyrus. She's on a different floor in another unit. They're taking good care of her. She's pretty beat up, dehydrated, and weak. But I think she'll be fine."

"When can I see her?" he repeated.

"Let her rest for a while. We'll let you know when you can see her."

As Dr. Miller turned to leave, Robert and John walked into the room. Robert said, "Doc, is it OK if we talk to Cyrus?"

"I suppose so, but don't stay too long. He's had a rough day," replied the doctor as he continued out the door.

Robert and John stood on either side of Cyrus's bed. John said, "How are you feeling, Cy?"

"How do I look?" asked Cyrus.

"Like shit, if you want to know the truth," replied John. "You know, that was a pretty stupid thing you did there. You should've waited for us. Things could have easily gone another way, and you two could be dead right now."

"I know, but it didn't go another way, did it? It went our way," Cyrus countered.

"You two were just damn lucky," said John.

Robert said, "We'll need a full statement from both you and Annie as soon as you're up to it. It can wait for now, though. Let's just get you back on your feet. That trailer was one hell of a frigging mess. I'm looking forward to hearing how it got that way."

"I wish I could brag about my heroism, but I'm afraid Annie is the real heroine here. If it wasn't for her, you'd be visiting me in the morgue right now. Have you seen her yet?" Cyrus asked.

"No, she's not ready for visitors yet. But they gave us a pretty positive prognosis. If I were you, I wouldn't worry, Cyrus. You should just concentrate on yourself right now, OK?" instructed Robert. Then he added, "Sheriff Bales is just about to be discharged, and he'll be coming in to see you. I don't know if he's going to hug you or slug you. Be ready for anything. He wasn't exactly overjoyed that you went after Patterson alone."

"Thanks for the warning," said Cyrus.

57

Cyrus was surprised that Tom never showed up to visit him at the hospital. That fact worried him greatly. He thought back on the entire incident, and though he hadn't exactly followed proper protocol, Cyrus was still convinced he had done what was necessary under the circumstances. Did Tom not understand that? Perhaps not. Cyrus knew that policies and procedures were important to the sheriff. Cyrus now wondered what he was in for. There was only one way to find out. When John came to take him home, Cyrus asked to be dropped off at the sheriff's office instead. Cyrus wanted to clear the air with Tom, and the sooner the better.

As Cyrus walked into the sheriff's office, Sarah immediately jumped to her feet and threw her arms around him. "Easy there," he said, wincing. "Don't hurt me now."

"Oh, I'm sorry. I'm just so glad to see you. How are you doing?"

"Better than yesterday, and a lot better than three days ago. Is Tom in?" he asked, nodding in the direction of the back office.

"Yup, go on back."

Before Cyrus could move, Tom appeared in the doorway of his office. "Hey, Deputy, I need to talk to you," he said.

The two stood for a moment looking at one another, Tom with his right arm wrapped to inhibit excess movement, and Cyrus with his left arm in a sling. Sarah looked at them both and joked, "Jeez, it looks like a triage line at a disaster site in here."

Ignoring her, Tom said, "Come on in, Cy, and have a seat." The two men sat down at the conference table.

When they had settled into their chairs, Tom said, "Cyrus, Robert will be here tomorrow to get a detailed statement about what happened on Tuesday out at the Chambers place. But I want you to lay it out for me right now. Give me the Reader's Digest version."

Cyrus thought for a moment and then began with the text Patterson had sent him with Annie's picture. He moved on to the call from Patterson, and the connection Cyrus had made between Patterson and Chambers. Then he described the entire timeline leading to Patterson's death in the mobile home. When he had finished, Cyrus simply looked at Tom and waited.

Tom said, "You do realize, don't you, that what you did was impulsive, even foolish? You could have been killed, and Annie could have been killed as well." Tom paused for effect, and when Cyrus nodded in agreement, he went on. "That isn't how law enforcement works, Cyrus. You should've let us handle it."

Tom looked down at the table and then up again. "However, under the circumstances as I understand them, I don't believe I would've acted much differently."

Cyrus, who had been staring down, not meeting Tom's gaze, now looked up at him, eyes wide in surprise.

"I want to thank you for saving my sister's life, Cyrus. No one knows how much longer Patterson would've let her live. Probably not much longer." Tom attempted to blink away the emotion that had begun to manifest in his eyes. "What you did may have been foolhardy, but it was remarkably courageous, Cy. And, most likely, it was absolutely necessary. Annie and I will be forever indebted to you."

Cyrus said, "I wasn't even thinking much at the time. I don't think it was courage as much as pure instinct. All it took was the right motivation. Annie was my motivation."

"You're a good man, Cyrus. Annie is lucky to have you in her life, and I'm glad to have you in mine as well." Then Tom added, "I hope, when you've fully recovered, you'll consider coming back to work for me. What do you think?"

"Boy, I don't know, Tom." Cyrus shook his head slowly. "It seems I made one fuckup after another in this case. First I lost my Glock to Patterson, then he made me give up my other handgun at the Brennan place, and then I lost my knife to him at the trailer. I'm just not very handy with weaponry, I guess. On top of that, I'd be dead right now if Liz Chance hadn't stopped Byron from killing me twice, and then Annie prevented him from killing me at the trailer.

"If I was a cat, I'd have only six lives left. Or maybe five if you count my encounter with Liz's two-by-four. I'm not sure I really did anything positive in solving this case. Instead, I just kind of got in the way of things."

Tom thought for a moment and then said, "Sometimes that's how crimes get solved. Just *getting in the way of things* can shake things up enough to bring a criminal like Patterson out in the open. Don't sell yourself short, Cy. You could be a really good officer—that is, if we can teach you to hold onto your firearms," Tom quipped. Then he got serious. "I want you to think about something. If you're interested, I'd like to have you go through some training so you could come back and join my department in a more official capacity. John and I can give you the necessary recommendations and any other help to make that happen. You don't have to decide now, but just think about it. I'd love to have you working with me. You have great instincts, you're smart, and you've proven that you're not afraid to confront adversity when the shit hits the fan. Will you think about it, Cyrus?"

Cy didn't offer a verbal answer, but he nodded as Tom got to his feet.

Tom added, "What I just offered you is all for my benefit, Cyrus. But there's someone else who would love to see you consider my offer and make this place your home. From what you've told me, you owe her that much."

Tom motioned with his good arm, and Cyrus walked toward the front of the office as directed. Standing at the front counter, Tom asked, "Are you going anywhere in particular right now?"

"No, not really. I just realized I don't even have a way to get home."

"I was thinking you and I might head over to the diner. I'll buy you some lunch and that piece of pie I owe you. Then I'll drive you home. Sound good?"

"Sounds great, Tom."

The two men walked out into the warm July sun and strolled through their quiet little Illinois town toward Annie's Place.

58

August had arrived with a vengeance in Illinois. The oppressive heat, accompanied by the high humidity, was great for growing beans and corn—but not so great for anything else. It was a Sunday afternoon, and Cyrus and Annie sat on the front steps of Cyrus's house, ignoring the compulsion to return indoors to the refuge of the air conditioning. About three weeks had passed since the incident, and they now simply sat together. No witty repartee, no silly jokes, no playful jabs between them. Just silence.

The shade of a large silver maple tree extended over the front steps, shading them comfortably from the searing sun, and a welcome summer zephyr periodically blew their way. Cyrus noticed a red-tailed hawk fly into view and deftly light upon a fencepost. He silently pointed, allowing Annie to follow his hand to the location of the majestic raptor, and they sat quietly admiring it. Cyrus couldn't imagine a more idyllic place on earth. Even in this oppressive heat, he couldn't think of anyplace he'd rather be right now.

"What do you think of my little piece of heaven?" he asked.

"I think you have it pretty nice out here."

After a moment, Cyrus continued. "You know, Annie? It's probably been obvious to you that I've been fighting some personal demons."

"You and me both, I think."

"Amid all of that, I've felt kind of unsettled, like I couldn't find my footing. That's made it hard for me to think about staying here for the long term. I guess that's why I've allowed a distance to remain between us. Over the course of the last few weeks, however, something has changed for me. I've now come to the realization that there's no other place I'd rather be."

"Well, that's good to hear, because I kind of like having you around. But why the change?"

"See that cloud of dust out there?" Cyrus pointed to a tractor working in a field about a half mile to the southeast. "That's Leo Kotaska workin' one of my fields over there."

"Isn't that your weird neighbor?"

"That's the guy. Anyway, Leo told me something just before I went to look for you that day. Something about the two most important days of your life: the day you are born and the day you figure out why.

"That day as I drove toward Chambers's place to find you, I think I realized the *why* of my life. I realized that everything else leading up to that point in my life had led me there for a purpose. Led me to you. You are the *why* of my life, Annie. I know that now."

"Me?"

"Yes. You, and this place. This town. All of it. This is where I have belonged all along. I feel like the emotional chains that have shackled me these past months have somehow worked themselves loose. Now, I feel lighter in a way. My vision clearer. My past more distant. Does that make any sense to you?"

"Not sure, but I think I like where this is going," Annie replied as she let her head come to rest on Cyrus's shoulder.

Cyrus reached around Annie and pulled her toward him as they again sat in silence, eyes trained on the crops across the road that were swaying in unison to the gentle summer wind. They watched as the hawk took flight and floated effortlessly on the air currents over the field, scanning the ground below for its next victim.

Cyrus and Annie sat now, holding each other close, basking in feelings of intimacy, contentment, and a tinge of desire. The emotional barriers separating them had fallen away, and as they gazed at the verdant cropland across the road, what they saw was not lush fields of soybeans and corn, but their future now coming into focus. It was a future of hope and promise; a future they now could envision sharing together.

Suddenly their euphoric moment was disturbed by the sound of a car approaching from the east. Cyrus watched it slow in front of his mailbox and then turn into his driveway.

"Hmm. I wonder who that is," he said, slightly annoyed by the interruption.

Not turning her gaze from the hawk, Annie said, "Oh, that's probably Mary Anne. She said she might stop by."

"Who?" Cyrus asked, and then, looking at Annie, he added, "And why?"

207

"Oh, you don't know her. I went to school with her. She's a really nice gal."

"Why is she here? She's not going to try to sell me something, is she? You see that old *No Soliciting* sign my dad put up by the front ditch years ago? I still stand by those words."

"No, she's not going to try to sell you anything," Annie said. Then she hesitated and added, "Well, not exactly."

Red flags were unfurling in every square inch of Cyrus's brain now, for he knew this small qualification probably portended an unwanted outcome. Annie stood up and walked toward Mary Anne's car, and Cyrus reluctantly followed her.

As Mary Anne got out of her car, out bounded a small, tan puppy that darted around her feet and then ran over and jumped up on Annie's shins, wagging its tail passionately.

"What a cutie! Isn't she darling, Cyrus?" Annie squealed as she scooped the puppy up into her arms and let it lick her face.

"Uh-huh," said Cyrus without a trace of emotion.

The woman extended her hand to Cyrus and said, "Hi, I'm Mary Anne Baker. I live about eight miles that way." She pointed.

"How can I help you, Mary Anne?"

"Well, my husband and I have a small business breeding Labradors. We've been doing it for years. Anyway, about eight or nine years ago, we sold Molly to your mom and dad. I think it was shortly before your dad passed. We kept one of the puppies from that litter for ourselves, too. She eventually had a litter of her own, and one of her puppies became the mother of this sweet little thing. I guess you could say this pup is Molly's grand-niece."

Cyrus knew what was coming next.

"Mary Anne thought maybe you'd like to have her," Annie said with hopeful anticipation, setting the puppy back on the ground.

Cyrus looked at the pup as it thrashed about at their feet, sniffing and wagging, wagging and sniffing. Finally, he said, "You two need to know something. For the last couple of weeks or so, there hasn't been a day go by that I haven't walked out past the barn," he pointed to the back of the farmstead, "and along that field, down the fence line, to Molly's grave under the mulberry tree. Most days, I just sit there. If you don't believe me,

I have the mulberry-stained jeans to prove it. I just sit there and think about how much I miss her, and the way she was taken from me by that monster. I don't think I can replace my memory of her by taking on another dog at this time. I just can't." Cyrus looked directly at Mary Anne to show her his mind was set regarding this matter.

Annie was disappointed, but she refused to show it, for she knew Cyrus had loved that dog dearly. She remained quiet, waiting for Mary Anne's response.

Mary Anne said, "OK, Cyrus, but if you change your mind, let me know soon. This pup is the last one I have from this litter. That's why I thought I'd offer her to you, knowing all the stuff you've gone through recently."

"Thanks all the same, Mary Anne. I appreciate the thought. I really do." Cyrus took a step back as if to indicate the conversation was at an end.

Right on cue, Mary Anne turned to leave. Then she stopped and said, "I hate to ask, but I was just on my way to get some groceries in town, and it's too hot to leave this puppy in the car while I'm in the store. Would you two mind watching her for about an hour? It shouldn't take me longer than that."

"No problem. Right, Cyrus?" said Annie happily.

"I suppose that would be fine," Cyrus reluctantly agreed.

"Great. I'll be back in a jiffy. Thanks," said Mary Anne as she got into her car and headed for town.

Cyrus watched her drive away and then said, "Now, where were we?"

Annie replied, "I think we were sitting on the steps enjoying a beautiful summer day."

With the puppy frolicking at their feet, Annie and Cyrus resumed their previous positions on the steps. This time, however, Annie seemed more engaged in playing with the rambunctious puppy than with either Cyrus or the beauty of the Illinois landscape. Cyrus watched her exuberance as she played with the pup on her lap, scratching its ears and stroking its soft coat. Her childlike glee made him imagine her as she must have been as a young girl. Cyrus smiled at that thought and turned to resume his survey of the carpet of cropland that stretched before him.

His view extended for what seemed like forever into the distance, dropping toward the horizon at a rate of eight inches per mile. Of course, Cyrus realized he was sitting with his eyes about five feet above the ground, and he knew that Geometry would put the limit of his visibility at about five kilometers. But he also knew that refraction helped to extend that limit, depending on atmospheric conditions, and he was certain he could just make out the top of the white water tower in Elby, some five miles away. Why was this all so important to him? He wasn't sure, but it was. He thought about this a while longer, and then let his thoughts return again to his own fields just across the road. These were his fields. His crops. This was his home. He reminded himself there was no need to search far into the distance for the things that were important to him. They were right here. Right in front of him.

After a long moment of wistful quietude, Cyrus again became aware of the sound of the puppy clambering about on the porch steps, and without looking in Annie's direction, he simply said, "You're going to make me keep her, aren't you?"

Annie replied impassively, "Sure am, Professor."

Acknowledgments

Many thanks to my wife, Tina, for all her encouragement and patience during the writing of this book. I would also like to thank all the other people who offered valuable suggestions, especially my daughter Jessica, who brought her considerable expertise to bear on the completion of this work. Her input had a major impact on the final product. Finally, I owe many thanks to Rebecca Rauff, my copy editor, and Kathleen Stevens, for her assistance with the law enforcement procedural elements of TWISTER'S WAKE. Thank you all so much.

About the Author

Randall Reyman is a musician, composer, writer, and professor at a private Illinois university.

Watch for his upcoming release of *The Path*, the second installment in the Cyrus Brandt Novel Series.

Read on for a sample from *The Path* . . .

The Path

1

The girl walked out of the school and boarded the school bus like she did every Wednesday afternoon. Like she did every Wednesday, she stared out the window for the entire six miles as the bus made its way toward town and stopped at the bus stop by the park. Like every Wednesday, the girl exited the bus at this stop, her backpack thrown over her shoulder. Every other Wednesday, she would've headed on foot toward downtown to start her shift at her part-time job. But this Wednesday she didn't do that. Instead, she stood quietly at the bus stop until the bus had driven away and all the students who had gotten off with her had gone their separate ways.

She walked into the parking lot of a nearby Dollar General store and stood waiting next to a blue U.S. postbox near the highway. She'd been told to watch for a gray minivan, so that's what she did. Five minutes later, she spotted the late-model Dodge Caravan entering the parking lot. It came to an abrupt stop in front of her. An unfamiliar woman was driving the Caravan, but the girl recognized the man smiling at her from the passenger seat. He waited a moment, watching her, before he got out of the vehicle.

"You can still change your mind, you know," he said.

"I know."

"The path you're choosing won't be an easy one, and it'll be difficult to come back to your old life."

"I won't be coming back. There's nothing for me here," she replied matter-of-factly.

The man studied her for a long moment, as if testing her resolve. Finally satisfied, he reached for the side door latch and slid the door open. Without a word, the girl stepped into the vehicle and plopped her backpack on the seat. Stone-faced, she fixed her eyes straight ahead as the man slammed the side door shut and slid onto the front seat. The Caravan left the parking lot and returned in the direction from which it had come.

2

Deputy Cyrus Brandt parked his Cane County Sheriff's Department cruiser in front of Annie's Place and grabbed his hat as he stepped out onto the street. It was a cool April day in the town of Elby. The sun was beginning to droop in the west, and traffic along Main Street was picking up as people got off work, heading for who-knows-where.

He glanced at his reflection in the car window and silently admitted to himself that he cut a fine figure in his new uniform. Cyrus had been an official, full-time deputy in the Cane County Sheriff's Department for only about a month. Two and a half years ago, when he'd moved back to his boyhood home outside of Elby, he'd had no idea what he would do with his life. The last thing he'd anticipated was choosing a career in law enforcement. Still, he knew that life often took unexpected turns, and he'd decided to simply lean into it to see where it would take him.

Prior to that, his life had been on a completely different trajectory. With a Ph.D. in hand, he'd finally managed to secure an adjunct teaching position at a small private university. At that time, he was certain his future in academia would play out as he'd long anticipated. But that had all changed when personnel downsizing at the college cost him his job, and his wife's sexual outsourcing cost him his marriage. It took his mother's unexpected death to offer him a second chance. As her sole heir, he'd inherited the small family farm in Central Illinois, and he now found himself living there, engaged in a career he'd never expected, and involved with the spunky brunette who owned the local diner. His life wasn't what he'd expected it to be, but he had to admit that it was turning out to be just fine.

Cyrus walked into the diner and took a seat at the counter. Annie watched him enter and said, "As many times as I've seen you in that spiffy uniform, I still can't really get used to it."

"That makes two of us, I guess. I bet it's kind of a turn-on for you though, isn't it? You know, the shiny badge, the big gun."

"Yeah, whatever you say, Deputy," she shot back, unimpressed. "Have you finished your training with Tom yet?"

"Not really. I doubt it'll ever be finished. He likes things done a certain way, you know. No deviations." Tom Bales was the sheriff of Cane County, and Cyrus's boss. He was also Annie's brother. It was a tangled web.

During the last couple of years, Annie and Cyrus had become very good friends, and eventually lovers. Their friendship was a complicated one, based upon the intersection of two troubled lives, each damaged by a lost love. Perhaps it was the pain of their losses that had drawn them together. Pain is more easily endured when shared.

"Hey, Annie, how about a cup of coffee? It's been a grueling day."

"Well, as far as I can tell, it appears you didn't shoot yourself or anyone else. I'd call that a successful day of law enforcement, right? Maybe you should reward yourself with a piece of pie. I made cherry this morning, and I think it'll meet your expectations."

"I don't see why not," Cyrus replied. "And maybe you can keep me company for a while before I head home."

"Sorry, Cyrus. The company part isn't going to happen. See all these people here? I've been working like a dog since six this morning, and one of my girls didn't show up for her shift this afternoon. I'm really dragging. You wouldn't want to help me wait tables, would you?"

"You know, Annie? Normally I would jump at the chance, but I don't think you want to incur the expense of all those broken dishes."

"Yeah, you're probably right," Annie said as she placed his pie ticket order on the sill of the food window. Without another word, she turned and scurried to the other side of the diner to take more orders.

Cyrus surreptitiously surveyed the patrons sitting around the diner. The place was starting to fill up with people who were either too lazy to cook at home or maybe were just addicted to Annie's pies like he was. Fruit pie was her specialty. Peach. Apple. Blueberry. Cherry. Oh, the cherry. It was exquisite. Cyrus had eaten a lot of cherry pie in his life. When he was a kid, his mother had made cherry pie from the cherries in their farm orchard. Ever since those days, his standard for cherry pie had been right up there with Marge Simpson's standard for hair spray.

As he grew up, he was surprised to learn that not everyone could make an acceptable cherry pie. In fact, very few people could come close to duplicating the scrumptious pies his mother used to make. The cherry pie people made these days was often so runny it drained out of the crust into a puddle in the middle of the plate, or else it had a rubbery consistency like some kind of coagulated, gelatinous cherry tofu. Annie's pie wasn't like that, though. Annie's cherry pie was always perfect, just like the pie Cyrus remembered his mother making. As he daydreamed about cherry pie, Annie grabbed his piece from the food window and slid it onto the counter in front of him.

"Does that look satisfactory?" she asked with her hand on her hip. She knew what was coming.

Cyrus gazed at the delicacy and prodded the pie filling gently with his fork before he spoke. "Hmm. It appears to be of an appropriate consistency, with a decent filling-to-cherries ratio. The color isn't bad, and the crust is prepared within the parameters of my acceptable specifications. Yes, it looks satisfactory. Thank you, Miss."

All Annie could do was roll her eyes, click her tongue, and stalk off. She'd been through this drill before. It always played out the same way. If she'd thought Cyrus was serious, there would've been hell to pay. But she knew it was just a game—a game she was willing to play. Whatever crap he dished out to her in these playful little scenarios, she knew she could respond in kind many times over. And she would.

Cyrus turned into his driveway about thirty minutes later. He was anxious to hit the shower and relax a bit before he drove back to town for his usual Wednesday pizza and beer night with Annie. He pulled up next to the house, and when he stepped out of his vehicle it hit him. The odor was unmistakable. He walked around to the front of his car to see if he had hit a skunk on the road. He crouched down and looked to see if it was lodged in the undercarriage. That would be a mess to clean up, he thought. No, there was no sign of a skunk under or around the car. That was a relief. He turned toward his house and that's when he spotted it. The skunk's bloodied carcass was laid neatly upon the first step of the stairs leading to the kitchen.

"Goddamn it. DOLLY!"

Cyrus could see the dog hiding beneath the steps. As he continued to call her, she finally crawled out of her hiding place and cowered on the grass in front of him. The yellow Lab struck a submissive pose, close to the ground, her ears down and tail hidden beneath her.

Cyrus winced as the stench from the dog wafted over him. "Jesus! This has got to stop!" he exclaimed, as much to himself as to the dog. Dolly had been a real handful since she was a pup, with a penchant for chewing on everything she could find. Cyrus had a closet full of decimated slippers and dog toys to prove it. Even his oak furniture bore the scars of Dolly's mastication.

For a time, Cyrus had banned her from the house and tried to engage her in more outside activities. While playing fetch with her, he soon recognized the extent of her zeal. With unrelenting energy, she was an expert at fetching anything Cyrus threw, no matter what it was or how far he threw it. He took to hitting softballs out into a nearby field. She would retrieve each one without fail. Last fall, Cyrus had hit a long fly ball far out into a soybean field across the road. Dolly had disappeared into the field after it and not returned for the rest of the day. Cyrus had found the ball on his doorstep the following morning.

His big mistake was when he took her hunting for quail in a recently harvested cornfield. He'd only downed two quail that day, but Dolly had expertly retrieved each one, bringing them to him proudly, cradled in her soft mouth. After that Dolly started leaving offerings on his doorstep. At first it was a small bird or a chipmunk, then squirrels, and then larger critters. One morning Cyrus stepped out of the house to find a rather large and very dead groundhog, left lovingly on the step by his mighty hunter.

But the skunk was totally unacceptable. As Dolly cowered on the ground, asking forgiveness for her *good* deed, Cyrus sensed that Dolly had known bringing the skunk to the house was a bad idea, but she simply couldn't help herself.

Cyrus stood there for a moment trying to remember the correct steps to take when dealing with a skunk encounter. He couldn't remember everything, but he knew that he needed to bury the carcass. This he did, as far from the house as he reasonably could. Next he grabbed some shampoo and a brush, and turned on the garden hose to begin work on the dog.

When he'd finished, he studied the pathetic-looking wet Lab and took a big sniff to ascertain the degree of his success. It was difficult for him to tell, since he wasn't sure if he was smelling the dog or himself. It'd just have to do, he decided. Then he headed into the house to get his own much-needed shower. He didn't want to be late picking Annie up for dinner.

3

The soul that aspires to worship God is plain and true; has no rose color, no fine friends, no chivalry; does not want admiration; dwells in the hour that now is, in the earnest experience of the common day.
(The Book of The Path)

The Dodge Caravan drove for nearly an hour before it turned onto a blacktop road heading south through the wide-open Illinois plain. The new spring growth of native flora was just beginning to show itself along the roadside, and Hattie watched as the shoulder whizzed by in a blur of browns and greens. She felt the vehicle suddenly swerve to the left, passing something moving slowly along the side of the road. She quickly looked back to see a horse pulling a small black buggy, half on the road and half on the shoulder. Two figures sat in the shadow of the buggy's roof. She realized they had entered Amish country.

When she was young, before her mother had left, they had sometimes driven to this area to observe the comings and goings of the Amish folk in their odd hats and simple clothes. She also remembered the sight of their horse-drawn farm implements out in the fields. The Amish led a very simple life, free of the modern conveniences most people took for granted. But she was somehow drawn to what she saw in an Amish community: The seemingly close-knit families. The idyllic rural existence. The traditions that eschewed any addiction to the superficial fluff of the capitalistic American society. The values that rebuffed any compulsion to purchase next year's model or the newest electronic gadget. She wondered what it'd be like to live like that.

She began to think about the life she was leaving. That life had generally treated her with indifference, even animus. As she thought about it now, she realized there was nothing she regretted leaving. Not her friends, if they really were her friends. Not her parents, who had never loved her. Not her teachers, who hardly knew her name. Nobody. The only thing that made sense to her now was the promise of this new path offered by Elijah, the man sitting in the seat in front of her.

Made in the USA
Middletown, DE
18 March 2019